Vintage Red

By the same author

Saturday Night Women
Glenroe – The Book

Vintage Red

Michael Judge

ROBERT HALE · LONDON

ISBN 0 7090 7620 7

Robert Hale Limited
Clerkenwell House
Clerkenwell Green
London EC1R 0HT

2 4 6 8 10 9 7 5 3 1

To Lil

Typeset in 10/14pt Bembo
by Derek Doyle & Associates in Liverpool.
Printed in Great Britain by
St Edmundsbury Press Ltd, Bury St Edmunds, Suffolk.
Bound by Woolnough Bookbinding Ltd.

ONE

When Babs McGuinness died there were no comets seen, but the stars of the select suburb of Silverglen came out in their glory to pack the Church of the Archangels for the funeral Mass.

Robert wore the off-black suit with the faint red pinstripe. He felt that the sombre colour emphasized the solemnity of the occasion and the vertical stripes made him look taller than his usual pudgy self.

He went in the mourning-coach with his daughter, Lucy, and his son-in-law, Derek Furlong. Had Miss Corr consented to travel with them, Robert would not have objected, but she had insisted that it would be more seemly to go by herself in her own car. On reflection, he had decided that she was probably right, as she invariably was in matters of etiquette.

When they arrived at the church, people were crowding the driveway. There was a contingent from the Knights of St Nicodemus in their splendid uniforms, cocked hats alert, epaulettes gleaming and shining swords at the ready. People crowded in on both sides of Robert's stately progress. Clammy hands sought his in silent sympathy. Subdued voices murmured equally clammy clichés. Friendly pressures were exerted on his arms and shoulders. Several kisses were pressed to his cheeks, accompanied by the whiff of expensive perfume.

Robert passed through the sympathizers, leaning on Lucy's arm, nodding his head in acknowledgement, returning the clammy handshakes, wafting his own sweet aftershave lotion, blinking back the furtive tear. He was the epitome of controlled manly grief.

Inside the church, a solid phalanx of clergy, led by the magnificent figure of

5

Canon Laurence Finnegan himself, flooded every available corner of the altar space, eddying and swirling against the mahogany communion-rail that divided them from the political dignitaries, the serried ranks of the Irish Countrywomen's Association, the Sodality of St Agnes, the Knights of St Nicodemus, representatives of the Chamber of Commerce and various sporting organizations, and lesser citizens from lesser associations and societies delegated to bid farewell to the dead wife of the most distinguished Christian in the parish, and the most generous sponsor of good causes.

'A veritable saint,' thundered Canon Finnegan, his white hair dancing around his red face, 'a wife, mother, parishioner, friend of the oppressed, uplifter of the downtrodden, almsgiver to the needy, lover of Jesus and His blessed Mother, a scintillating example to us all. Never in the limelight, never self-seeking or self-advertising, always remaining in the background, going about her duties with the silent diligence and devotion of a Martha.'

He paused, wondering what else he should say. There really was nothing to be said about Brigid Mary McGuinness beyond the fact that she had lived and was now dead, and that she had been the wife of Robert McGuinness. She had never really *done* anything on her own account, certainly nothing in the public eye. The august bodies that were represented at the funeral were there purely for the sake of Robert McGuinness and, of course, for the sake of his brother, the Bishop of Tamishni. A great pity that the bishop had not been able to come home from Africa for the occasion, but he *had* sent a message and a blessing.

The canon tried to picture Babs McGuinness, but found the image elusive. A small red-haired woman, he remembered, with a broad accent from somewhere in the west of Ireland, passably good-looking, but always self-effacing and shy, providing tea or whiskey while he and Robert were ensconced in two comfortable armchairs in the lounge of Twin Cedars, discussing the affairs of the parish, the Church and the world. What could he possibly say about such an unobtrusive personality? Then, in a sudden flash of inspiration, he remembered Lucy Grey.

'A violet by a mossy stone half hidden from the eye,' intoned the canon, almost in triumph. 'Fair as a star. . . .'

He hesitated. Was this pushing it too far? Oh dammit all, the woman was dead and the bishop was her brother-in-law!

'Fair as a star, when only one is shining in the sky. Today, sadly, she has gone from us, never to return. Yes. We bid farewell to Brigid Mary, with tears, yes, but also in the confident hope that we all may be reunited with her again in that paradise where she now surely resides.'

'Amen,' murmured the congregation, stealing surreptitious glances at the dignified bowed head of Robert and marvelling that he could be so strong in his grief. Like the canon, very few of them could remember Babs's face or the sound of her voice, but they felt that a husband as faithful and devoted as Robert McGuinness must surely be suffering acutely in his bereavement.

'We extend our deepest sympathy to her grieving husband,' the canon continued, now on surer ground. 'Robert McGuinness is one of our own in the best sense of the word – born, bred and reared here in Silverglen.'

This wasn't strictly true, as the suburb of Silverglen was the product of a recent housing development and had not existed when Robert had been born. However, the ancestral home of the McGuinness family had been a cottage on a hill a few miles away and Robert was one of those worthy citizens whose investments had made Silverglen possible, including the fine church in which they now were, so the canon felt justified in what was no more than a slight distortion of the truth.

'A Christian *par excellence*, a Knight of St Nicodemus, a benefactor of the Church, a businessman of probity and piety, an employer of integrity and even-handedness, a faithful husband, a loving father, a man, in short, of whom we can truly say, "Whence comes there such another!" Yes.'

The final 'yes' was unfortunate, but it had slipped out almost before he was aware of it. He put it behind him and paused for applause. It duly came, scattered and tentative at first, but swelling as the congregation became aware by the movements of his hands that he really wished them to clap. Normally he would not have tolerated any such noisy demonstration within the sacred precincts of his church, but obviously today was not a normal day. The applause continued for fifteen seconds or so. Then the canon's hands changed their position and indicated that silence was now required.

Silence returned.

'Yes,' said the canon approvingly. 'You are quite right to show your appreciation of Robert McGuinness, not only for the way he has upheld the Christian tradition of the McGuinness family, but also for his unceasing and very generous contributions to the welfare of this parish. Today he has suffered a grievous blow, his life-partner and helpmeet has been snatched from him, and today we shower him with our heartfelt sympathy. We ask the good Lord to give him comfort and strength to carry the cross that now lies heavily across his broad shoulders. Yes, Robert, you have our deepest sympathy. And more than our sympathy. I think I may safely say, on behalf of all of us here present, that, yes, you have our love.'

The canon paused again, feeling that the word 'love' was a good note on which to end, even though he found it difficult to believe that many people in the parish, or indeed in the world, loved Robert McGuinness all that much. They admired him, perhaps, certainly envied him for his business acumen and his obvious wealth, and very often praised him for his contributions to the community. Love, however, was another day's work But no doubt Babs had loved him for himself. That would suffice for now. So, with the help of the amplification system, 'love' hung quivering in the air for several impressive seconds and pervaded all the secret recesses of the packed church.

The canon glanced across at Father Doherty, who was in charge of the rubrics, and was disturbed to see that the curate had turned his back on the congregation and was mouthing something in his direction. Good heavens, what was that idiot Doherty fussing about now? Then the penny dropped.

'Of course,' said the canon, as if he had intended saying so all along, 'we must not forget Robert's daughter, the lovely Lucy, who bears her own share of the burden of grief. To her we say, "God is good and will give you the strength to carry your cross. And, yes, in time, this burden too will pass away." '

Lucy started to weep and those nearest to her clucked in sympathy. Derek placed his arm around his wife's shoulders and produced a white handkerchief for her use. There was something almost magical in the way Derek always seemed to have a clean white handkerchief available. Lucy had cried a lot since her mother's death, but Derek never failed to have the requisite piece of linen in his hand at the appropriate moment.

Robert shifted himself another few inches away from his weeping daughter, in an instinctive effort to protect his off-black suit with the faint red pinstripe. He was glad to note that Derek was mopping up the tears and keeping them away from his father-in-law. Derek was all right, though a bit of a slob, perhaps. His pink face was a picture of concern for the distress of his wife. His handkerchief was working away like a dryer in a laundromat.

A pity Lucy wasn't a tad stronger, thought Robert, more like Babs herself. Especially as she looked so much like Babs, the younger Babs, before her fine brown-red hair had been bleached white by the passage of time and the suffering of her later years. Lucy had the hair in all its glory, with the green eyes to match, but there was another strain in her, a sort of dreamy weakness, which didn't sit easily with her physical appearance.

Babs had been a strong woman, who had always seemed capable of dealing with the vicissitudes of life. She never – *had* never – looked for sympathy, had never cried, or come whingeing to him, even when he had been rather less than kind to her. It was one of the reasons why he had married her. Of course, there were other reasons, but her strength had certainly been high on the list of her desirable attributes.

'Receive her soul, oh you Holy Angels, and present it to God the Most High.'

The cemetery was cold. A fresh wind blew in from the sea, made an unholy mess of the canon's white hair and flapped the pages of his Prayer Book. It also raised the skirt of his surplice and disturbed the regalia of the knights who clustered around the grave.

The Knights of St Nicodemus had now been drawn up in a formal guard of honour. All the other representatives had apparently reached an amicable accommodation on who should stand where. The canon was glad that the competitiveness displayed by some of the august bodies as the cortège was setting out from the church had been modified to suit the occasion.

Robert McGuinness regretted that he had not brought his overcoat. Like Silverglen itself, the cemetery was a new development and the management forbade the erection of standing tombstones and trees. Consequently there was nothing to shelter the mourners from the sharp wind.

He shivered slightly and was immediately conscious of the concern in Miss Corr's eyes. She stood across the grave from him, behind the colourful robes of the knights and their elaborate headdresses, her hands clasped, the wind pressing the material of her trim tailored beige suit against her firm breasts and long thighs. Robert's gaze momentarily met hers. Neither of them gave the slightest outward sign, but there was an almost palpable exchange of warm sympathy between them.

Robert felt immediately comforted. That was how Miss Corr had affected him from the first moment that she had come to work at ORMAX.

He closed his eyes, remembering that day, nine years earlier.

Although she had been engaged as his personal secretary, Robert had not himself interviewed her for the job. In the light of subsequent events, he was glad of that. No one could legitimately accuse him of having an ulterior motive in the choice, or of having succumbed to her obvious charms rather than to her equally obvious qualifications.

Myles Cassidy, his Personnel Manager, had found Miss Corr for him in his usual passionless methodical way. A bulky, dull man, he had brought Miss Corr into Robert's private office on that fateful day and had presented her to Robert as he might have presented a new piece of office furniture.

'This is Miss Corr, Mr McGuinness.'

'Who?' said Robert, without lifting his eyes from the document he was perusing. He rarely found it worthwhile to look at Myles Cassidy.

'Your new private secretary, sir.'

'Oh,' said Robert. 'Right, Myles.'

He carefully put the cap back on his gold pen. Babs had given it to him the previous Christmas and, because she had paid for it from her generous household allowance, Robert deemed it worthy of conservation. He lifted his head.

Miss Corr stood there. She wore a soft yellow clinging dress with a gold buckle at her waist and gold ear-rings to match. The ear-rings were shaped like little stars. Funny how he remembered that small detail. He seldom remembered women's clothes and certainly not their accessories, not even the presents from himself that he expected Babs to wear on the infrequent occasions he took her out to his business dinners.

But Miss Corr's golden buckle and golden ear-rings were immediately indelibly etched on his mind.

Miss Corr stood there. There was an ineffable softness about her. Her deep blue eyes looked kindly at him. The office seemed full of warmth and comfort and understanding. A faint scent of some very agreeable perfume emanated from her and wafted over Robert.

Myles was saying something, but Robert couldn't hear him. He waved his hand in dismissal. Myles placed a folder on the desk and melted away.

'Please sit down, Miss Corr.'

Miss Corr sat. The yellow dress rode up her long slim legs and for one awful moment Robert thought he was going to faint. He bowed his head and looked at the folder. It seemed to contain some sort of curriculum vitae of Miss Orla

Corr, with added comments from the Personnel Department. Robert could make no sense of the words, except for the name Orla. The golden one. It was music.

He cleared his throat. 'I gather you have already been hired by Mr Cassidy.'

She nodded, smiling at him.

'So they tell me, Mr McGuinness.'

Her voice was throaty and soft.

'He has an unerring eye for the genuine article. I hope you'll be happy working for me.'

'I'm sure I shall, Mr McGuinness.'

He raised his eyes and drowned in the blue depths of Miss Corr's.

'Dad.'

Lucy was tugging at his elbow. The wind across the cemetery brought reality like a cold douche.

'Are you OK?'

'Yes, of course.'

Robert realized that the graveside ceremony was over, apart from the business of the roses. With Lucy on his arm, he advanced to the edge of the grave. The coffin looked surprisingly small, but then Babs was not – *had not been* – a large person, and she had got progressively smaller during the latter stages of her illness. It was no doubt adequate for her small frame. And it was an expensive coffin, one that she would never have sought, but which Robert felt was demanded of a man of his social standing. Even he himself would ask for no finer casket when the time came to make his descent into the earth.

One after the other, the two of them dropped their single red roses into the grave, then stepped back as the gravediggers moved forward to place in position the green cover with its piled wreaths and bouquets of flowers.

There were commands. The swords of the knights flashed in the sudden burst of sunshine that unexpectedly illumined the scene.

TWO

Séamus Creedon very rarely followed a strange woman in the street. In fact, he couldn't remember an occasion when he had done so since the days of his youth, on his way home from the October evening devotions with his pals.

October had always been a magical month. The days became dark, the streetlights were switched on earlier, and there was a sharp hint of frost in the air. Best of all were the evening devotions, the Rosary and benediction in the seminary chapel, where the priests, dressed in golden robes, led the prayers and elevated the golden monstrance containing the Body and Blood of Jesus Christ in blessing over the bowed heads of the congregation, while the seminarians, assembled on both side of the incense-shrouded altar, sang hymns in sonorous, mysterious Latin.

He and his friends were not normally allowed out after dark, but an exception was made for the devotions. When the ceremony was over, they invariably seized the opportunity to follow, and sometimes to shout at, the groups of giggling girls who linked arms and swaggered ahead through the darkened streets. They had been innocent times. Nothing much had ever happened on those nocturnal excursions, but they had exuded possibilities of exciting events just around the next corner, hanging like the golden apples of the sun and the silver apples of the moon on unimaginable trees in dark and mysterious places.

All that had been many years before and, being the serious-minded studious type of man he liked to think he was, he had not since followed a strange female anywhere at any time.

Also he had grown a beard. This had started out both as a defensive weapon to fend off ridicule (he was a slight, timid man and wore glasses) and as an offensive ploy to gain a hearing from people, particularly university lecturers, who tended to take one look at his appearance, say 'yes, yes' and turn their attention elsewhere. During tutorials he had found himself isolated and ignored, even when he had more to say and more intelligent opinions to offer than most of the big louts who managed to dominate the gatherings by thrusting themselves forward and shouting their inanities.

So he had grown a beard and the beard had worked wonders. The tutors found it impossible to ignore a man with a beard; words emerging from a mouth surrounded by hair were universally considered more meaningful and erudite than the very same words from a hairless orifice. He was now quite proud of his beard and tended it affectionately morning and evening. It was black, was cut spade-like on the lower end of his narrow face and lent him a gravitas that nature had unfortunately neglected to supply.

Now, a bearded man, with gravitas, should certainly not be following a strange woman along a Dublin street. Yet he could not help himself. The whole incident had a certain inevitability about it that was almost literary. In fact, take away the literary overtones and there was nothing at all there.

To call it an 'incident', of course, was really overstating the case. There had been no 'incident' in the dramatic sense of the word. He had merely heard a voice, or rather an *accent*, and had been riveted by it. And the situation, Nassau Street, and the fact that he had come back to Dublin with the intention of writing about Joyce, struck him as being so coincidental as to be a stroke of Fate, with a capital letter.

He heard her clear Galway accent, lifted his eyes and saw her thick red-brown hair and was unable to move for what seemed like an age. She said goodbye to her companion, a nondescript female person in dark clothes, then turned and walked away towards Grafton Street. The other woman crossed the street, but he had no idea where she had gone. He had eyes only for the red-brown hair and, as if pulled by an invisible thread, was drawn irresistibly after it.

As he walked down Nassau Street, he took careful note of the woman in front of him. She was small. This was a good thing – if they ever got to a ballroom together he could dance with her without feeling inadequate, not to say ridiculous. She wore a light summer dress with a green pattern on it, silk stockings and brown-and-beige sandals. Fine. Her legs were shapely. Fine again. Her steps were firm and decisive, her shoulders were square and her back was straight. Her figure wasn't noticeably voluptuous and that suited him too.

Voluptuous women were dangerous, or so those of his friends who had extensive experience had assured him. Voluptuous equalled exciting-but-dangerous, they said. He had had very little experience himself, but the truth of their assertions seemed to him to be self-evident. Most females, even non-voluptuous ones, looked dangerous to him.

Many times during the next few hundred yards he told himself that he was an idiot, that it just wasn't *seemly* (he could hear his mother's voice ringing in his ears) to be following a strange woman, like some sort of a stalking pervert. A man with a beard engaged on any sort of romantic adventure always looks highly suspect.

On the other hand, he countered, it was a pleasant summer day and he had nothing much to do at that particular moment. He had spent the morning working in the National Library and carried under his arm a blue folder containing the notes he had made on Joyce's early years at university. He needed a rest, a bit of diversion, an exhalation.

All the same, this adventure was verging on the ludicrous. He decided to follow her only as far as Grafton Street. Anything else would be out of the question. If she turns left into Grafton Street, he thought, I'll turn right towards Westmoreland Street and revert to my previous state of relative sanity.

But when she turned up Grafton Street and he saw her small figure disappearing in the crowd, he had no option but to hurry after her. Like Martin Luther, he felt he 'could do no other'.

He caught up with her outside Switzer's Department Store. She had paused to look into one of the windows at some ladies' underwear. Turning sharply right, he positioned himself at another Switzer window a few yards away, but around the corner in Wicklow Street, from where he could observe her through the angle of the glass. He pretended to be looking at men's ties as he stole surreptitious glances at her.

Her face was a strong one, not pretty exactly, but certainly not unattractive. She had a straight nose, full lips and wide eyes. And her expression was pleasant, definitely kindly, even when she frowned and puckered her lips at the price tags on some of the garments. Only once did she turn her eyes in his direction and then it was no more than a passing glance that drifted over him and was gone. There wasn't time even to notice what colour her eyes were, though he felt sure they must be green. She spent a further moment or two looking at the clothes and then turned away and continued up the street.

After a discreet pause he followed. But when he turned again into Grafton Street, she was nowhere to be seen. Panic gripped him. She had disappeared in the crowd. Then he caught the flash of the green patterned frock in time to see her turn into Bewley's Oriental Café.

Bewley's was a familiar coffee house to him, a home from home, a place of refuge in the city where he could hide himself away and eat cheaply when he felt alone and abandoned. Savouring the tingling scent of coffee, now made more pungent by the excitement of the chase, he followed the woman through the foyer. She took a brown plastic tray and joined the queue at the counter. He found his own tray, added himself to the queue and in his turn selected a sticky bun and a mug of coffee. When he turned from the cash desk, he saw that she had taken her position over against the wall and was sitting under one of the stained-glass windows. He drifted towards her in what he hoped was a nonchalant fashion, found a table close by and sat down to observe her.

What happened next came as a total surprise. She picked up her tray and walked over to where he sat.

Her strange green eyes surveyed him.

'Do you mind?'

He shook his head silently. Carefully placing her tray down on the table, she sat opposite him. When she had tasted her coffee and rearranged the bun – she too had a sticky bun on her plate! – she slowly lifted her head.

'You're following me, aren't you?'

'What?'

'Oh come on. Don't act the innocent. You've been following me for the last ten minutes. All the way down Nassau Street. Isn't that right?'

There seemed nothing for it but a full confession.

'Yes.'

'Why?'

'It's very complicated. I mean, please don't think that I've any evil intentions, or anything like that.'

'I should hope not.'

There was a pause, while she stirred her coffee and took a bite from her bun. He was relieved to see that she wasn't angry, but he didn't quite know where to go from here. He looked at his own bun. Then he sipped his coffee.

'Well?'

'Huh?'

15

'Aren't you going to tell me why?'

'Yes, of course. It's just that it's complicated.'

'You said that before.'

'I know. But I feel very foolish. I don't know where to start.'

'It can't be *that* hard.'

'Well, you know how it is when you get an idea for a story. It's great in your mind. Inside. And then you make the mistake of telling it to someone else. And the minute it's out in the open, it's like a dead cat that you roll over and suddenly discover all the dreadful things that run about under its dead body. That's the way I feel at this point. What seemed plausible in my diseased mind is now revealed as utterly implausible, stupid even. It has families of working-mother woodlice beavering away under it. Though maybe woodlice don't beaver. Beavers beaver. Woodlice . . . I wonder what woodlice do.'

'Do you write stories?'

'No. Not really. I'd like to. Well, I do occasionally. But I've never sold any. Maybe I will someday.'

'I've never met a writer before.'

'For God's sake don't call me that, or you'll drive the ambition right out of me.'

She laughed.

'You're a funny yoke, do you know that? All those woodlice and beavers.'

'That about sums me up.'

There was another pause. She munched her bun.

'Come on, tell me.'

'Well . . . I've just done a degree in Galway. Last September. English and History.'

'*You're* not from Galway. Your accent's pure Dublin.'

'Oh yes. I'm from Dublin. Over on the north side.'

'What brought you to Galway, then?'

'I thought I'd like it there. Way out in the Wild West. Beyond civilization. And it was easier to get into. Also it was far away from home. Now I've got a place teaching in a secondary school, after the holidays. But in the meantime, I thought I'd have a stab at an MA. On James Joyce. Something like that.' He patted the folder lying on the table. 'So I've been reading Joyce like mad and looking through the archives in the National Library. It's still all pretty vague in my mind.'

16

'You must have the life of it.'

'Oh it's hard work, I can tell you.'

She looked at him in disbelief.

'Anyway. A short while ago I left the library and walked down Kildare Street, to catch a bus back to Drumcondra. I crossed over Nassau Street to the Trinity side. And then I heard your voice.'

'Oh God, that must've been a disappointment.'

'No. Absolutely not. It was wonderful. Here I was, thinking about Joyce and here was this lovely Galway accent. And then I looked up and all I could see was red-brown hair.'

'Manky!'

'Wonderful. Do you realize that Joyce met Nora Barnacle for the first time just about where *I* heard *your* voice for the first time?'

'Tell you the truth, I didn't. Who's Nora Barnacle when she's at home?'

He leaned across the table and spoke intently.

'The love of Joyce's life.'

'Ah, will you get out of that!'

She had coloured under his concentrated stare. He sat back in his chair and nibbled contritely at his bun.

'You know what I mean.'

They ate in silence for a few minutes.

'It all seems very fishy to me.'

'I'm not trying to pick you up.'

'Now the compliments are flying! Who'd want to pick *me* up, anyway.'

'Believe me—' He paused. Then he added, 'Do you have a name?'

'I do, but I'm not going to tell you.'

'I'll have to call you something.'

'Who says you've got to call me anything! When I finish my bun I'm going to walk out of here and I'll probably never see you again.' Then she laughed and he admired her strong white teeth. 'Tell you what. Why don't you call me Nora? And I'll call you James. That way no milk gets spilt for the cat to lick up.'

'Done. Nora. Only she always called him Jim.'

'Right, Jim.'

'And please don't walk out when you've finished your bun.'

'Not picking me up, he says. That sounds very like a pick-up to me.'

'Joyce picked up Nora. Or maybe it was the other way around. Opinion is divided on the subject.'

'When was that?'

'June the tenth, 1904.'

'What day of the week was it?'

'A Friday.'

'Well, that cooks it for a start. This isn't June the tenth. It's the sixteenth. And it's 1976, not 1904. And it's a Wednesday.'

'It's close enough. We can't have everything.'

'*We*! Will you listen to the man! This is all in *your* head, not mine.'

'They made a date for the following Monday, but she never turned up.'

'Now *that* sounds more like *my* Nora.'

'But they *did* meet again a few days later, probably on June the sixteenth. Nobody knows for sure. But years later, when Joyce wrote *Ulysses* he set it on June the sixteenth. It was probably his way of commemorating that first date. So you see, June the sixteenth is a good date too. Better, in fact.'

'Romantic, wasn't he?'

'Oh yes. He was very romantic. But so was she.'

'Where did they go?'

'What?'

'On their first date. Where did he take her? Some nice restaurant? I don't suppose they'd pictures in 1904.'

'For a walk.'

'A walk?'

'Down to the harbour near Ringsend.'

'Oh God, what a stingy!'

'He was stingy all right. He was a genius at scrounging money. He could have scrounged for Ireland at the Olympics.'

'Some lad, your Joyce. I suppose all he was after was a bit of a hoult on the cheap.'

'You *could* say that. At least at the beginning.'

'And did he get what he was after?'

'A bit more than he bargained for.'

'And what does that mean?'

He waved his hand helplessly.

'I can't tell you that.'

'Why not? Oh, you're shy! I suppose it was something dirty. All you men are the same, aren't you?'

'They lived together for the rest of his life. They even got married later on. So it was a lot more than just a quick hoult in Ringsend.'

'I'm sure *she* was the one decided what happened afterwards. About the marriage and so on.'

He said admiringly, 'You've got *that* right, anyway.'

They finished their buns in a companionable silence. He watched her covertly while she dabbed her mouth with the paper napkin. No lipstick, he noted, but then her lips didn't need any. They were full and red enough without any artificial aids.

She sighed and pushed back her chair.

'Well, I've got to go now.'

'Ah please.'

'Please what?'

'I'll buy you another coffee and bun if you stay for a while.'

'Just to prove you're not stingy, I suppose?'

'Just to keep you here a little while longer.'

'What for?'

'I'm enjoying talking to you. Aren't you enjoying it too?'

'Listen to him, will you! You don't think I'm going to answer a question like that, do you? No, I've got to go now.'

'Can I walk with you to the bus, then?'

'Who said I was going on the bus?'

'I just presumed.'

'For all you know, the chauffeur could be waiting in the Rolls at the bottom of the street. You just sit where you are and no harm'll come to you.'

'Will I not see you again?'

'Dublin's a small place – we're sure to bump into one another sooner or later.'

She stood up. He stood too.

'Is that all the hope you can give me?'

'Maybe it's hope you want!'

He held up a finger and thumb.

'Even that much would be better than nothing at all.'

'You're serious, aren't you?' she said, looking straight into his eyes.

Suddenly he realized that he was.

'Deadly serious.'

'All right, then. This time Wednesday next. Here. And I'll stick you for a sticky bun.'

'I'll buy you two.'

'And then I'll get fat and you'll run a mile when you see me.'

'Never.'

'Goodbye, Jim.'

'Goodbye, Nora.'

She smiled at him as she turned away. Watching her walk out of the café he hoped she would turn around, but she did not.

THREE

Robert McGuinness shifted uneasily in the armchair. It had been a long and tiring day and he wanted to lie down and rest. But the brandy bottle was still nearly half-full and the canon droned on and on.

They sat together in the lounge of Twin Cedars. It was a big room, because Twin Cedars was a big house, bigger than anything else in Silverglen, and had been built specially for Robert McGuinness. It was an ugly, pretentious house, with porticoes and pillars and balconies, inserts of red bricks and white corner-stones, and two enormous eagles spreading their wings on the overweight gate pillars. It squatted in its own grounds on a height on the northern end of the development – Silverglen was some distance above being a mere 'estate' – and glared down across the city at the sea and the islands beyond. But it was impressive, it made an unequivocal statement that here resided wealth and power and importance, and it dwarfed the houses nearest to it.

The furniture in the sitting room was weighty and covered with dark-red brocade, the walls were hung with heavily embossed paper, and the drapes on the tall windows tumbled ponderously to the deeply carpeted floor. There were two dull paintings in oppressive gilt frames, reminiscent of the School of Rembrandt at its most gloomy, one over the marble fireplace and another on the wall facing the windows. Robert liked to be surrounded by grave, depend-able things that dressed a room without demanding to be looked at.

Sally and Pat, the two maids, had just finished clearing away the last of the glasses and plates that the departing guests had left behind them, while Mrs Kirwan, the housekeeper and cook, was taking her ease with a bottle of sweet sherry after her labours in the kitchen.

An hour earlier, Twin Cedars had been full of people, the tinkle of glasses and teacups, and the smell of cigar smoke. Now all the guests had gone about their business. Lucy and Derek had returned to their own new home in Howth, which glowered back across the bay at its senior partner. Robert's two sisters, both of whom had planes to catch, had left with their spouses immediately after the funeral. The employees of ORMAX, as soon as they decently could, had taken themselves off to salvage what was left of their unusual free day before it escaped from them. The various knights and dames had gone to remove their cumbersome regalia and revert to their everyday guise of businessmen, professional people, academics, bridge-playing housewives and *nouveaux-riches* shopkeepers.

Robert fervently wished that the canon also would disappear and leave him alone. But the canon was in full flight. He liked the comfort of the armchair and the Hennessy VSOP, and he felt it was his duty to stay with Robert in the dying hours of what must have been a harrowing day for the widower. Besides, he was growing old and his feet ached. He wished to rest them before retiring to his celibate bed.

'What you need is a purpose in your life, Robert,' the canon intoned, conscious that what he was saying was rubbish, but unable to help himself. 'You must mourn your beloved wife, of course, but keep a sense of proportion about it, keep it in perspective.'

'Oh, I know that, Canon.'

The canon cupped the brandy glass in his two hands and slowly swirled the golden liquid.

'After all, when you really think about your dear wife and ask yourself what she would wish you to do, what answer do you come up with? I'll tell you, Robert, my old son. Yes. Brigid Mary, were she alive here talking to us, would tell you to get on with your life.'

'True, true.'

Robert essayed a brave smile. The canon averted his eyes from the disagreeable sight and sought other words to fill the gap.

'She would indeed. Yes. And so would His Lordship. We must not forget His Lordship in all this. Toiling out there in the jungle, bringing the Word of God to all those poor savages so ravaged by paganism and AIDS.'

He regretted using the two words 'savages' and 'ravaged' in such discordant juxtaposition, but it was out now and there was no going back on it. To disperse the memory of that unmemorable phrase, the canon mentioned a matter of practical importance.

'Ah . . . have you thought of a suitable inscription for the headstone?'

Robert remembered a suggestion made by Lucy as they were leaving the church.

'Fair as a star.'

'Eh?'

'You said those very words in the church.'

'Did I? Ah yes, of course. Wordsworth. Most apt. A fine poet of the old school.'

The canon finished the last of the brandy in his glass and paused. Robert, a little uneasy at the idea that he might be expected to discuss Wordsworth, felt obliged to reach for the bottle.

'Thank you, thank you. One thing that nobody can take away from you is your generous spirit, Robert. You shame us all with your liberality.'

'If you have it you should spend it, Canon.'

'A sound axiom, but, alas, there are people in this parish whose material wealth almost equals your own, but whose generosity falls far short. No names, Robert, but I think we understand the score well enough.'

Robert groaned inwardly. He knew that if the canon got on to his favourite topic, the parsimony of his better-endowed parishioners, the homily could stretch into hours.

'Excuse me, sir.'

Blessed relief in the form of Sally had entered the room.

'Yes, Sally?'

'There's a woman here to see you.'

Robert rose, trying not to show his pleasure at the interruption.

'You'll have to excuse me, Canon.'

'Of course, Robert, of course.'

'I won't let her hold me. In the meantime, feel free to have more brandy if you wish.'

The canon waved his hand deprecatingly at the suggestion.

'I'll be back as soon as I can.'

The woman who was waiting in the small reception room was blocky and dark. As Robert entered, she sprang from her chair and stood to face him with the stance of a karate expert. She held a briefcase under her arm. Her body language seemed to warn all and sundry, men especially, that she was not a woman to be trifled with, and that one false move could have disastrous consequences. Robert disliked her instinctively.

'Mr McGuinness?'

'Yes.'

'I'm Kate Hanley, of Hanley and Patterson, Solicitors.'

The name meant nothing to him, though it was spoken like an imperial edict.

'It's very late for a business visit.'

'I apologize for that. I waited until all the guests seemed to have gone. And on behalf of the firm, I'd like to offer you our deep sympathy on the death of your wife.'

Robert could detect no vestige of sympathy in her voice and whatever emotion was in her eyes was certainly not warm and friendly. In fact she seemed to dislike him as much as he disliked her.

'Thank you, Miss Hanley.'

'I am here to inform you, as a matter of courtesy, that our firm, and I personally, have been appointed executors of your late wife's will.'

'Her what?'

Miss Hanley stared implacably at him.

'Her last Will and Testament, Mr McGuinness.'

'I don't understand.'

Miss Hanley produced from her briefcase a pink folder and held it up. Robert could see quite plainly the words *Last Will and Testament of Brigid Mary McGuinness* typed across the front of it.

'Sit down a minute,' he said.

As she perched herself warily on one of the armchairs he noticed that her legs were fat and unattractive. He had anticipated that they would be; everything about her was confrontational and threatening. Even her shoes were solid and black, like a policewoman's, and were evidently chosen for defending herself against truculent clients and other male aggressors. He felt sure that her underwear was made of thick black tweed.

He tried to maintain the gentle tone of a recently bereaved man.

'I don't follow this at all. My wife and I made our wills together a year ago, so I don't see how this document could be genuine.'

Miss Hanley brought her knees together with a snap. Her face darkened still further.

'I sincerely hope, Mr McGuinness, that you are not impugning the integrity of Hanley and Patterson!'

'No, no, of course not,' Robert said hastily. The sudden movement of her knees had startled him. 'But there must be some mistake. Babs and I had no secrets from each other.'

Miss Hanley's lips twisted into a grimace that might have been intended as a smile, but came out as quite otherwise.

'I can assure you that this will was properly made out, signed and witnessed, just a little over six months ago, here in this house.'

Robert was astounded.

'Here?'

Miss Hanley almost licked her lips in satisfaction.

'Mrs McGuinness rang me at my office in Leeson Street and asked me to come here.'

'Six months ago?'

'The date on it is Tuesday, the eighth of February 1999. The time of the actual signing was 3.25 p.m.'

'My wife was very ill six months ago. She was confined to bed.'

'I realize that. We did the signing at her bedside. But while she may have been physically ill, she was certainly *compos mentis* when she called us in. No doubt about that. And she made this will and appointed us as her executors. It was witnessed by one of the maids and by the nurse who was in attendance. I have all the documentation here for your perusal. Naturally, it supersedes all other wills made by our client prior to this one.'

Robert stared at her.

'But she had nothing to leave.'

Miss Hanley's pseudo smile deepened, showing more of her irregular teeth. It signalled that her deepest fears concerning Robert had been fully realized – obviously he had stripped his poor wife of all her assets before consigning her to the earth.

'She had at least one thing.'

'Nothing.'

'Her motor car.'

'Motor car?' Robert started to laugh. 'You mean the old Morris Minor?

That heap of rubbish?'

'Mrs McGuinness thought very highly of her car. She told me that she didn't wish to change anything in her previous will, except in respect of the car, which was apparently not specifically mentioned in the other documents.'

'Women!' snorted Robert.

Miss Hanley's face darkened several shades. He stiffened defensively. For a moment he thought that she was going to jump up and hit him.

'You know what I mean! Women really know nothing about cars. That old banger doesn't deserve another fill of petrol, let alone mention in a will.'

'That wasn't Mrs McGuinness's perception of it.'

'I think we must make allowances for my wife's state of health when she called to your office.'

'She was perfectly logical and most precise in her requirements.'

'But emotionally unstable.'

'We saw no evidence of that, Mr McGuinness.'

Robert bared his teeth again at this unpleasant woman.

'I think you will accept that I would know more about my own wife after a lifetime of marriage than you and your associates could possibly find out in a few minutes.'

'I don't intend to argue with you on that point,' said Miss Hanley with finality. 'In fact, my only reason for coming here was to let you know about the existence of the will. And now that that has been done . . .'

She stood up.

'Hold on a minute.'

'Yes?'

'I think I'm entitled to know exactly what is in the will.'

'Of course. This copy is for you.' She laid the folder on the occasional table. 'You can read it at your leisure. It's quite short and to the point. We have already put the advertisement in the appropriate newspaper.'

'Advertisement?'

'Mrs McGuinness wished to have the car sold after her death.'

'Sold?'

Robert realized how stupid his repetitions must sound to the Hanley monster, but he was unable to help himself.

'Sold,' repeated Miss Hanley, with evident satisfaction. 'She was very insistent on it. She even gave us the exact wording for the advertisement. Do you wish to hear it? I know it by heart.'

Robert nodded dumbly. He felt she had taken considerable pleasure in committing it to memory.

'I quote: "The vintage car that toured the little towns in Connacht, fuelled with love, is now for sale. The first bidder to reach the reserve price may drive the car away. Contact Hanley and Patterson, Solicitors, Leeson Street, Dublin 2".'

'That's it?'

'That's it. Short and sweet. And unambiguous. The notice appeared in yesterday's edition of the *Connacht Tribune*. There is a copy of the advertisement and the receipt in your folder.'

'Only in the *Connacht Tribune*?'

'That was the instruction from Mrs McGuinness.'

Miss Hanley snapped her briefcase shut as definitively as she had closed her legs.

'And that concludes my business with you, Mr McGuinness. Unless, of course, you have any questions.'

'Questions can wait until I've read the full documentation and taken legal advice.'

Miss Hanley's smile indicated that she knew full well the futility of any course of action he might consider.

Later, when the solicitor had stamped her way out of the house, as if in search of other aggressive males to demolish, and the canon had finally been prevailed upon to leave, Robert sat alone in the drawing-room. He was tight with rage. The idea that the will had been signed behind his back in his own house appalled him. He picked up the folder and looked at the copy of *The Last Will and Testament of Brigid Mary McGuinness*. The two witnesses had signed their names as Sarah O'Byrne and Esther Whelan. He presumed the Esther Whelan must have been the nurse on duty at the time. He had no memory of her. The Sarah O'Byrne undoubtedly was Sally, the maid.

Robert summoned Sally.

'I remember signing something, sir.'

'What was said to you at the time?'

'The lady just asked me to write my name as a witness that Mrs McGuinness's name was really hers.'

'Did you read the document?'

'Oh God, no, sir.'

Robert dismissed her, thankful at least that the girl knew nothing about the will. Then he sat for a long time trying to compose himself, before he found the necessary impetus to walk out into the garage.

The Morris Minor stood silently between the silver Mercedes SL600 and the blue Volvo T5, like an impecunious cousin at a wealthy wedding. It was red in colour and weathered in appearance, but it was clean and polished. Babs had always seen to that.

Robert walked around it slowly. He felt calmer just looking at it. It was like Babs herself, he thought – solid, dependable, not unattractive, though certainly not beautiful, with none of the style of the other two cars. Just as Babs had had none of the style of someone like Orla Corr.

Not her fault, Robert told himself. Orla Corr was exceptional. And Babs couldn't be blamed for being a simple country girl. He had always made allowances for that, had never made her feel inadequate, not even when he had gone up in the world and she had been called on to play hostess to important people. In spite of whatever faults he might have, no one could say that he wasn't a fair-minded man. He remembered with thankful pride that he had never raised a hand to her in all their married life.

He got into the Minor. The leather upholstery shone and exuded a faint perfumed smell. It squeaked gently as it took his weight. There was not a speck of dust to be seen anywhere. But that was Babs. She had always kept the house immaculate, especially in the early days when money had been scarce and the idea of hiring a servant had been unthinkable. A good woman, no doubt about it. An excellent wife within her own limitations.

A lump came into his throat. A tear pricked his eye. He bowed his head. He hoped that God would be good to her – and to himself, when his time came to go. He had done his best; nobody could take that from him.

Then the mileometer caught his attention. He blinked and bent to study it more closely. The figure it showed was 176,335 miles. Robert considered this with some surprise.

Ten years ago, when Orla Corr had first wrapped her long legs around him in a bedroom in Paris, he had bought the car for Babs. In his magnanimous way he had felt that he owed her something for his infidelity. The car was second-hand, though he had been quite prepared to expend money on a new one. She had chosen it herself. It was a good buy – one previous owner, an old lady who had run up only 18,000 miles in nearly double that number of years. Babs's delight and gratitude at the gift still warmed his heart. God rewards a good man with a grateful wife.

But 176,335 was still a considerable mileage. It meant that Babs must have covered about 160,000 miles in ten years, or 16,000 miles a year, over 300 miles a week. How could she possibly have managed that? Certainly not by trips to the shops. Or taking Lucy to school. Their daughter had been a boarder in Athlone for most of that time.

How then?

He realized that he had no idea how Babs had spent her days while he was away, as he frequently was. Her private life, if she had any, had never interested him. He had always assumed that she just pottered about the house, cooking or planning meals, looking after Lucy, making sure that things were exactly right for him on his return. As they always had been.

Sitting in the car, his hands on the steering-wheel, feeling her presence, smelling her smell, he felt very troubled at having discovered a mystery about the woman who had shared his house, if not his life, for nearly thirty years.

FOUR

When Wednesday came he felt like a young boy going out on his first date.

That morning, standing in front of his mirror, in the cheerless bathroom of the house in Drumcondra where he had a room to rent, he combed his beard morosely.

She won't come, he thought. No way. I'm mad to imagine that there's the slightest chance.

He selected from his meagre wardrobe a white shirt, a pair of grey trousers, a light jacket and black shoes. The shoes were his only pair, a present from his mother, so he had no option but to wear them, despite his aesthetic aversion to black shoes with grey slacks.

As he walked down Kildare Street, he saw no reason to change his mind about the feeling that fate had him by the short and curlies, was somehow pushing him along willy-nilly and that nothing he could do would alter the course of events by one iota.

She wouldn't come, of course. Nobody in her right sense would keep an appointment made with a complete stranger in Bewley's Café, especially with an unprepossessing stranger, who had followed her in the street. An ugly stranger. A man with a face like a crinkled Bluebeard, the sort of face to be seen on the covers of cheap nineteenth century novels in the second-hand stall outside the Dublin Bookshop. A skinny man, an uninteresting man, who talked about the activities of woodlice and beavers in the same breath, not to speak of the same sentence.

Ah well, one could but try to overcome one's limitations.

It was another pleasant day. The streets were full of direct copies of those people who had been there the previous Wednesday, all going about their

30

obscure business. Only their names had been changed, to protect the innocent. He mingled with the crowd. They accepted him into their midst as one of their own. No one challenged him or asked for a means of identification. He revelled in his anonymity as he made his way towards Grafton Street.

It was its usual busy self. He paused at Switzer's window in Wicklow Street where he had paused the week before, but when he looked through the angle of the two windows, the view was different. She wasn't there. A fat lady in a navy-blue coat was in her place, staring hopelessly at the frilly pieces of lingerie in the window. She was like a stand-in for a star who was elsewhere, resting or putting on her make-up. Or sleeping with the producer. But the star was nowhere to be seen.

He looked at his watch. He was right on time, give or take a couple of minutes, so it wouldn't do to be hanging about. He walked the few yards to Bewley's, took his stance just inside the door and watched the customers come and go. He held his blue folder as a man on a blind date might wear an identifying carnation. Even if she had forgotten what *he* looked like, she would surely remember the folder.

Large women, small women, overweight women and thin women, young women and old women and women-in-between swirled and eddied about him as he stood there. Several times he saw green dresses approaching and his heart lifted with his gaze, only to find that there was no matching red-brown hair and green eyes.

Interminable minutes passed, then a quarter-hour. It was hopeless, as he had known it would be. She wasn't coming.

'Ah well,' he said aloud.

There was a light touch on his arm. A beautiful accent fell on his ears.

'Hello, Jim.'

He swung around and met her green eyes. The red-brown hair was piled on her head in a different style from what he remembered, but there was no mistaking the smile. Her dress too was different – it was white with green trimmings. She had a white shoulder bag and white sandals, and she smelt of summer and fresh air.

'Hello, Nora.'

'I'm sorry I'm late.'

'Oh no. Don't even think about it. I was early.'

'Did you imagine I wasn't coming?'

'No. Well, yes. But not because you were late. Which you weren't.'

'I was late.'

'No.'

'If I say I was late, I was late.'

'All right,' he surrendered, hands up, 'but I've been thinking since early this morning that you weren't going to come.'

'I always do what I promise.'

'I have a feeling that you do. But I always anticipate the worst. That's the way I am. It saves me disappointment later.'

She smiled at him.

'You're an odd fish.'

'You don't know the half of it.'

They looked at each other in silence.

'Well? Are you going to buy me that sticky bun?'

'Oh yes. *Yes*.'

As they walked into the restaurant, he didn't know whether to take her arm, or not. In the event, he didn't touch her. He walked to her right and a little behind her, admiring her hair, feeling as happy as a sandboy, whatever that was.

'What's a sandboy?'

'What?'

'A sandboy.'

'I don't know what a sandboy is.'

'That's what I'm as happy as right now.'

Again her smile gleamed at him and it seemed to light the whole restaurant. They didn't speak again until they had selected their sticky buns and found a table as near as possible to the one they had shared a week before. In fact, they didn't speak until they both had stirred and tasted their coffee.

He raised his eyes then and looked at her.

'Well?'

'I shouldn't have come.'

'Why?'

'Just shouldn't. I turned back twice in Nassau Street.'

'Why? Is there an impediment?'

There was a pause. She said nothing, but kept her head lowered, staring at her hands.

'I let you pick me up. I'm a brazen hussy.'

'So was Nora Barnacle.'

'I know. I've been reading about her.'

He was absurdly glad that she had taken the time.

'I'm sorry. I shouldn't have said that. About Nora Barnacle. She was OK. She stuck with a difficult man all her life.'

'I know that too.'

'You're OK as well.'

'Eat your bun.'

They ate in silence for a while. Then she dabbed her mouth with her napkin and faced him, holding up her left hand.

'That first time, I don't know why. Just that morning, coming out, I left it off. It was a sort of an impulse. No real reason behind it. I wasn't coming out to pick up a man.'

'Are you trying to tell me that you're married?'

'Sort of.'

'How can you be "sort of" married? You can't be sort of married.'

She looked at him very seriously.

'Are you married?'

'No. Not even "sort of".'

'Then how could you know anything about it!'

She didn't sound angry, just thoughtful.

'I'm sorry. I shouldn't have been prying.'

'That's right. You shouldn't.'

'I promise it won't happen again.'

'Yourself and your promises! Easy enough for you to give promises that you don't intend to keep.'

'I'll keep this one, I promise.'

'Promises to keep promises. You're some article.'

There was a pause.

'This isn't going the way I intended,' he said.

'What way did you intend it to go?'

'I don't know. Not this way.'

'Would you rather I got up and left?'

'No!'

She was surprised at the passion in his voice.

'Oh my, we *are* getting very narky, aren't we!'

'Yes.'

'Was Joyce narky?'

'Very. But he had a lot to put up with. His sight, for one thing. And he suffered a lot from toothache. And a chronic lack of money.'

'What do *you* have to put up with?'

He thought about that for a long while before he answered.

'Things. There's a tap in my place that won't turn off. And the chap in the next room sings very badly and very loudly all day long. And part of the night. He also tries to hog the bathroom. I have to employ strategies to best him. And I'm cursed with an inadequate intelligence. I know what I want to do, what I want to *think*, but I don't have the equipment to do or think these things. So mostly I have to put up with myself.'

'Pity about you.'

'Indeed. Then there's this beard of mine.' She stared at him. 'I have a lot of trouble keeping it trimmed.'

'Why did you grow it then?'

He told her why he had grown the beard. In a little while the wonder went out of her face, to be supplanted by laughter. The gates of Heaven opened. She *understood*.

'God, you're an eejit.'

He felt his heart become warm in his breast. This was unimaginably *right*.

'Did Joyce have a beard?'

'No. Look, if you wish me to cut off the beard, I'll do it. Would you like that?'

She shook her head.

'I wouldn't recognize you. I'd be liable to pass you in the street.'

'I'll bring a razor and remove it in front of you. Then you'd be in no doubt who was hiding behind it.'

'Ah no, I like your beard. It's part of you.'

'Part of my charm?'

'I wouldn't go so far as to say that, Jim. We'll just say that it was there when I found you and leave it at that.'

He was delighted to hear her use the word 'found' to describe their meeting.

'I have this vision of getting married. I bring the wife home to a very respectable neighbourhood in a small town and carry her over the threshold in full view of all the neighbours. Then, during the night, I shave off the beard and next morning a totally different man comes out of the house and causes everlasting scandal in the valley of the squinting windows. My only regret is that it would have to be a one-off. Unless I used a false beard once a month. But I really don't think I could do that. Whatever may be said about this one, it's the genuine article. And it's mine.'

They laughed so much that their coffee went cold and they had to buy a second cup each. This time she paid. Despite his protests she told him that she *had* to pay and he could see the justice in that.

Later they walked in St Stephen's Green. She suggested it.

'Could we go for a walk?'

'Oh yes. If you're sure?'

'Why wouldn't I be sure?'

'I thought maybe . . .'

'Don't think.'

They walked up Grafton Street together, not touching, but close enough to show they were together. Suddenly it started to feel like a real date.

'Let's go into the Green.'

They crossed the busy road and he touched her elbow lightly as they negotiated the traffic. She didn't pull away, he was glad to notice. But he presumed nothing further.

The Green was full of people sitting on the seats or on the grass, sunning themselves.

'We Irish are a funny lot,' he said. 'We're so surprised when we see a bit of sunshine that we lose the run of ourselves.' He paused. 'We're going to have to talk, you know.'

'I thought we *were* talking.'

'I mean about serious things. About us. Who we are.'

'Why?'

'You know we have to.'

'All right.'

She turned suddenly and slipped her arm through his.

'We'll talk when it's right. Just let's enjoy the sunshine for a minute.'

They found a vacant piece of grass near the duck pond. He put the blue folder down on the ground.

'You can sit on James Joyce,' he said.

'The grass is dry.'

'I don't want to see your white dress getting dirty. And James Augustine will be honoured.'

She sat on the folder. He stretched himself on the grass beside her.

'Was Augustine his middle name?'

'Yes.'

'Sounds like a monk.'

'He was no monk, I can tell you. Though he once did think of becoming a priest.'

'That's hard to imagine.'

'Oh the strangest people *think* of becoming priests. I even thought it myself once. Not for long, mind you.'

'I'll bet.'

They sat for a while without speaking.

'What are we doing here?' she said.

'Looking at the ducks.'

'I mean *really* doing.'

'I know what *I'm* doing.'

'Tell me.'

'I'm doing what Joyce was doing when he went out with Nora Barnacle. I like being with you. Tell you the truth, all week I was thinking that I'd never see this Wednesday, that I wouldn't *live* to see it. Or, if I did, that you wouldn't turn up and that it all would be over. Now I'm here beside you and I'm out of my mind with happiness. And I'm waiting to see what is going to happen. What are *you* doing?'

'I couldn't begin to tell you.'

He looked up at her in surprise. Her hands were tightly clenched and there were tears in her eyes.

'You're crying!'

'No, I'm not!' She said it fiercely, as if she were determined to make it count for herself as much as for him. 'I'm not crying. I've cried enough. I'm done crying. It's just that I don't know what I'm doing. I shouldn't be here. It's wrong.'

'It doesn't feel wrong to me.'

'Nor me. But it *has* to be wrong.'

He didn't know how to respond to that. He put his hand on hers and she didn't push him away. They sat in silence.

Two small girls came to the water's edge with a bag of broken bread pieces and started to throw them to the ducks. The ducks grew wild with excitement, pushing and shoving each other aside, grabbing and gobbling with indecent haste whatever fell within reach of their beaks. The children became as excited as the birds. They jumped up and down and screamed encouragement and abuse at the quarrelling ducks.

'Go on! Go on, you! Leave him alone! Oh you dirty glutton! Stop it!'

'Worse than hooligans at a football match.'

'They're lovely.'

The voracious ducks soon devoured the bread. The two girls gazed disconsolately at the empty bag and then threw it away. They ran off screeching together.

'Mammy, Mammy, can we get more bread?'

'If I was their mother,' he said, 'they'd get a clip on the ear before they got any more bread. And I'd make them pick up the empty bag.'

'Schoolteacher.'

'It's in my genes.'

'Don't you like children?'

'I'm neutral. Someday maybe when I have my own, I'll get besotted with them. I've seen it happen to otherwise sensible men. But at the moment I can take them or leave them.'

'Aren't you the lucky man!'

'Am I?'

'No ties. Nothing to bother you all day long. Making your own decisions without having to get permission from anyone else. Traipsing around the city in the middle of the day and following women through the streets when the fancy takes you.'

'It's a great life.'

'There you go again.'

'Are we having a row?'

'I don't know.' She stood up suddenly. 'Yes, we're having a row.'

He stood up too.

'Our first lovers' tiff.'

'Oh stop it. We're not lovers. We're just two strangers who've had a cup of coffee together.'

'Two cups. Three, if you count last week. And they were mugs, which probably counts as six.'

'Don't you ever talk seriously about anything?'

'Are we talking seriously at long last? Hooray for that.'

She turned and walked off along the path. He picked up his folder and followed her. When he caught up with her, he laid a restraining hand on her arm. She didn't shake him off, as he had expected she would, but instead stopped and faced him.

'Will you take me somewhere connected with Joyce?'

He was surprised at the sudden change in her. Although she was still breathing heavily, her face was composed.

'All Dublin is connected with Joyce,' he said. 'All these streets. He was at university over there. He went to school in Belvedere College in Denmark Street. That's only up a bit from the Parnell Monument at the end of O'Connell Street. He once managed a cinema in Mary Street. It was called the Volta. Leopold Bloom lived in Eccles Street.'

'That's enough,' she said. 'Could you take me out to where they spent their first date?'

'Ringsend?'

'That's the place.'

'We'll take a bus.'

'No. I want to walk. Like Jim and Nora.'

FIVE

Robert McGuinness lay back on the pillow and stared at the ceiling. Sunlight streamed in through the tall windows framing the sea, flooding the bedroom with golden lustre. It was a very pleasant room elegantly furnished in yellow and white. Orla Corr had supervised the decoration. She had impeccable taste. And he, Robert, had the money that allowed her to indulge her impeccable taste. A fair enough bargain.

He looked at her as she lay in sleep beside him, the golden hair strewn across the pillow, one arm flung above her head, one naked breast lying in soft luminous beauty where the duvet had fallen aside. Perfection. Myles Cassidy had chosen well when he chose Orla Corr. It was a pity that subsequent events had forced Robert to sack Myles, with his dull face and ponderous way of speaking, but even a fool like Myles can know too much. Robert had no intention of ever allowing an employee to gain a position from which he might do harm. Not that Myles had ever threatened harm to Robert. Merely having the potential was enough.

He remembered with distaste how Myles had pleaded with him not to sack him, whining about his wife and family, and reminding Robert that he had spent the better part of his life with ORMAX. The man had no dignity.

Robert rose from the bed and walked naked to the window. The view across Scotsman's Bay to Dún Laoghaire Harbour and the smudged coastline of Dublin to the west and Howth Head to the north had its own peculiar charm. The sea was calm and very blue. Some little boats already on the water looked innocently quaint. The white shoebox of the car ferry, newly arrived from Holyhead, manoeuvred its cumbersome bulk within the harbour as it prepared to dock. A lone white-headed man, brown in body and clad in a skimpy pair of undershorts, jogged patiently down the East Pier. His familiar presence was a reassurance that all was right with the world.

Robert sighed with satisfaction. Now that Babs was safely tucked in her cosy grave, it would soon be possible (after a respectable period of mourning, of course) to bring Orla in as mistress of Twin Cedars. Sleeping in the penthouse was no punishment, but it did entail a certain amount of irritating subterfuge and discretion, and he hated being forced to lie to people and to risk being found out. Leaving it would avoid the possibility of humiliation. It would also save him the arm and a leg he was at present paying in rent for the place. Of course, he didn't begrudge it to Orla Corr, but economics were economics. Only a fool would continue to shell out so much money on an avoidable expense.

He looked at himself in the sliding mirrors of the wardrobe. His big white face was still handsome enough and the thick black hair still showed no sign of thinning as it curled across his forehead. Turning himself sideways, he hefted his belly in his two hands. Pudgy, no doubt about it. Too pudgy. The doctor had said so, when Robert had first gone to enquire about the pain in his arm. Angina doesn't like excessive weight. Since then he had been trying to lose a few pounds, but with indifferent results. Below his belly his limp penis lay quiet and docile between his hairy thighs. Nothing much wrong with *that*. It had been well-satisfied and now wished for nothing more than the chance to rest.

He heard a stirring from the bed.

'Oh? You're up, darling?'

'I'll have to go in to the office today.'

'Surely you can take another day or two?'

'I have things to do.'

'There was nothing important in the diary.'

'I have to solve this bloody car problem.'

'Oh *that!*'

'That! If I can't have the sale called off, I suppose the only thing I can do is buy the damn thing myself.'

'Why bother about it at all?'

'Because it was Babs's car.' She looked at him with her big blue eyes. Was there a flicker of amusement in them? He hadn't told her about the mileage on the Morris. In fact, he had kept that disturbing information strictly to himself. Should he tell her now, or let her go on thinking that he was merely

fussing about an old car? 'I'm not entirely without a heart, Orla. I don't want
any Tom, Dick, or Harry driving around in it. So I've decided to buy it myself.
First thing this morning I'll ring that Neanderthal solicitor and tell her. In fact,
I'll do it right now.'

'It's only seven, Robert. Solicitors don't get out of bed till the streets are
well aired.'

'Well, I'll do it when I get to the office.'

'If you must, you must. Do you want *me* to go in today?'

'Not unless you want to.'

She yawned lazily and swung her long slim legs out of the bed. He gazed
admiringly at her. A fine-looking woman. Intelligent too. He had been lucky
to get her. No wonder he had turned away from poor mutilated Babs to this
golden, tanned beauty. Any red-blooded man would have done the same. Not
that Orla Corr had been the first infidelity in his life, but she was the first that
had counted for anything more than a bit of bustle and sweat in a bed.

They had been lovers for almost eight years now and the physical passion
showed no sign of diminishing. Not on his side, anyway. And she too seemed
satisfied with their relationship. Moreover, she understood him and his business
affairs, and had an encyclopaedic knowledge of all the important contacts in
his life. She was a very valuable asset indeed.

Robert had carefully kept the liaison secret from everyone else, especially
from Babs, because he had not wished to hurt her. He liked to think that he
was not a cruel man. Babs had never known about Orla, she had gone to her
grave sweetly ignorant of the duplicity of the man she had worshipped all her
married life. He was glad that he had done that much at least for her.

And duplicity was too strong a word for what he had done. God dammit,
he had nurtured and coddled Babs for as long as he could have been expected
to. Longer, in fact. No man could have done more. His mother had been right
when she had objected to the marriage. She had foreseen that his inevitable
rise in the world would make an ignorant country girl more unsuitable as a
wife with every passing year. No matter what he had done to try to train Babs
in the ways of society, she had never come up to scratch. In fact, her death had
been a blessed release for her, not only from her physical suffering, but also
from the mental strain of trying to be what she could never be.

Orla walked across the cream coloured carpet. She put her arms around his
neck and her naked body against his.

'I think I'd like a day off, if it's all the same to you, darling.' She nuzzled his neck. 'Why don't you stay here with me?' His body hardened under her caress and she smiled. 'I think somebody else would like to stay too.'

'The minister may call today,' he said, without conviction.

She bent her head to look into his face.

'Who? Which minister?'

'Kerrigan.'

'Did he make an appointment?'

'No, I hear a whisper in the wind.'

'Isn't he still in Strasbourg? That was his excuse for missing the funeral.'

'He's due home today. So I expect he'll be on the blower to pay his respects.'

'Do you think he'll have any news?'

'Who knows. But it'll come eventually, don't you worry. That bugger owes me too much to shove me around for much longer.'

'You really want the job, don't you?'

'I want it.'

And he did. He wanted the Gallery more than he had ever wanted anything else. It was not the money. He had more than enough money to do him for the rest of his life – and beyond, if what the canon said was anything to go by. 'Make friends of the Mammon of Iniquity, Robert, old son, and they will receive you into everlasting dwellings.' Finnegan was always coming out with some such nonsense. 'Give, give, old son, to the poor and to the Church, until it hurts; and God will not be outdone in generosity.' Robert had no intention of being quite so generous with his money on such a tenuous premise, but he gave a reasonable percentage to charity, especially when it was tax deductible, and he presumed that, if there was a God and there was any justice in the world, he would get some recompense for spreading the slush around.

No, it wasn't the money. It was the prestige, the international recognition such an appointment would bring him, the sheer *stature*. Papal knighthoods were all right in their way and, though he hadn't received one yet, he reckoned that it was only a matter of time. However, entrée to the artistic dining-rooms of Europe would be a horse of quite a different colour.

He clutched Orla to his now fully tumescent body and vowed silently that she would one day share that honour with him. As she took him by the hand, he made no protest.

Later, she remained in bed, while Robert showered and dressed. He drank some coffee and ate a slice of toast. When he looked into the bedroom to enquire if she wanted breakfast, he found that she had fallen asleep again. He left the apartment quietly, so as not to waken her, or to signal his going to the other occupants of the block. The Volvo was waiting in the underground garage and he moved it out with the minimum of noise.

He drove citywards along the coast road through the burgeoning sunshine and then across the East Link Bridge to the edge of the Liffey in the heart of Dublin. The ORMAX Tower stood cheek by jowl with the Irish Financial Centre, matching it in imposing splendour. The sun continued to shine on the city as he parked his car in the private car-park.

The ORMAX staff were surprised to see him back so soon after the funeral, though they knew him to be a man devoted to his work, who spent as little time as possible away from his desk. For his part he noted with satisfaction that no one had taken the day off on the chance that he might not turn up. The junior clerks respectfully hid their heads as he passed through to his private office, but some of the more senior personnel rose to shake his hand. He acknowledged their greetings and their renewed condolences. Robert prided himself on being an approachable employer. Any one of his staff could speak to him, provided he had the time to spare.

Seated at his desk, with the vast panorama of the city stretched before him, from the yellow Liffey beneath his feet to the distant blue-black shoulders of the Dublin mountains, he called through to his secretary. There were no messages for him, according to Delia Reed, whose job it was to monitor such things in Orla's absence. This annoyed him. He hoped that Kerrigan wasn't dragging his feet on the Gallery job.

He rang Hanley and Patterson, Solicitors, in Leeson Street. Her hateful voice came loudly in his ear.

'Hanley and Patterson. Kate Hanley speaking.'

'This is Robert McGuinness.'

The minimal warmth in her voice fell several degrees.

'Yes, Mr McGuinness. What can I do for you?'

'About my wife's car. My late wife's car. I do *not* wish to have it sold.'

'I'm afraid there is nothing I can do about that, Mr McGuinness.'

'You're not listening to me, Miss Hanley. I am telling you now not to sell the car.'

'I *am* listening, Mr McGuinness. But the car isn't yours. Mrs McGuinness didn't leave it to you in her will. Her instructions were quite explicit. I have no power to alter them in the slightest.'

There was malicious satisfaction dripping from every syllable. He controlled himself with difficulty.

'Very well. If that is the attitude you're taking, we'll do it another way. I wish to put in an offer for the car myself.'

'There is a reserve on it, remember.'

'Whatever that reserve is, I'll meet it.'

'You don't understand, Mr McGuinness. The reserve has nothing to do with money. The reserve is a special object.'

'What *special* object?'

'I can't tell you that.'

'What the hell do you mean?'

'There is no point in shouting at me, Mr McGuinness. I am merely following my client's precise instructions.'

'What object is required to buy the car?'

'*You* haven't been listening to *me*, Mr McGuinness. I'm not at liberty to divulge the nature of the object required.'

'Do *you* know what it is?'

'Of course.'

'Then tell me!'

'No.'

'God dammit—'

'Please stop trying to bully me, Mr McGuinness. My hands are tied on the matter. Whoever has the object will know what it is, so Mrs McGuinness told us. As *you* obviously don't know the nature of the object, it is clear to me that you are not the person to whom Mrs McGuinness wished to sell the car. I hope that is clear to you too?'

'Go to hell,' snarled Robert, slamming down the phone. 'Shag off,' he shouted to the silent office in which he sat. 'Damn you, damn you. And damn your partner too!'

There was a discreet knock on his office door.

'What?'

Delia Reid put her head into the room.

'Well, what do you want?'

'I thought I heard you shout, Mr McGuinness.'

'Do I usually shout for you when I want you? Do I?' His face was livid with anger, but his voice was soft. 'This button on my desk is for calling you. I press it and I speak – *speak* – into this gadget when I want you. I don't shout. Am I right?'

'Yes, Mr McGuinness. I'm sorry.'

When Delia Reid had gone, Robert sat glowering for some time.

What the devil had Babs been up to, wanting to have the car sold after her death? Why had she sent for that dreadful Hanley woman in the first place? Why had she kept the whole thing secret from *him*?

What was she trying to do to him!

He had been turning the matter over in his head all the weekend and the more he thought about it the stranger it all seemed. Babs had never deceived him in her life. She would never even have thought of doing such a thing. Not the woman he knew. Not the *Babs* he knew.

But who *was* the Babs he knew?

He had casually asked Mrs Kirwan if Babs had used her car much over the years and had been disturbed to hear that she had made regular trips down the country to visit her friends and relations. The only relations of Babs that Robert was aware of were some cousins in Achill that she didn't much care for and would certainly not have visited regularly, if at all.

The thought that there might be another, *unknown* Babs caused the pain in his arm to grow more acute. He reached into his pocket, took out the little pump and sprayed glyceryl trinitrate under his tongue.

SIX

When they reached the drawbridge on Ringsend Road, he stopped to point out the view towards the south-west, across the little canal harbour with its backdrop of the sunny Dublin mountains.

'Somebody once said that it was a bit like Venice,' he said, 'but I think the operative word is *bit*. The only *bit* of Canaletto here is the canal.'

'It's nice all the same.'

'Yes. But that's only because it's a sunny day and I'm here with you.'

They stood in silence for a moment.

'You must think I'm stupid, Jim.'

'Good Lord, no. I never follow stupid women in the street.'

'You must. A sort of a culchie eejit with turf mould in my ears.'

'No. I can't see anything stupid about you, except that you're here with me.'

'Shut up a minute, will you. Just look at me.'

'I could look at you all day long.'

'Ah Jim, stop it! Here I am seven years in the city and I still don't really know anything about it.'

'Seven years?'

'You've shown me this and you've pointed out that, and it's all new to me. I'm like a real thick of a tourist nodding my head like an almighty gawm. Do you want to know something about me?'

'I'd like to know everything about you.'

'No, you can't.'

'I'm willing to live off scraps, if it'll guarantee that you'll keep meeting me.'

'I can't even guarantee that much.'

'Then tell me what you can.'

'I come from Galway, but you already know that. I've been living in Dublin for seven years; since I got married. I'm twenty-four years old.'

'You were married at seventeen?'

She started to walk again. He fell into step beside her. She took his arm, which pleased him inordinately. It felt right.

'I don't get out very much. Well, I didn't. It never seemed worthwhile going out. I had the house to look after and it took up most of every day. Last week was very unusual, me to be wandering around town, waiting to be picked up by any Tom, Dick or Harry who happened to be passing the way. This week is even more unusual.'

'For me too.'

The pressure on his arm was very comforting.

'Have you no friends?'

'There's a married woman lives a few doors from me I meet in the shops. We often have a chat. And a girl called Kate I bumped into in the library. I like her. She comes round for a cuppa tea sometimes when my husband's away. She's going in for the law. She's the one was with me last week when you started following me.'

'I never saw a bit of her.'

'There's nobody else really. It's probably my own fault not getting out more. All this is boring you, isn't it?'

'I don't find it a bit boring. Go on.'

'There isn't anything else.'

'That can't be all your life – two girlfriends and a cuppa tea when your man's out.'

'I wish I could tell you more. I'd like to tell you all about me. I'd like you to know every little thing about me.' She paused. 'You believe that, don't you?'

'I believe you.'

'I'd like to be able to say whatever it was that Nora said to Joyce on their first date. I really would. But I can't.'

He smiled at the idea.

'She probably didn't say very much that night. Probably didn't have a chance to get a word in. *He* was the talker. And don't forget they spent a lot of their time having a bit of a hoult.'

'Well, *we're* not having a bit of a hoult. So you'll have to do the talking for the two of us.'

'OK. I'm twenty-three.'

'Ah, God, you're only a babbie!'

'Quiet. I'm Dublin born and bred. I have a sister and a brother. Both now married. I'm the youngest. My parents live in a little town in Mayo.'

'Mayo? Where in Mayo?'

'A one-horse place called Maaclee.'

'I don't believe it!'

'Oh it exists all right. I've been there.'

'I *know* it,' she laughed. 'I *know* Maaclee!'

'Nobody knows Maaclee except the few people who live there.'

'I passed through it with my da once. He was going to buy a cow at a fair in Castlebar and he took me with him. He got a lend of an oul rickety lorry from a friend of his. I must've been about nine. I got an ice-cream cone in the little shop beside the church. It had a red front. The name over the window was Molloy. Right?'

'One hundred per cent. It's still there.'

'I remembered that ice-cream for ages afterwards. Not that I didn't often get an ice-cream. Well, if the truth be told, I *didn't* often get an ice-cream. But somehow, that day, being all the way up there with my da on my own made it stick in my mind.'

'Do *you* have brothers and sisters?'

'I was the only one in the litter. My Ma died when I was a toddler. And now my da is gone too.'

'I'm sorry. I'll lend you mine, if you like. He's still hale and hearty.'

'Is he *from* Maaclee?'

'No. But his grandmother came from around there, and Dad decided to return to the place when he retired. A sort of a sentimental journey back down to his roots. Or up the family tree. Whichever you like. I thought it would take only a couple of months in the sticks to drive him back to the city, but he seems to like it, solitude and all. Mind you, there's a nice lake for fishing in.'

'I saw the lake when we were going by. What about your mother? Does she like it there?'

'Oh she does whatever Dad says.'

'What was he?'

'A teacher.'

'That explains it.'

'Explains what?'

'Why your mother follows him about like a lamb. It wouldn't be me, I can tell you.'

'Don't worry, I won't ask you to.'

'You won't get the chance.'

It was some time before either of them spoke again. They walked along Bridge Street and turned right into Irishtown.

'It must have been somewhere around here,' he said.

'What?'

'That Joyce and Nora came that night.'

'It doesn't look very much now, does it? I mean, to take a girl on your first date?'

'It was seventy-two years ago. I suppose it was different then. Anyway, it was dark and they must have found a nook for themselves. You know what Kavanagh says?'

'What?'

' "Gods make their own importance". Dates do the same. Bewley's will always be important to me now.'

'Yes. Me too.'

'I'm glad to hear that. And I'll go down to Maaclee and look at Molloy's shop with the red front and think of a little girl with red hair dribbling ice-cream down her chin.'

'Disgusting!'

'Beautiful. You in any pose at all.'

'You're out of your tiny.'

But she was pleased, he could see that. Her face when she bent to blush was the prettiest thing he had ever seen in all his born days. He wanted to put out his hand to touch her cheek and he knew that she wouldn't mind if he did, but he held himself back. When that came, it would have to be somewhere private, not out here in the public street, with people walking and cars going by.

'Let's walk on down to Sandymount Strand.'

'*Ulysses*.'

He stopped to look at her.

'Don't tell me you've read the book?'

'Don't *you* sound so surprised! I *can* read and write. Even big words like marmalade. No, I didn't read it. They say it's very hard. I got a book about Joyce in the library, that's all. And it mentioned Sandymount Strand. So I just thought I'd show off my superior knowledge to impress you. I'm really for the fairies. My Da used to tell me I was a born liar.'

'No.'

'Oh I was. As a kid I was forever making up stories about all sorts of people. A born liar.'

'Tell me about your "sort of" marriage.'

'No.'

'Why not?'

'You said you wouldn't pry. Anyway, hearing about it wouldn't do you any good.'

'I want to. Make it up, if you have to. I won't mind.'

'I don't have to make it up. It's real, Jim. There's no iffing or butting about it. I'm married. Before God and the law, as they say. That's why today is going to have to be our last day together.'

'Our last day? Ah no, don't say that! We've only met, for God's sake.'

'It isn't right to be taking up your time like this, with nothing in it for you in the heel of the hunt.'

'Look.' He put his face close to hers. 'Let me be the judge of that. Let me decide whether you're wasting my time or not. I've got loads of time. I could spend it all just walking along here with you. I wouldn't ask for anything more than just this.'

'Of course you would.'

'No!'

'You wouldn't be natural if you didn't. And I wouldn't be natural if I didn't want you to. But, you see, it's no good. There's no end to it. No happy end, anyway. I'm married and I'll stay married, and you'd be better off going and finding yourself another woman who wouldn't be coming your way with a heap of baggage on her back.'

'I'll carry your baggage for you, if you'll let me.'

'You couldn't. And I wouldn't let you.'

'Please.'

'No!'

They became aware that they were standing very close together on the pavement and were beginning to attract curious looks from those passers-by who had to circumnavigate them.

'We'd better move on before they arrest us,' he said.

As they resumed walking, she slipped her arm again in his, just as if they had been married for years and had had a bit of a spat which didn't affect their relationship in any way. At least, that's what he thought. He wondered what she was thinking.

After a while she spoke.

'I'm married all right. But he doesn't love me. That's the pure holy all of it. He probably never did love me, though I used to think he did. It's not his fault he doesn't love me. It must be something in *me*.'

'Oh for God's sake!'

'No, listen. I'm not just feeling sorry for myself, or belittling myself. I'm just telling the plain God's truth. He's not a bad man. He doesn't beat me, or anything like that. He just doesn't love me, no more and no less.'

'He must be mad not to love you.'

'That's only *you* talking! He's not mad. He's maybe too sane.'

'Does he have other women?'

'I don't know. Yes, I *do* know. He does sometimes. I usen't to think so, because he's so religious. But I know now he does. I found some things. You know what I mean. That's when I knew for sure. Apart from that, he's OK. He keeps me well, keeps the house well. There's no shortage of money. And I do my best for him. But he doesn't love me.'

'I don't understand any of this.'

'I told you it would do you no good asking me.'

'If he doesn't love you, you could always leave him.'

'No.'

The finality of it crushed him momentarily. He could feel himself droop. She tightened her hold on his arm, as if to hold him up.

'How could I possibly leave him? Where could I go? I've got no family to run home to.'

'You could always come and live with me.'

'Talk sense, boy.'

After a while she added, 'This will have to be our last day, Jim. Let's make it a good one. We'll go to Sandymount Strand. And then maybe afterwards you can take me out to Sandycove to see Joyce's Tower.'

'Afterwards? You mean, you're not running off the way you did last Wednesday?'

'I can stay as long as I like, if that's what you want. Is that what you want?'

'Oh yes, I *want.*'

'Well, then, come on.'

'But what about. . . ? I mean, won't there be anyone looking for you?'

'Who'd be looking for me? He's away to Paris, or somewhere. He often goes away on business. All I know is he won't be back tonight. Maybe not even tomorrow. That's the way of him. Coming and going, trying to make more money.'

'Are there no children?'

'No children. Don't even talk about children.' She pulled him along by his arm. 'Oh God, this is a lovely day, isn't it? Look at that sea.'

He allowed her to lead him. As they walked she became very animated, chattering away about all sorts of inconsequential things. When they passed a van selling ice-cream, she made him buy her a cone. He felt lost and despairing, but at the same time full of enjoyment that this strange adventure was happening to him.

They walked on Sandymount Strand. They did more – they *ran* on Sandymount Strand. He discovered that she liked to run. The moment they could gain access to the beach, she was off like a child, her skirt flapping about her knees, her strong legs flashing in the golden light of the sun. He followed as best he could, holding his blue folder under his arm, concentrating on the red-brown hair bobbing in front of him, catching the excitement that emanated so vividly from her that he could almost see it.

She took off her white sandals and paddled her feet in the water. His black shoes and socks were heavy by comparison, but he bravely bared his feet and trundled into the waves after her. The cold of the water took his breath away. She screeched and ran to kick water at him. He backed away in panic, holding his shoes in one hand and the folder in the other.

'Have pity on an old man!'

'Will you listen to him! What sort of a cissy are you at all!'

He fled and she pursued him, both of them laughing as if they had only just discovered how to do it. A great transformation seemed to have occurred in the entire day. Everything was suddenly different.

Later they sat on the sand together and let their feet dry in the sun. He was overwhelmed at how straight and well formed her tiny feet were. Not a bit like Gerty McDowell's.

'Why the sigh?'

'I was thinking about poor Gerty McDowell.'

'Who?'

He took a tattered paperback from his folder. It was a copy of *Ulysses*, well thumbed and dog-eared.

'Would you like me to read to you the bit about Sandymount Strand?'

'Yes, please.'

So he read some of the story of Gerty McDowell and Leopold Bloom, how she had sat on a rock showing off her legs while he looked at her. They had played out their little drama together in almost this very spot, he told her, with the Martello Tower over there, the church there, the sound of sacred singing, the pictures in Gerty's head, the bell ringing out as the Host was raised in benediction over the congregation and the surrounding community. And then came the fireworks and the lights in the sky and the Roman candle bursting over their heads. And the stillness of the end, as Gerty limped off down the strand and Bloom watched her go, realizing her plight and his lack of worth in the whole episode.

She listened very carefully, saying nothing until he had finished.

'God love the poor girl, showing off her knickers like that! She must've been desperate for a bit of notice.'

'Well, you have to remember that she was crippled and she felt in her heart that she would never get a man to love her. And what was going on in her head was a lot different from what *he* was thinking about.'

'He wasn't only *thinking*. He was *doing*. He was crippled too, wasn't he? In his own way.'

'We're all crippled in our own way.'

'God, aren't we getting very deep all of a sudden.'

'I'm sorry about that. In time you'll get used to listening to me waffle.'

'I've told you this is going to be our last day.'

'I'm hoping you'll change your mind before the day is out.'

'Not a hope.'

She lay back on the sand. Before her head touched the ground he gently slipped his folder under it. She smiled at this, but kept her eyes closed. He lay down beside her, locking his hands behind his head, and stared up at the sky.

This is the strangest day I have ever experienced, he thought. Here I am lying on Sandymount Strand with a married woman. Technically, I could be committing adultery. Certainly in my heart I'm committing adultery. Thinking things. Bad thoughts about her body. Impure thoughts. A mortal sin. That's what I learned at school, anyway. Every sin of impurity is a mortal sin, and adultery is the impurity of impurities. I'm damned. But I don't care. She's a strange woman. This is only my second time to meet her and yet I feel that I've known her for ages. I could lie here for the rest of my life and never want for anything else. If Heaven really exists then it must be something like this. Contentment. That's what it is. Resting in the Lord. Resting in Nora.

'Don't be bloody stupid,' he said aloud.

'Jim.'

He raised himself on his elbow to look at her.

'Yes, Nora.'

'What are you thinking about?'

He told her, but left out the bit about committing adultery, technically or otherwise. He stared at her closed eyes all the while. Although she didn't open her eyes, she blushed as if she could feel his gaze on her face.

'That's nice. The last bit of it, anyway. Do I bring you contentment?'

'Contentment and disturbance at one and the same time. What am I going to do tomorrow and the day after that, when you've disappeared out of my life?'

'Offer it up for the holy souls in purgatory.'

Then she sat up suddenly and looked at him, her face full of remorse.

'I'm sorry. I shouldn't have said that, Jim. But you haven't known me the length of a wet Sunday yet and you'll forget all about me just as soon as I'm out of your sight.'

'I won't forget you. I know I'll never forget you. Or this day in this place. Never as long as I live.'

She put her hand on his cheek and he took it in his own, pressing it to himself.

'You're a sweet boy. And I know I'll never forget you either. But look, if we have only this day—'

'We could have many more, if you would—'

'We can't! We *can't*, Jim. So let's make the most of what's left of it. Come on, put your shoes on.'

She slipped into her sandals. He struggled with his laces, hating his black shoes, wishing he were as free and mobile as she seemed to be.

'Now, listen to me,' she said. 'This is what we're going to do and I don't want any arguments from you. Right?'

'Whatever.'

'We're going to Dún Laoghaire and I'm going to buy us something to eat. No, don't even think of arguing with me. I'm starving. And it's my treat. I've got the money to pay for it.'

'I've got money too.'

But all he had in his pocket was a fiver and some loose change. Coffee and sticky-bun money. He hadn't reckoned on taking her out to dinner.

'Maybe you have and maybe you haven't, but it doesn't matter anyway. This is my treat. Either that or I leave you now and we go our separate ways. So make up your mind.'

'All right. But you're making me feel like a kept man.'

'Enjoy it while you can.'

SEVEN

Robert McGuinness met Brigid Mary Needham in July 1969 at a dance in Salthill in Galway. Robert was twenty at the time and worked for VKI, an investment firm run by a Vincent Kenny and Son. That summer he went with Joe Doolin, a fellow worker, to Galway for the races. They hadn't much money in their pockets when they left Dublin and had even less after a couple of days spent backing the wrong horses. The weather was windy and wet and the boarding-house they were staying in left a lot to be desired.

Inevitably they fell out. Joe Doolin arrived back one night flushed with drink and lust and told Robert that he had the solution to all their financial problems. He had picked up two beautiful American girls who were living in a caravan on the campsite at Barna. Joe's one was called Dee and the other one, designated by Joe as Robert's, was Cathy. He wanted Robert to join in and make up a foursome.

'They're loaded, Bobbie. Bagsful of money. Bloody lovely dollars. We can live it up for the rest of the week and we won't have to put our hands in our pockets. And they're mad for a ride! They want me to go and stay with them in the van. That means you too. It sleeps four. Think of it – no more staying in this poxy kip. And I tell you again – they're crazy for it. We can have *everything* you've ever dreamed about. *And* get paid for it.'

Robert, who hated to be called 'Bobbie', refused. In the first place, he hadn't seen the Americans yet and had only Joe's word for it that they were beauties, especially the one allocated to him. In the second place, he wasn't anxious to get involved with a couple of wild ones from a distant land, who might have odd sexual habits that he knew nothing about. In the third place he was fed-up with Joe's company anyway.

His refusal annoyed Joe.

'God, you're a terrible stick! Will you not even come out and give it a try! Come on, for God's sake. Just one night. If you don't like her by then you can call it off. The least you can get is a good ride.'

'I don't want a good ride.'

'Every normal man wants a good ride.'

'I'm not into that sort of thing.'

Joe was furious.

'You're not *normal*, then! God, what *are* you? A *queer?*'

'I'll forget you said that.'

'You're a prissy bloody prude. A holy bloody Mary. I don't know why I ever bothered coming to Galway with you.'

Next day Joe left the boarding-house and took all his belongings with him. They didn't see each other for the rest of the holiday.

Later that evening Robert found himself at a loose end in Salthill. He was wandering around morosely, dodging the frequent showers, when he was attracted by the sound of music. He followed a steady stream of people into a ballroom.

It was a crowded place, full of noise and thick with cigarette smoke. A crystal ball hung from the ceiling, flashing its reflected light over the dancers. A showband in brightly coloured costumes pranced about on the stage and dispensed loud music. It was not the sort of place Robert usually frequented. All that kept him in the hall was a reluctance to waste the price of the entrance ticket.

And then he noticed one particular girl.

She had red hair and she was dancing with another female, a jiving dance with a lot of twisting and turning. He admired her quick assured movements and the swing of her blue skirt, and he decided he would ask her for the next dance.

Because there were far more females than males present – most of the men were still in the pub getting their courage up – she was glad to see him. They danced a slow foxtrot, not his particular *forte*, nothing connected with dancing was his *forte*, but he steered her through the crowd without doing any spectacular damage to her shoes. She felt light and small in his arms. And she sang along to the music.

For years afterwards, Babs always spoke of the song *Wonderful World*, which she said was the first tune they had danced to. Robert couldn't remember that. There was a lot going on in the world at the time. Apollo 11 landed on the moon that same month and Neil Armstrong made his famous gaffe about big and small steps and leaps for man and mankind. There was also the explosion of violence in Northern Ireland that was destined to grow and continue for the next thirty years. Those were the important things – not tunes at dances.

But Babs remembered the songs that the band played. *Gentle on My Mind, Those Were the Days, Release Me, The Last Waltz*. She remembered especially *Wonderful World*, because it was the first tune they had danced to. She sang it as if it were somehow very precious.

Robert found himself attracted to Brigid Mary Needham. She was small, pretty enough and very lively. She aroused in him a pleasant sort of lust, easy to control and, therefore, easy to indulge in. They danced several times together that night. She was cheerful and laughed a lot, though Robert didn't find her particularly bright in the upper storey. But that suited him well; he wasn't in the business of taking up with someone smarter than himself. They agreed to meet again the following evening.

Next day the weather had improved, so they went for a walk. His interest in her increased when she told him she was the only child of her widower father and lived with him on their small farm. A few days later she took Robert home to Ballinkrale on the outskirts of Galway, where she had been born and reared. He met Ben Needham, a frail old man who peered myopically at him and bade him welcome. Robert took great care to ensure that they got along well together, by making himself as agreeable as possible and by evincing great interest in Ben's life. He was good at that sort of thing, because it was part of his business technique.

Ben showed him around the fifty acres of the farm and Robert decided that here was a piece of property with the potential to become very valuable at some future date.

During the rest of his holiday he went out a lot with Babs. It didn't cost him much. In the interests of female equality, he allowed her to pay her own way, which she was anxious to do. She was a very innocent girl, so there was no possibility of sexual hanky-panky between them, but then Robert wasn't seeking any. It was a time in his life when he was being ostentatiously moral, diligently performing his religious duties and ingratiating himself with the clergy.

At the end of the holiday, he parted from Babs without too much regret, though they did promise to write to each other. Well, she said she would write and he more or less agreed to answer any letter she liked to send.

Back in Dublin, Robert made some discreet enquiries in VKI about development possibilities in the Galway area, what planning applications had been made and by whom and so on, storing away the information thus gained in the corner of his mind for possible future attention. In the meantime, he maintained a desultory correspondence with Babs, though he didn't think much of her rather chaotic letters. Trying to get on in VKI and ferreting around for useful connections in the property world left him with little time for romantic exchanges with a girl living on the other side of the country. He was seriously contemplating calling the whole thing off, when her letter arrived at the end of August telling him of the death of her father.

Because he had a client to see in Galway, he went to the funeral.

Babs was tearful and vulnerable, a tiny figure in her mourning black, and something stirred within him, a protective feeling, fatherly almost, though still mixed with the rather pleasant lust. He put his arms around and told her not to worry anymore, that he was here now to take care of her. Relatives and neighbours, gathered at the graveside, were extravagantly pleased and gratified to see that 'little Babs' had someone from Dublin to look after her, especially such a fine-looking, plump young man in a lovely grey suit driving an expensive car. (Robert neglected to tell them that the car belonged to VKI and that he had merely borrowed it through the good offices of his immediate superior, whom he had had the good fortune to catch with his hand up the skirt of one of the typists.) He relished the affection and hospitality shown to him by all those concerned, most of whom presumed that this was an altar-bound love match. By the end of the day, he was more than halfway towards accepting that presumption as fact.

After the burial, there was a reception in the Needham house in Ballinkrale for those special friends who had attended the funeral. The small house was crowded and there was plenty to eat and drink. Before he died, Ben Needham had taken great care to set aside sufficient money to ensure that he wouldn't be disgraced in front of his neighbours by neglecting to look after them properly. As the afternoon passed, the gathering turned into a party, as was usual on such occasions, and people began singing songs and telling stories.

Some relatives of Babs had come from Achill Island to see their cousin safely off on his journey to the next world and also to discover what Ben's will said about the future of his piece of land. One man in particular, a tall, dour character called Arthur, persisted in trying to get Babs into serious conversation on the subject. She spent most of the evening dodging him.

Eventually, she took Robert by the arm and asked him to come out for a breath of air. In the cool of the evening, as they strolled together from the house and across the fields of the Needham farm, Babs told him that she had never seen the Arthur character before in her life and that it was very funny how people like that always turned up whenever there was property to be disposed of.

'Where there's a will there's a relative,' said Robert. 'Is he a genuine cousin?'

'Everybody says he is, so I suppose he must be. But all he's interested in is the bit of land.'

'What's going to happen to the farm?'

'What do you mean?' There was real surprise in Babs's voice. 'I'm going to keep it, of course.'

'You mean it's all yours?'

'Of course. Who else's?'

Standing there surrounded by all the land, which seemed huge to his city eyes, Robert, moved by drink and the feeling of self-importance induced by the adulation of the neighbours and friends, not to speak of a surge of the pleasant lust, proposed on the spot. Babs sealed her acceptance with the first really passionate kiss they had ever shared.

That was a turning point in Robert's life.

When they broke the news to the people gathered in the house, the general joy was unconfined, apart from the Achill Island relatives, especially Arthur. *They* left almost immediately after the announcement, but not before Arthur took the newly engaged man aside and, putting his face up unpleasantly close to Robert's, hissed, 'I'm on to you, you bloody fat little city sleeveen!'

Robert hissed back, 'Shag off, you long culchie git!'

He was now irrevocably committed.

They married in October of the same year in the little church of Ballinkrale, a stone's throw from the Needham house. Even though Rose McGuinness did not at all approve of her eldest son's throwing himself away on some simple, no doubt uneducated, little country girl, Martin, his father, thought it was a smart move on Robert's part, and said so.

'Property, Rose, that's what the boy's after. Property. And more luck to him. Nothing like a few acres of muck in this country to get you a bit of respect. And that girl's all right. She'll be a good wife. Most good wives are a bit thick. You wait and see.'

Rose gave him a caustic look, but decided against open warfare over this reference to the correlation between thickness and wifely excellence.

On her wedding day, Babs wore one of the new fashionable maxi frocks and a long overcoat to match, her head of brown-red hair complemented by the bottle green of the coat. She looked particularly fetching and was obviously head over heels in love with her new husband. They held the reception in a Galway hotel and all her friends and neighbours turned up, though the Needham contingent from Achill were conspicuous by their absence.

Robert's parents stood them a fortnight's honeymoon in Glengarriff. It was agreeable enough in the hotel. If Robert seemed in no great hurry to consummate the marriage, Babs took this as an indication of his kindness and consideration. Eventually all was safely, if a trifle awkwardly, accomplished.

They returned to Dublin to live in a modest semi-detached house in one of VKI's investment developments on the north side of the city, which Robert rented on very favourable terms. Babs was delighted to be able to make the farm over to him. She saw it as her 'portion', or dowry, which any self-respecting girl was expected to bring into a marriage and to give to her husband.

Robert was now a man of property. With the help of the same superior who had lent him the car for the journey to Galway, he started to climb the ladder at VKI. Old Vincent Kenny had had a stroke and had lost his enthusiasm for the market-place, while his son, Vincent junior, was more interested in girls than in gilt-edges.

Clever with figures, and with a sensitive nose for a speculative bargain, Robert was quite unscrupulous in dealing with clients, though very careful to keep within the letter of the law. He also had no compunction about cheating on his colleagues, when it suited him, by withholding information or stealing ideas from them. In time he was making most of the major decisions within the company. One of his earliest was to sack Joe Doolin. This gave him a great deal of personal pleasure.

He held on to the farm until he judged the time to be ripe. As he had foreseen, the day came when the land was desperately needed for a new development. With the help of a few venal councillors on the local county council, who were persuaded by some gifts made to them on Robert's behalf, the land was re-zoned from agricultural to housing/industrial. Robert then sold at a highly inflated price and netted a substantial profit.

By now he had enough capital to start out on his own. Saying goodbye to VKI, which was being steered rapidly downhill by old Vincent's son, he took with him all the inside information he had garnered over the years, as well as those clients he had carefully fostered during the same time. ORMAX was born and rapidly grew from a lusty baby to a strong adult.

From such small beginnings, he thought with justified pride, I have, by my own efforts, made the journey to where I am today.

Babs was an amenable and undemanding wife, who kept the house clean and tidy, cooked good plain food, though not very well (whenever he fancied a really decent meal he ate out) and was always there to welcome him when he came home. She encouraged him in his work, told him continually what a good man and provider he was, how proud she was of him and how lucky she was that he had come to Galway and found her there just waiting to be taken into his arms and swept around the ballroom to the strains of *Wonderful World*. He agreed with all of this, except perhaps for the tune, which he still couldn't remember, no matter how hard he tried.

He set about educating Babs in the ways of the world and particularly in the ways of the sophisticated world to which he was more and more aspiring as his fortunes improved. There was nothing extravagant about his instruction and his admonitions, he told himself with justifiable pride; the discreet head-shake here and the judicious cough there were sufficient to let her know when she was stepping outside the bounds of acceptable behaviour and to steer her back into line. He brought home books for her to read and then questioned her on what she had learnt.

Babs, for her part, was very willing to be instructed. She wanted to improve for his sake, and if she sometimes felt hurt and humiliated by a frown or a corrective gesture, especially in front of company, she was always able to laugh it off and carry on as if there were no pain inside.

However, there was one major point of disagreement between them. Babs wanted children, but Robert did not.

They had no real rows about it – Robert would not have tolerated rows in his happy home – and he explained to her as he might have done to a child how unfortunate it would be to bring a baby into such a small house. They both needed time, he told her. He was busy trying to get on in the world, for her sake as well as his own; she was still striving towards domestic competence. A family could come later, when the conditions were appropriate, and when that happened she would understand how right he had been all along.

Babs, who had expected to become pregnant on the honeymoon, was bitterly disappointed. He could sense her hurt, which he thought quite unreasonable, though she never openly complained. Sometimes he found her crying during the night, but he always managed to comfort her by holding her in his arms and telling her not to be silly.

Life had gone on like that for several years, while Robert set about the task of making more and more money. He worked very hard and spent more and more time out of the home and even out of the country. On one of these trips abroad he was introduced to some of the sexual pleasures available in foreign cities to businessmen like himself, and found the experience extremely pleasurable. Although the moral code he adhered to at home forbade such adventures, he rationalized these transgressions as being essential to the well-being of a red-blooded young man forced by circumstances to abstain from marital sex for long periods of time. So he confessed his sins, promised to give them up (they were always spur-of-the-moment incidents that he really intended to avoid for the future) and promptly forgot about them, until the next time.

He made influential friends in higher and higher places. By judicious observation he came to recognize those politicians who were willing to listen to a good argument when it was accompanied by a pecuniary offering disguised as a political donation. Gradually there gathered around him what he liked to call his 'little stable', a group of team players dedicated to helping him fulfil his ambitions. He devoted much time to investing in tax-free offshore accounts on behalf of his stable, thus ensuring that they always had sufficient cash to indulge in the finer things of life while they were running the affairs of the country.

His stable included, at different times, a Taoiseach, several cabinet ministers and a gaggle of Opposition politicians. They were flattered by his estimation of their worth in the great scheme of things and they accepted his financial help with gratitude and appreciation. For his part, he knew that he could always rely on their co-operation and assistance whenever legislation was needed to further his economic plans, which were, after all, devoted to the well-being of the country as a whole.

So they benefited from his financial expertise and he grew wealthy from their political influence. It was a fair exchange in Robert's eyes and not too difficult to square with his conscience.

He did not, however, buy a new house and so the embargo on a family continued.

And then God took a hand.

Because of his religious beliefs, Robert would never countenance the use of any artificial means of contraception, so he and Babs relied on the so-called 'natural' method of discouraging potential babies. His acquaintances told him that he was mad, that the 'safe period' was about as safe as a parachute descent over a lake infested with crocodiles, but Robert refused to listen to them. God, he said, knew exactly what He was doing when He invented a woman's menstrual cycle, and one had only to obey the laws of nature and of the Church to ensure for oneself happiness in both this world and the next.

And it worked very well, until God, out of the blue, broke the rules of the game. Despite all the precautions, Babs became pregnant.

Robert couldn't believe it. His first impulse was to blame his wife. Her calculations must have been awry. She must have misread the calendar. He came to the brink of raising his voice to her, but was forestalled by public reaction to the news. His parents were delighted. His brother, Declan, now an ordained priest working in the foreign missions, sent home hearty felicitations and multitudinous tribal gifts from Africa. The local clergy called around to offer their congratulations and one of them managed to organize a blessing from the Pope himself. Even the Nuncio paused to lay a hand in benediction on Babs's bump.

Robert was forced to smile and keep his mouth shut.

He made a point of being kind to Babs while she was pregnant. If his visits abroad increased during the nine months, that was only to be expected. A man is a man and the strength of his desires is preordained and understood by the Almighty.

In time, Lucy arrived.

The fact that she was a girl almost knocked Robert off his perch, but he kept his panic to himself. He had lately been inducted into the Knights of St Nicodemus and it would not have been proper for a knight to refuse to welcome such an obvious gift from God. So he put on a smile, accepted the congratulations of his parents and colleagues, and settled into the business of parenthood.

Twin Cedars was built to celebrate his patriarchal status and he moved his family into the affluence of Silverglen. The new house had to be looked after in a fashion beyond Babs's capacity, so Robert hired some staff: a very accomplished and well-recommended housekeeper/cook, two efficient maids and a gardener-cum-general dogsbody. The man was an ex-soldier and was extremely useful as a bodyguard, whenever a bit of muscle was needed.

Robert now spent more and more time away from home, but Babs didn't seem to mind. She was extremely happy with her daughter. Life bloomed again in her face, the lightness returned to her step, the sound of her laughter filled the corners of the house with unrestrained joy. She seemed to miss Robert less and less, when he went away on his business trips.

When Lucy was twelve she was sent to boarding-school. This was difficult for Babs, but Robert had decided that these things were necessary for the well-being of the child, so she put up with it for the sake of her family. She felt her own inadequacies as a mother too keenly to argue with her husband. Besides, she wasn't well that year and spent several weeks in hospital. It was better for everyone that the child should be removed from the distressing realities of illness.

Orla Corr arrived on the scene at almost the same time. She descended upon ORMAX like Pallas Athene springing from the head of Zeus. She crossed her legs in front of Robert and displayed hitherto unimaginable beauties for his delectation.

He bought the Morris Minor for Babs.

From then on his absences from home increased in frequency. The penthouse in Dún Laoghaire was rented and the key given to Orla. Meetings and conferences took up more and more of his time, he explained, making it necessary for him to sleep away from home, even when he was not actually out of the country. Babs, in her own trusting way, never questioned the truth of what he told her.

Whenever he felt the occasional prick of conscience, Robert consoled himself with the thought that his wife was well taken care of. She had more than enough money to spend, she had her little car to run around in, the house was being efficiently managed for her, and she could devote as much time as she wished to her daughter.

When death finally took a hand and Babs was gone, he knew it was a happy release for her and a great convenience for himself. Some kind of natural cycle had been gone through and life was now ready to enter a new phase. Everything in the garden should be increasingly lovely from now on.

In fact, he had every reason to be happy – if it wasn't for the sorry business about the car.

That irritated him beyond measure. It more than irritated him, it made him feel threatened. He liked his life to be ordered, to know where everything was. He liked to be in control. God dammit, he *was* in control. Yet the thought that there might be some person, unknown to him, who possibly knew private things about him, was profoundly upsetting, even more upsetting than that his wife had friends of whom he was unaware.

The preposterous idea that Babs might have had a secret lover was no more than an obscene joke.

EIGHT

The weather was so gentle when they reached the main road that they decided it would be a shame to waste it sitting on the top of a bus, so they walked the couple of miles to Dún Laoghaire, past the bird sanctuary at Booterstown, through Blackrock and out along the coast road by Seapoint and Salthill.

They talked about everything and nothing. They held hands as if they were real lovers. She was bright and cheerful and he responded to her mood. She told him stories about Galway and her life on the farm. He told her about being the son of a schoolteacher in Dublin and about his minor escapades as a young student in UCG. There wasn't much to tell. He had kissed a few girls and got drunk several times.

'You don't have to apologize for being good,' she said.

'Oh God, you make it sound really bloody bad.'

'I was a good little girl too. You don't get much chance to be anything else, when you're keeping house for your father and feeding the chickens and milking the couple of cows. Well. I suppose you can always find the chance for *anything*. But I didn't. And I didn't mind. I liked looking after animals. Animals are safe things. They're honest. They might bite you, but they won't ever lie to you. Not like a lot of people.' She paused and then added, 'I was a virgin when I got married. It never entered my head to be anything else. That was the way things were, the way they were meant to be. Being a woman was being like the Blessed Virgin, who didn't have sex even *after* she was married.'

'That's why they always made Joseph look like an old man. He must've felt old all his life.'

'I was taught that it was up to the girl. If she was pure, she could keep the boy pure. Vessels of purity, that's what they called us, when I was in the Children of Mary. And if you went out on a date and he had bad thoughts, it was all *your* fault. I was afraid of my life that I might damn a boy to Hell for all eternity. Do you believe in that stuff?'

'Not even a little bit of it.'

'My husband does. But he's very religious. Are you religious?'

'Not so as you'd notice. I believe in God, sort of. And I go to Mass on Sundays when I'm at home, because it pleases my mother. But I don't really think about it all that much during the rest of the week.'

'Me neither.'

'All that nonsense about the girls being responsible for everything is a load of rubbish. Adam invented that, when he blamed Eve for giving him the apple. Then celibate men carried it on. It's a way of helping them stay away from women and of shifting the blame from themselves, if they slip up. Though, mind you, we're all responsible for one another in one way or another.'

They found that they agreed about a lot of things. There was the marvellous fact that the movement of each of their lives counterpointed the other – she had left Galway to come and live in Dublin, he had left Dublin to go and study in Galway. Of course, this was only a minor sort of coincidence, but they felt that it was important all the same. It displayed some sort of pattern. Little incidental things became significant. A red shop-front they passed reminded them both of Molloy's shop in Maaclee and set them wondering what he might have been up to while she was busily sucking her ice-cream cone. He decided that he was almost certainly swimming in Clontarf Baths on that sunny day fifteen years before.

'We used to walk out there from Drumcondra, to save the penny we got for the bus.'

'And what used you spend it on?'

'A cigarette and a match.'

'Silly eejit.'

'I know. But I was only a kid.'

They compared birthday dates and were pleased to discover that hers was the 4 December, while his was the 12 April – 4/12 against 12/4. This was surely remarkable, another example of pattern.

In no time at all they had put the couple of miles behind them. The day waned.

They found shabby, genteel old Dún Laoghaire bathed in the glow of the setting sun while the quiet of the evening drifted in across the sea from Howth. Harbour Road was busy with holidaymakers strolling about. Half-a-dozen cormorants sat on a large rock with their black wings outspread. Little boats with red sails were running back into the harbour as the day's activities came to an end; bigger boats with white sails were still fussing about outside the sea wall. Two ice-cream vans were parked near the entrance to the East Pier, both of them doing brisk business.

They walked hand in hand down the pier and watched the car ferry ease away on its evening sailing to Holyhead. The sound of its siren sent the sailing boats scurrying out of the way.

'We could be on that,' he said. 'We could go to England, change our names and live happily ever after.'

She just looked at him, smiling and shaking her head.

A man was playing a banjo down beside the lighthouse. A small crowd had gathered to listen to the music. They too paused for a while. When the banjo played *Summer Days* they both joined in the singalong.

'Our one summer day is drifting away too soon,' he said.

'Oh don't be such a gloomy puss. Isn't the sun still shining and the place full of music! What more do you want?'

'Permanence.'

'You want jam on your egg!'

They walked up the stone steps to the upper level and out on to the sloping rocks to look out across the sea. The mail boat was now only a distant smudge on the horizon. The Kish lighthouse, seven miles out, was struck by a ray from the setting sun and glowed brightly through the gathering dusk.

'I've never been here before,' she said.

'You can have a wish so.'

She closed her eyes and screwed up her nose in concentration.

'What did you wish for?'

'Can't tell you that, or it wouldn't come true.'

'Has it anything to do with me?'

'Can't tell you that either, so stop fishing for compliments.'

She it was who decided on the restaurant. When they had walked back to the road and she saw the illuminated sign, she seemed to know instantly that that was where she wanted to go. She led him by the hand down some steps, along a little path and through a doorway hung with coloured beads. Inside there was a small room with about fifteen tables. They picked one near the front window from which they could watch the activity outside.

The waiter lit a candle on their table when he brought them the menu. They studied it together, their heads almost touching. He ordered lamb chops, she preferred poached salmon. She also insisted that they have a bottle of red wine, a Merlot that glowed darkly in the candlelight.

'Merlot, by God! You must be a connoisseur.'

'Sarky! But we *do* have it at home from time to time. I make a note of what's on the bottles.'

To the waiter he said, 'Is this a vintage wine?'

'Absolutely, sir.' She looked knowledgeably at the label on the bottle and tasted the red liquid with great seriousness, before giving the waiter the nod to pour.

'Chancer.'

'Will you stop, or I'll burst out laughing.'

They toasted one another solemnly.

'Here's to a perfect day,' she said.

'Amen to that.'

They clinked glasses and looked at one another in the half-light.

'I wish that this could go on forever, Nora.'

'So do I, but it won't. It can't. We have to be sensible, Jim.'

'I hate being sensible.'

The food arrived and he suddenly realized how hungry he was. As they ate, the restaurant gradually filled up with other diners, mostly couples like themselves. Lights began to appear on the promenade and on the black bulk of Howth across the bay.

The dark-red wine induced in him a feeling of infinite possibilities. He began to concoct an elaborate plan for smuggling them both out of the country on a cargo boat to northern Spain. Santander, or somewhere like that. It involved dyeing their hair and dressing in Spanish costumes, a flat black sombrero and tight trousers for him, and a mantilla and a long skirt for her, and pretending to be a couple of flamenco dancers who had been displaced from their homeland during the Franco regime. This would entail learning how to dance flamenco, but because of their natural ability and innate sense of rhythm, it should present no real problem.

'Won't we be expected to speak Spanish?'

'We'll tell them that we've been so long away from home that we've forgotten the language, apart from a few handy phrases that we've picked up from a phrase book. '*Quiero algo para un resfriado*', for instance.'

'What does that mean?'

'I want something for a cold.'

'That won't impress anyone.'

'It will, if we both cough a lot.'

'They'll only deport us for bringing in an infectious disease.'

'Did anyone ever tell you that you're a terrible pessimist?'

'My father was a Galway farmer.'

'Ah, that explains it. I don't suppose *he'd* recognize a flamenco if it blew up his nose.'

She got such a fit of the giggles that the waiter came over to enquire if there was anything they needed. He felt expansive enough to put his last fiver on the line.

'Another bottle of the plonk. And this one is *my* treat.'

He handed his fiver to the waiter.

'Will that cover it?'

'Just about, sir.'

'Well, keep the change.'

'Thank you, sir.'

The waiter went off to get the second bottle.

'Are you trying to get me drunk?'

'Absolutely. Not that you're far off it already.'

'So that's what's wrong with me? Thank God for that. Do you know what I'm going to tell you, Jim? I don't think I've ever been tight in my life.'

'What does it feel like?'

'It feels blooming marvellous.'

'It won't feel so good in the morning.'

'Hump the morning. This is tonight and I'm enjoying myself.'

'Me too.'

'I hope so. Oh, I hope so.'

She reached across the table and took his hands in hers.

'Whatever happens tomorrow, or next week, or next year, I just want to say . . .'

She paused.

'Yes?'

She turned his hands over and brought them to her lips, kissing each palm in turn.

'Is that it?'

'That's it.'

'Nobody has ever said anything as nice as that to me before.'

'You only think that because you're jarred too.'

They dawdled over the second bottle of wine and, by the time that they had finished it, the darkness outside was complete.

She looked out the window.

'Oh lord, I won't be able to see the tower at all.'

'We can always come back another day.'

'You know we can't.'

She called the waiter with a sudden urgency, paid the bill and then led him out.

The air was cooler now, the crowd thinner, the movement on the street a little less animated. They went along the seafront towards Sandycove, both a trifle unsteady on their feet. She had her arm tucked firmly into his and he could feel her breast nudging against him as she walked. It was a most comfortable intimacy that moved him strangely. He wanted to shout with joy that he was walking here with this wonderful woman on his arm, experiencing her nearness in this most inexplicable way, and at the same time he wanted to howl his lamentations that when this day ended he would never see her again.

As if she understood his thoughts, she stopped suddenly and drew him over to the low wall at the edge of the water. They stood there, looking out across the sea. The lighthouse threw its lazy arms across towards Howth.

'I'm drunk, Jim.'

'Me too.'

'But it's not just the wine: it's just this whole day.'

She turned to him, put her hand on his cheek and kissed him on the mouth. Her lips were soft and wet. He held her gently, afraid to spoil the

moment by any roughness or over-enthusiasm. He smelt her skin and the richness of her hair.

In a moment she pulled back her head and smiled at him.

'Let's go and see this famous tower.'

At the end of Otranto Terrace, just past a grove of trees, they turned left
towards the little beach of Sandycove. The water rolled gently in small ripples
on the sand. In the gloom they could see shadowy couples sitting on the strand
or on the low wall, whispering, merging together, kissing.

'There's a lot of activity going on here,' he said softly.

'It'd be nice to go for a swim now, wouldn't it?'

'We're both so tight, we'd probably drown.'

'It'd be a lovely way to go.'

' "Now more than ever seems it rich to die".'

'What's that?'

'Keats. I'm full of these useless quotations. Comes with the job.'

'It's lovely. Rich to die. Do you think dying will be rich?'

'I don't know. I've never done it. But it'll probably be bloody expensive.'

'You've got no soul!'

They turned right up the hill. Somewhere out of sight the waves pounded
on the rocks of the Forty Foot bathing place. *Gentlemen only*, said the notice.
She peered over the chest-high wall.

'Would there be anyone down there this time of night?'

'I don't know. There could be.'

'Can we go down and see?'

'There could be all sorts of ould fellas in the nip.'

'Gentlemen, how are you! We had a parish priest in Galway once was at the
same sort of thing. One beach for the men, another for the women. Hadn't he
little to be occupying himself with? I'll have a go, if you will.'

'You're mad. And I'm not going to take you down there. It's too dark. Too
easy to fall and break a leg. And I've no intention of risking you like that.'

'You're a careful Peter, aren't you!'

'Only where you're concerned. Come on and look at Joyce's tower.'

The bulk of the tower stood before them, black against the lesser blackness
of the sky.

'It's ugly,' she said.

'It wasn't built for beauty. If we'd been earlier we could have gone inside.

It's a museum now. Lots of his stuff in there, including his death mask.'

'Yuck.' She made a little moue of disgust.

They stood close together, arms entwined.

'I'm going to miss you,' he said.

'I know.'

'I mean, *really* miss you.'

'I know what you mean.'

She kissed him again, pressing herself against him. He hugged her tightly, tasting her. Again she was the first to break away.

'Come on,' she whispered. 'Let's find somewhere.'

They found a patch of grass sheltered by a wall. He went first and then lifted her down, feeling her body stretch along his as she slid into his arms. They kissed again and then lay down on the dry grass together. The night and the world disappeared in a mad swirl of emotions. He had never known anything so sweet, so exciting, as her melting mouth and her glowing body. There in the dark, with his head spinning, he discovered her breasts, the soft skin of her thighs. Her hands freed him and then drew him down on top of her. They kissed deeply and then deeper still, until they were both lost. He plunged into the dark tunnel, searching his way up and up. He could hear her giving a little cry and it was all wonder and ecstasy and the whole world exploded in light and he thought he was going to die with happiness.

Later there was stillness and the gentle touch of her hands on his back and in his hair. She crooned softly in his ear.

'My darling. My own sweet darling Jim.'

'Oh Nora, I'm sorry. I didn't mean to—'

'Sssh. Did you like that?'

'Oh God it was wonderful.'

'Then just hush and hold me.'

Later still she stirred in his arms.

'We must be going. Have you got a hankie?'

The banality of the request startled him. He fished in his jacket pocket and gave her his handkerchief, hoping it was clean, trying to remember when he had changed it. She disappeared into the darkness with a whispered warning to him to stay where he was. He tidied himself. His mind was a jumble of conflicting emotions as he fastened his belt. Then he searched for and found the blue folder.

In a few minutes she was back. She took his hand.

'Come on, love. We have to get back into town.'

They caught a bus and sat close together on the top deck, holding hands. There seemed to be nothing left to say. He stole a glance at her. She was glowing and beautiful. She turned under his gaze and gave him a smile of pure joy and contentment.

'My darling Jim.'

When they alighted in O'Connell Street, she allowed him to walk her to the corner of Middle Abbey Street before she stopped.

'This is where we part, love.'

'Let me see you to your bus.'

'No.'

'But you just can't go like this.'

'I have to. If you saw me get on to a bus, you'd know where I live, and you'd only be bothering yourself trying to find me. Here.' She reached into her bag and took out a little gold cross on a chain. 'I've had this since I was a child. It's not real gold. But take it anyway.'

He took it reverently.

'I'll guard it like the Crown Jewels. But I've nothing to give you.'

'You've already given me enough. I dumped the hankie in a bin in Dún Laoghaire.'

'Unless you'd like the book.'

'I'd love the book.'

He took *Ulysses* from his folder.

'Hold on a minute.'

He produced a pen from his inside pocket and wrote on the flyleaf.

'That's my name. And the school where I'll be teaching after the holidays. Just in case you want to get in touch with me.'

'I won't need your name. You'll always be Jim to me.'

'Just in case.'

'Anyway, that's a Cork name. It's not from Mayo.'

'One of my ancestors was caught sheep-stealing and was driven out of Cork in the seventeenth century.'

She leaned close and kissed him again.

'God, you're a terrible chancer, but this has been the most magical day of my life.'

'I love you, Nora,' he said, the words out before he realized. 'It was my first time.'

'I know. And *I* love *you*, Jim. I really do. Now look over there and don't turn till I'm gone.'

He turned obediently and stood staring at a neon sign that flashed on and off, on and off. It said, *Guinness is Go d for you.*

NINE

'Who?'

The word was snapped out. Noel Kerrigan was not a happy man.

For one thing, his feet were acting up again and had been ever since the bloody flight from Strasbourg. Why the hell couldn't the airlines provide an air system that didn't play havoc with his feet, even in first-class! You'd imagine a foreign minister travelling first-class could be guaranteed against swollen ankles and aching joints! But no! It happened to him all the time lately, no matter whether he took morning or evening flights. And he was getting more and more claustrophobic even in first-class aeroplane seats. He had arrived back in Dublin like a wounded hippopotamus, shaking all over, barely able to drag his bulky body through the VIP lounge.

As if all that wasn't bad enough, his eczema had flared up again during the past few days He hated his eczema. It woke him up in the middle of the night with an urgent desire to scratch, as if he were surrounded by a whole galaxy of itches competing for his undivided attention, like importunate constituents at one of his weekly clinics. It made him irritable, he who was renowned for the bellow of his laugh in the Dáil bar and the pungency of his wit. He snarled at his personal secretary and close friend, the efficient Aoife Langan, whom he normally treasured for the sterling performer she was in all her capacities. He shouted at poor Mollie, his wife of thirty years, as dependable and uncomplaining a woman as any man could wish for, when she said to him, 'Be sure and don't scratch, Noel – you'll only make it worse'. Christ, he *knew* that he shouldn't scratch, that scratching was what the treacherous eczema was aiming for, but he couldn't help it.

And now, here he was, just back from Strasbourg, trying to relax in his favourite armchair with a glass of whiskey in his hand, his ankles swollen and his whole body itching, when Mollie brought him the unwelcome news that a guest had arrived.

'Who?'

Mollie hurriedly closed the door.

'Hush, he'll hear you.'

'Who'll bloody hear me?'

'Mr McGuinness.'

'Oh Christ,' said Kerrigan, with all of the fervour, if none of the devotion, of an eremite in the desert being assaulted by temptation. 'That fat bollocks! Throw him out!'

'You know I can't do that, Noel!'

Discretion and the shock on Mollie's face forced him to rethink.

'I suppose you'd better show him in.'

He didn't want to see Robert McGuinness. He didn't want to see anyone just at the moment, but particularly not McGuinness. He wanted to unwind and dull the itch of a thousand spots with a little Jameson. He knew what Robert would be on about and he really wished to avoid the subject if at all possible.

However, he put on an expansive smile and heaved his bulk out of the armchair to greet his guest. Robert McGuinness came smoothly into the room, a man sliding on the grease he spread about his world.

'Robert, good to see you!'

'Thanks, Noel. Good to see you too.'

'You'll have a drink?'

'Why not.'

Kerrigan filled the glass himself. Mollie hovered.

'I don't have to tell you how sorry I was—'

'We both were,' said Mollie.

'—to hear of the death of your good lady, Robert. And how I hated not being able to attend the funeral in person.'

'I know, I know.'

'But I *did* send the Secretary. I hope you noticed that.'

'Indeed I did. And thank you for the kind gesture.' Robert took the glass from Kerrigan and sat down. 'You've put a lot of whiskey in this, Noel.'

'Go on, get it into you. It'll do you good.'

'Do you want some tea after?' asked Mollie.

'I don't think so,' said Kerrigan, settling back in his armchair.

'Not for me, either. Thanks, Mollie.'

'I'll leave you, so.'

When the door had closed behind the departing wife, Robert took an envelope from his pocket and laid it on the occasional table.

'A little something for yourself, Big Fella.'

'Thanks, old man.'

Kerrigan knew what was in the envelope, but protocol demanded a certain ceremony. He stood up, took the envelope and put it away in the bureau that stood against the wall. Then he sat down again.

'You're a generous man, Robert.'

'You are entirely welcome.' Robert smiled a mirthless smile. 'Consider it a political donation for the party.'

'Of course, of course. It'll be put to good use. Here's to your good lady. May she rest in peace.'

'Amen.'

They drank and observed a moment's silence in honour of the dead. Kerrigan felt that he should add another tribute or two to the departed wife, but he couldn't think of anything to say – he couldn't even remember her name – and he realized what an almighty gaffe it would be to misname her to her grieving husband.

'But life has to go on,' said Robert. 'At least so Canon Finnegan tells me.'

'And there's no man better up in these things.' Kerrigan had met the canon once in Robert's house and decided that, although he undoubtedly was a canon and entitled to respect, he was a pompous old bluffer who should have been put down long before they had accepted him for ordination.

'How was Strasbourg?'

'Oh, you know. The same old stuff. Sometimes I wonder why I ever got myself into the job. It's not worth all the bother.'

'Somebody has to do it, Noel, and your country has decided that you are the man for the job.' He knew that Kerrigan liked to hear such platitudes. 'How did Aoife enjoy herself?'

'Oh fine, fine.' Kerrigan threw a nervous glance at the door. He was infuriated at this reference to the health of his secretary, who performed other duties on the occasions they found themselves away together. Just like the bastard

McGuinness to bring it up, he thought, here in my own house, with the wife in the next room. And it was especially inopportune in that things hadn't been going so well between himself and Aoife since the arrival of the eczema. She had become increasingly nervous every time he took his clothes off, even though he repeatedly assured her, and had medical certificates to back him up, that it wasn't contagious.

'That's good,' said Robert. 'A fine woman,' he added by way of letting Kerrigan know that he had sufficient material in his armoury to blast out of the water any minister who was unable to see reason. 'Strasbourg is a good place to take a good-looking woman. Plenty to spend your money on. I know a lot of people there.'

The last piece of information was given with an innocent air, as if it were merely throwaway trivia, but the minister knew that Robert was telling him that he had spies everywhere. When a camera flashed in the foyer of the hotel, or in the nightclub visited after the day's business was over, one could never be sure whether the Press, an innocent bystander, or someone more devious was behind the device. Kerrigan could feel his eczema reach boiling point. He decided that it was time he changed the direction of the conversation and adverted to the subject that he knew had brought McGuinness to his house.

'I know you've been looking for word about the Gallery job.'

'I half-expected a call from you this morning.' Robert smiled his mirthless smile again.

'Sorry about that. I meant to ring you, but the plane was delayed and what with this and that it just wasn't possible to get in contact. However, you need-n't think that it's been forgotten. I've been working my socks off on your behalf.'

'I take it that it's still on the cards?'

'Oh God, yes. Absolutely. No doubt about it. It's just . . .'

He paused.

'Yes?'

'It may need a little more time.'

'Why should it need more time? The building was completed six months ago and I was told then that the director would be appointed without any further delay. And it's your choice, Noel. No one else's.'

'Absolutely. And I've chosen your good self.'

'Then why should it need more time?'

'There are wheels.'

'Wheels?'

'Within wheels.'

'Let me be clear about this. What wheels? Are you getting any flak from Europe?'

'No. Well, not much. I've been round most of the ministers and they're all willing to go along with our suggestion. I just have to tie up . . .' For a moment he considered naming a couple of countries to lend credence to his statement, but decided that it might be inadvisable to be too specific. '. . . a few loose ends and the job's right.'

'How long will that take?'

'A couple of weeks at most.'

'A couple of weeks?'

Kerrigan sensed the menace in the question. It increased the torment of his eczema.

'Maybe not even that long.'

'Well, that's that, then. As long as it is no more than a couple of weeks.'

'The real problem is with the opposition here at home.'

'With a small or a capital O?'

'Both. There'll be questions in the Dáil.'

'Fuck the questions in the Dáil.'

'Well, yes.' Kerrigan gave a nervous laugh. While he often indulged in such coarseness himself about the sacred assembly in Leinster House, he hated being expected to give tacit acceptance to it by a non-member. 'But they can create a lot of noise. And the media aren't going to help. Especially the *Indo* and bloody RTE. Then there's that woman painter who seems determined to see you get the job over her dead body.'

'I'm sure that could be arranged.'

Kerrigan feigned a laugh. He hoped it was no more than a joke, though with McGuinness you could never be sure.

'I agree with you there, off the record. But she has backing from that new group called Friends of Civilization and they're likely to look for a judicial review in the courts the minute I make the announcement.'

'Friends of Civilization, my arse. That crowd of Masons with their Protestant archbishop of a patron. We all know where they're coming from. Pay no attention to them. Tell them to get lost. Their day is over in this grand little

Catholic country of ours.'

'True, true.' Kerrigan's eczema was getting itchier and itchier, as it always did when he began to feel stressed, and he wished to God he didn't have to discuss such unpleasant matters with McGuinness. Why the devil couldn't the man want something reasonable, like the governorship of the Central Bank, for instance, instead of having this hankering after a place in the pantheon of the fine arts, of all things.

Kerrigan poured more whiskey for himself. He offered the bottle to McGuinness, but he refused. The fat little bastard's too cute to drink too much, thought Kerrigan. He always has his wits about him, which is why he's made so much money during his life.

The foreign minister deeply regretted the day when, as a gauche young counsellor, he had first accepted money from McGuinness and had thus allowed himself to be drawn into the net of deceit and compromise and dependence so skilfully cast about him by the businessman. It had all seemed so easy at first – take the few bob, vote the correct way, get the planning application passed and give the wife and kids a holiday in the Canaries. All more or less Mickey Mouse stuff. But, of course, the stakes had not remained small. As he progressed up the political ladder larger favours were asked for and, almost imperceptibly, the day arrived when he found himself in a position where refusal was no longer an option. He was too far in to back out without bringing political ruin down on himself and disgrace on his family and the party. Over the years his dependence on McGuinness and his hatred of the pudgy little crook had grown in equal measure. Damn him to hell, thought Kerrigan. If there's any justice in the world, God will strike him dead one day as he's marching up the church to receive Communion, with his hands piously crossed and that insufferable look of sanctity on his face.

But he had no real faith in the justice of God, at least in this life. McGuinness and his sort would continue to flourish and amass more and more wealth, until they were put in their coffins to the blowing of bugles and with the blessings of the Church.

He sat back heavily into his armchair.

'Believe me, I'll pay them no attention,' he said, 'but the papers will. And the TV and radio.'

Back in 1989 the idea of a European Art Gallery to house works of art created in the EU since its inception had been the brainchild of the French president. He had naturally expected the building to be situated in Paris, the cradle of European civilization, under the direction of some eminent Frenchman. Unfortunately, the German chancellor, a Bavarian, while agreeing that such a Gallery was definitely a Good Idea, believed that the Bavarian capital, Munich, was the obvious choice. The Italian premier, despite strong reservations in the Vatican, where his socialist government was viewed with disfavour, insisted that Rome had better claim to the honour than either of the other two. At this juncture Madrid was put forward by the Spanish Government (with a minority vote from Catalonia for Barcelona) and this was immediately followed by a Portuguese nomination for Lisbon.

The argument had continued for almost ten years, with no sign of a resolution, and the European Parliament was on the brink of calling off the whole project, when the newly elected Irish Taoiseach, Éilís Ní Snodaigh, had pulled a masterstroke. One fine Easter Sunday, in 1998, dressed in a long flowing gown reminiscent of Maude Gonne in her heyday, and in front of all the TV cameras that could be commanded or bribed to attend, she ostentatiously laid the foundation stone for a new gallery in the heart of Dublin. It was to be situated on a prime site in Merrion Square donated by a consortium of Irish businessmen, led by Robert McGuinness. How this consortium had acquired the site in the first place remained a mystery, as it had for thirty years been earmarked to hold a Catholic Cathedral and had been jealously clung to by successive Archbishops of Dublin. When it passed out of Church hands there were rumours about the involvement of the Papal Nuncio in a secret deal, though nothing had ever been proven. Shortly afterwards the Nuncio had resigned for reasons of health and had gone back home to St Lucia di Piave to prepare his soul for the next life. Many heads were shaken wisely, but no hard evidence was ever brought to light.

Taoiseach Ní Snodaigh, in a broadcast carried on all the major networks around Europe, named the new building The European Gallery of Arts and Culture and announced that Ireland was prepared to foot the cost of the project, since the other EU countries seemed more concerned to bicker among themselves for narrow national gain than to put up the money and get on with the job. Faced with this well-publicized challenge to its generosity and lack of political will, and recognizing that there were better prospects for the acceptance of Dublin as the site of the new Gallery than any of the contentious major cities, the European Parliament had hurriedly reconvened from holiday and passed a Bill naming the Irish project as the definitive one, praising the Irish initiative in the matter and voting a large sum of EU money to help defray the cost.

So the magnificent new Gallery had risen in Merrion Square and was acknowledged all over the world as a building of architectural brilliance, if a little awkward in some of its aspects, and a fitting repository for modern works celebrating the arts and culture of the EU nations. Ní Snodaigh had trailed her long gown around the capitals of Europe and it was universally agreed that the structure would be an enduring monument to the vision, perspicacity and, not to put a tooth in it, *genius* of the first woman to hold the position of prime minister in Ireland. The President, a woman also well versed in the arts, was understandably miffed at being so cleverly outmanoeuvred by the Taoiseach, but was forced to grin and bear it.

A twelve-member Executive Committee, drawn from the member states of the EU, began the work of assembling a collection of appropriate artefacts and manuscripts. This proceeded apace, the day of the official opening drew nearer and nearer, and all seemed to be going as merry as a marriage-bell, much to the gratification of the Irish Government.

Then a large and unexpected fly landed in the political ointment.

Robert McGuinness approached Foreign Minister Kerrigan with the request that he be appointed director of the new Gallery. He made it clear that refusal would be inadvisable. Kerrigan immediately started phoning around his cabinet colleagues, looking for support.

Because Robert was the main financial contributor to the whole project, because his request was accompanied by gifts of more than usual generosity to a wide variety of ministers (apart from the Taoiseach herself, who guarded her integrity jealously), and because it was widely appreciated in political circles that a thwarted Robert might use the ammunition he undoubtedly possessed to do real damage to many reputations, the government gave serious consideration to its choice of candidate. It was decided that Robert McGuinness was indeed an ideal person to be the first director. Though a little light in artistic appreciation, there was no denying that he was a good *manager* (or 'cute hoor' in the local dialect) as was evidenced by the prosperity and continued expansion of his many projects, particularly ORMAX, the flagship of his empire. The Church, having taken a lot of criticism for failing to back the Italian bid, was happy to weigh in on the side of this most eminent of her sons. He had demonstrated by his life and works that being a devout Christian, and there-fore bound for Heaven, was no barrier to making a lot of money, and he had always been more than generous in giving assistance to all sorts of worthy causes dear to Christ's Mystical Body.

The decision had already been quietly passed at cabinet level. Noel Kerrigan, having spent several months canvassing his colleagues in the EU, was expected to make the announcement publicly in the near future. Then the Minister for Arts and Culture, who belonged to one of the junior parties in the coalition, and who clearly felt that the honour of making the announcement should rightly have been his, leaked the name of the proposed candidate to the media. Immediately there were rumblings of opposition from all over the country.

'You know what you can do with the media,' said McGuinness. 'They'll whine no matter who gets the job. And if that uncouth paint-splatterer chains herself to the railings, or those Protestant bigots decide to go to court about it, I know a few judges who owe me a couple of favours.'

The thought of buying the law genuinely appalled Kerrigan. He was an old-fashioned kind of politician. He firmly believed that politicians were inherently corruptible and were permanently available to be solicited by dona-tions in brown envelopes. This was the nature of the business and had been so since time immemorial. On the other hand, bishops and judges were of another class entirely. Kerrigan loved to kiss the ring of a bishop and would go out of his way to find one, that he might bend the knee and the head before it. And his respect for the law, at least in the abstract, was total. Entering a cour-thouse was to him like entering a cathedral. Had the judge had a ring, Kerrigan would have kissed it, both coming and going.

He knew, of course, that there were crooked judges and less than perfect bishops, because he had met some, but he sincerely considered them to be disgraceful departures from the norm, whose existence served only to point up the general integrity of the two professions.

To hear a dishonest little pig like McGuinness call into question the unim-peachability of both the law and the Church made him want to vomit. It also set his eczema hammering away like a demented organist struggling with a Bach fugue.

But there was nothing he could say in that vein without incurring the wrath of this most valuable sponsor. So he promised to take on the Opposition and the media, and whatever hostile public opinion those two adversaries might generate, and to make the announcement at the earliest moment feasible.

'That's good,' said McGuinness, 'and tell Lizzie Snoddy that I won't forget it to her.'

Kerrigan had no intention of telling 'Lizzie Snoddy' any such thing, because he knew that McGuinness's use of the English version of the Taoiseach's name was quite deliberately demeaning and would certainly induce a state of near-apoplexy in his leader. However, he said he would convey the message to her ears.

When Robert McGuinness had departed, Kerrigan poured himself another drink and sank deep into his armchair, trying to conjure up a possible scenario that would enable him to work his way out of the dilemma he was in. But he could think of nothing feasible, nothing that would please both his constituents and his patron. His ankles throbbed and his eczema itched.

The black cloud loomed over him as it did with increasing frequency in his more desperate moments. He added yet more whiskey to his glass and sucked it into his veins in an effort to dull the misery that threatened to overwhelm him.

'One of these days, McGuinness, I'll swing for you.'

TEN

The morning had started badly.

Séamus Creedon was late. It wasn't his fault, it was never his fault, but that never seemed to matter when he had jumped off the bus and was running up the hill, around by the Distillery, past the small group of shops, across the square and finally was climbing the steps to the heavy brown-grained door.

It was locked. Solidly and implacably locked. He leaned his forehead against the brown gloss paint, spent, panting. His first impulse was to turn and go home, back to his room, and then to ring in sick. Or better still, get his land-lady, Mrs Maher, to ring in for him. It wouldn't be a lie. He really *was* feeling sick, especially after the run from the bus stop. That was it. Mrs Maher would-n't mind telling the white lie. She might even consider nursing him in bed, if he felt that he needed the attention. He had observed certain signals to that effect emanating from her lately. All he had to do was to turn around, slip down the steps again, and make his way quietly back along the square.

But what if somebody sees me? he thought. Somebody will be sure to see me. The whole building is a veritable warren of squinting windows. Brother Clarke has armed outposts located on the roof of the school at both ends and in the middle, commanding a field of observation east, south and west. Radio links already have informed the head, the deputy head, all holders of posts of special responsibility, and the provincial of the Order in his bunker out in Booterstown. The airwaves are literally full of information about a delinquent teacher observed *trying to escape*. Very probably the Special Branch has been notified. Although I can't hear it with the traffic, a helicopter is certainly hover-ing somewhere above, recording my every move.

There was only one thing for it – dignified surrender. He wished he had a sword and a hat with one side of the brim turned up, so that he could stand there like Pádraig Pearse before General Lowe.

'In order to prevent the further slaughter of innocent teachers, and in the hope of saving the lives of teachers yet unborn, I have agreed to an unconditional surrender to you, General Clarke, Commander-in-Chief of the massed forces of the Christian Brothers' Army.'

He rang the bell.

The door was opened by a grinning denizen of second year, who were stabled in the classroom closest to the front door. This boy, a particularly obnoxious specimen called O'Reilly, bared the gaps between his teeth in what was obviously intended to be a smile.

'Good morning, sir,' said O'Reilly, expanding his grimace still further as he recognized the identity of the latecomer. Séamus Creedon nodded briefly in return and swept past the exultant gatekeeper. He left the hallway through the double doors, crossed the corridor leading to the head's office (thank God nobody was visible there) and ran up the stairs.

O'Reilly shut the door and slithered back into his classroom to spread the glad tidings that old Creedo was late again and would probably be sacked this time.

Séamus could envisage the scene in his fifth-year English class. The adolescent hoodlums, whose voices deepened in inverse proportion to the expansion of their brains and understanding, would be whiling away the time assaulting one another, retailing dubious jokes to the accompaniment of raucous laughter, or merely kicking their heels and their desks with the paradoxical indifference and destructive intent of the bored teenager. He knew the noise would be indescribable once he came within earshot.

However, when he turned the landing of the third floor, he was struck by something even more awful than the expected hoarse bedlam. The silence was absolute.

He briefly considered hurling himself through the landing window on to the railings beneath, there to hang like a bloody rag and create a shrine, a place of pilgrimage for future generations of misunderstood and persecuted teachers. Instead he paused, recalled a yoga class he had once attended, took several deep breaths, squared his narrow shoulders and mounted the remaining steps to the clamour of silver trumpets and brass bugles. 'And what is else not to be overcome? That glory never shall his wrath or might extort from me.'

He opened the classroom door.

Fifth-year English was like a still-life painting. On one side were the immobile figures of twenty students, all bent over their *Anthology of English Poetry* books, heads bowed, each one encased in an invisible bubble of utter stillness; on the other side stood the statuesque figure of Brother Clarke, locally known as the Clarinet, because of the height to width proportions of his long black figure. As Séamus entered the room, the Clarinet looked at him with unconcealed distaste, inclined his head in a brief bow of acknowledgement, and performed an unhurried glissando out the door.

'I love you too,' said Séamus, but he said it under his breath, to avoid giving scandal to the innocents before him.

As the door closed behind the Clarinet, the innocents immediately relaxed. An audible sigh went round the room, feet were pushed out or pulled in, books were closed, backsides were moved and a frisson of relief agitated the collective corpus. There was even a small fart delivered from somewhere at the back of the class. An appreciative murmur ensued.

What had been a bad morning improved beyond measure. They plunged into an examination of Yeats's *The Circus Animals' Desertion* and from thence the discussion diverted to hacking around in the jungle of poetic inspiration and the dark night of the creative writer's soul when the black block descends.

When the bell went, he felt pleasantly exhausted. His usefulness in the scheme of things had, to some extent, been validated. He descended the stairs to the staff room and the prospect of a few minutes' respite before tackling Six B, who had a reputation for driving teachers to an extreme form of madness.

The staff room was empty, except for Bill Clancy, the physics teacher, who was standing awaiting him with the phone in his hand.

'For you, Séamus,' he said. Then he covered the mouthpiece and whispered, 'A mott. A culchie, by the sound of her, you cute hoor, you.'

Séamus took the receiver.

'Hello?'

'Hello, Jim.'

He felt as if he had been hit in the stomach by a bus.

'What? Oh merciful God! Nora?'

'I suppose you thought I'd never ring you.'

He was speechless for one of the few times in his life. Her tone was somehow accusatory, as if he had been deficient in trust. What in God's name did she think he thought!

'It's been over a year.'

'God, you don't have to tell me. Sure, haven't I been thinking of giving you a call for the past couple of weeks. How are you?'

'I'm fine.'

'That's good. I'm fine too, now that you're asking. I was just wondering would you be able to meet me somewhere? I've got something I want to show you.'

'Meet?'

'Yes. I'd love to see you again. Would you like to see me?'

'Oh yes, of course.'

'All right. When? What time do you finish there?'

'It changes from day to day.'

'Tomorrow?'

'Ah . . . my last class ends at ten past three.'

'You teachers have the life! Would you be free to come and meet me in Stephen's Green tomorrow? At about half-three-twenty-to-four?'

'Not Bewley's?'

'No. The Green.'

'I'm sure I could manage that.'

'You don't sound jumping for joy.'

'You've taken me by surprise. I don't know where I am.'

She lowered her voice. 'Truly, Jim, I'm dying to see you. You don't know how much.'

He managed, 'Me too.'

'Half-three then. Beside the duck pond. Where we sat that day. Do you remember?'

'I remember.'

'We can keep all the gossip till then. 'Bye so.'

' 'Bye.'

He hung up.

'By God, Séamus,' said Clancy, 'That sounded pretty heavy. Are you all right?'

'What?' He hardly knew which side of him was up. 'Oh yes, of course, Bill. I'm fine.'

'You look a bit shook. There's a cup of tea in the pot, if you're interested.'

'Right. Thanks.'

'I'd love to stay and hear the story, but I've got to earn my crust. You can give me all the dirty details later on.'

Séamus poured himself a cup of the treacly liquid and sat down to digest the unprecedented happenings of the past couple of minutes.

It was now September 1977. She had last said goodbye to him in June 1976. Since then he had heard not a word from her. For the first few weeks he had lived in hope that each day might bring a phone call, but none had come. Gradually he had accepted the fact that there would never be a phone call, that she had meant it when she had said she would never see him again, that it was all over. Whatever 'it' meant. The affair? The adultery? The story of Nora and Jim? Fade to the sound of violins and a slowly dying sun. Ride away to the west, hunched in the saddle, rolling a cigarillo with one hand, pulling the tobacco pouch closed with his teeth.

Whatever it was, it was over.

He had buttoned himself up on that fact, just as he had buttoned himself up when the action had finished that night beside Joyce's Tower, and got on with his life without his handkerchief. The idea that he might do an MA on Joyce had gone out the window. He had no heart for it anymore.

He went down to Maaclee in August and spent a couple of weeks with his parents. Every day he walked past Molloy's shop with its red front and visualized what she must have looked like standing there eating her ice-cream cone. Sometimes he went into the shop and bought himself a cone, so that he might stand outside where she might have stood and eat it as she might have eaten hers. He had never mentioned her to his parents, even when he had found his mother looking rather anxiously at him and wondering out loud why he wasn't off mixing with young people of his own age instead of spending his time so quietly with them in such a small village.

Niamh Creedon was a woman of the old school – almost literally. She had been a schoolteacher herself, just like her husband. She had fixed ideas about the growth and development of children and she had succeeded admirably in putting these into practice with the first two.

However, there was something vaguely disturbing about her second son. Séamus was a bit of an enigma to his mother. For one thing he had chosen to go to Galway University instead of remaining at home and attending UCD.

And he had grown that ridiculous beard, something she would never have allowed had he been living under her roof. All her attempts to get him to shave it off had met with a stubborn resistance she hadn't known he possessed. But most disturbing of all was his devotion to James Joyce. Joyce was not a character that any self-respecting young Irish Catholic should be devoted to. Of course Joyce was a writer of genius, she was willing to admit that, but of wasted genius. His antipathy towards the Church was enough, in Niamh's eyes, to have him excluded from the company of those artists worthy to be enshrined in the pantheon of Irish geniuses.

As for Nora Barnacle, words failed her!

Séamus on one occasion had tried to explain the situation to her.

'Look, Mam, don't be worried about me. I'm all right.'

'You're twenty-four years of age.'

'That's nothing to be worried about.'

'Who says I'm worried about you?'

'I've seen you looking at me.'

'Does this mean I can't look at my own son?'

'Well, just don't worry.'

'Why should I worry? I'm not worried.'

'I just want to tell you that I'm not homosexual, or anything like that.'

Niamh Creedon blessed herself.

'Don't you even mention that word in this house.'

So the previous September he had gone back to teaching in St Fiachra's. In a fit of religious guilt he had confessed his sexual encounter with a married woman. The priest had admonished him to give up this occasion of sin and he had promised that he would. He didn't tell the priest that he had no choice in the matter. She was gone and the temptation was gone with her along with his handkerchief. He was free of the sin and the occasion of sin and he was completely miserable.

Ah well, he told himself, you can't have everything.

His reverie was interrupted when the maths teacher, Sally Carmody, entered the room with another female teacher, both of them in search of tea. Sally was a jolly sort of young woman, very pleasant and outgoing, but meeting her always made him feel uncomfortable ever since an incident which had occurred in a local hotel at the school staff dinner the previous Christmas.

During the evening, when several bottles of wine and many pints had been consumed, Séamus had made his unsteady way to the Gents to relieve his kidneys. On his way back he had bumped into Sally in one of the dimly lit corridors. Without any preliminaries she had thrown her arms around him, pulled him into a corner, pressed her body to his in the most suggestive way and kissed him, shoving her tongue down his throat. He had been taken by surprise and had stood there gagging, while his organs reacted in the conventional way to the close proximity of her feminine softness. This movement appeared to encourage Sally to even greater effort and she began moaning and straining herself against him more and more, even to the point of taking his hand and guiding it to one of her ample breasts. It occurred to Séamus that something more was expected of him, so he transferred his other hand to her waist. Sally immediately pushed it down along her thigh and he could feel the edge of an undergarment under his fingers. Her tongue extended further down his throat.

How it might have ended was anyone's guess, but fortunately Fidelma Quinn, the geography teacher, had chosen that moment to approach, coughing loudly as if driving out devils. Sally had immediately released her grip on Séamus and pushed him away, saying loudly at the same time, 'God, you're an awful divil, Séamus!'

She had then gone off laughing with Fidelma, a rather desiccated lady of indeterminate age, who wore a cynical look of 'I didn't think you were like that!' on her face.

Now when she arrived in the staff room, and he was thinking about his rendezvous with Nora, he found he couldn't face Sally, and so he immediately fled. The two women, he was sure, were laughing behind his retreating back.

The ringing of his alarm clock made him leap out of bed. It was seven a.m.

After his shower he dressed himself in his best clothes. He found a clean handkerchief and put it in his pocket and doused himself in a new kind of aftershave that a fellow lodger had conveniently left in the bathroom. Of course, the very word 'aftershave' was a mockery, a mere euphemism for 'perfume'. He had dickied himself up with perfume because he had a date with Nora. It was pitiful and degrading, but then nobody was perfect.

Mrs Maher smelt him over the cornflakes and gave indications of being consumed by overpowering lust. She was a lately widowed woman, who clearly was missing her usual ration of conjugal bliss and was nosing about for a substitute. Séamus fended her off and made his escape from the house. For once, he was early for school.

When the bell rang at ten past three, he was out the door like a greyhound from the traps. He ran to the corner of the square, past the shops and the Distillery and down the hill, and caught a bus to Stephen's Green. He could have walked the distance in ten minutes, but he felt he shouldn't leave anything to chance. In the event, the bus journey took fifteen minutes.

Because it was late September there were fewer people about. There was a hint of rain in the air. He went to the duck pond and found the very spot where they had sat a year before. He had been there, of course, many times during the shifting year, perhaps hoping that she might reappear, but she had never come.

He decided that the grass was too damp to sit upon, so he found a vacant bench nearby and sat there watching the ducks. After a moment he lay back and closed his eyes, trying to picture how it had been the year before – the two children playing and her white dress and the way she had sat on James Augustine and how her eyes had filled with tears for some unaccountable reason. He began to drift off.

'Hello, Jim.'

It was like heavenly music. She was standing over him, head bent, smiling into his face. Her long, dark-green mackintosh, made of some sort of shiny material he hadn't seen before, looked very expensive. Around her neck there was a light-coloured silk scarf. Everything about her seemed more expensive than he remembered from the last time they had met. The boots on her little feet had gold buckles and matched the rest of her apparel in richness. Her eyes were bright and shining.

'Hello,' he said.

She looked plumper than he remembered, fuller in the face. She reached out a hand and touched his cheek.

'My dear Jim,' she said softly.

He stood up and she stepped back, as if she were afraid that he was going to embrace her.

'It's all right. I know my place in public.'

'Please, Jim, don't be cross with me.'

'I'm not cross. I'm just trying to keep my hands off you.'

'It's lovely to see you again. I've thought about you such a lot over the last year. Did you think of me at all?'

'Of course I thought of you. I thought about you every day. It's just that – you look different somehow.'

'I *am* different.'

'Your clothes are different.'

'You don't expect me to wear the same clothes all the time, do you?'

'God I've missed you.'

'I've missed you too. You don't know how many times I've picked up the phone to ring you.'

She paused. He was staring fixedly past her.

'What is it, Jim?'

He pointed a shaking finger.

'What is *that*?'

She turned and looked behind her.

'That's a pram,' she said.

ELEVEN

When Lucy and Derek arrived at Twin Cedars for lunch, they found Robert McGuinness in the garage prowling around the Morris Minor. Lucy ran through the door in her usual fashion and threw her arms around him.

'Oh Dad, how are you!'

Robert told her he was fine and somehow the words repelled her. She insisted he couldn't be. He admitted that he wasn't *fine* in that way, but only in the sense that he was getting on with life as best he could. He became conscious of the fact that she was probably weeping on his suit and he sent a mute appeal to Derek over her shoulder.

Derek immediately produced one of his white handkerchiefs and moved in to the rescue.

'Get away from me,' said Lucy fiercely. 'I'm not a child!'

The two men looked at her in surprise. She was not crying. For a moment Robert thought he had caught a fleeting image of Babs in her face. Once or twice in their life together Babs had flashed at him like that. Not often, it had to be said. He had never given her cause to be angry with him, he prided himself on that, and to her credit she had never sought an excuse to be so.

Now, seeing this echo of his dead wife in Lucy's face, he felt a sudden burst of nostalgia, a longing for the old days when Babs was alive and knew her place, knew that she owed everything to him and never had the slightest inclination to be secretive or disobedient. Life had been much simpler then. The thought that she might somehow have been different from his conception of her filled him with despondency.

'Put away your handkerchief, Derek,' said Lucy, remarkably dry-eyed. 'I'm perfectly all right.'

'Of course, love.'

Derek made the offending linen square disappear like a conjuror's rabbit.

'Dad, Derek and I have been thinking. You need a holiday. In fact we all need a holiday. We should go away together, get this place out of our minds for a month or so.'

'I don't think that would be possible.'

'Of course it's possible, Dad. Everything's possible. You're the boss. All you have to do is to delegate a little authority for a while. We'll find some place in the sun where we can relax. You can choose. Where would you like to go?'

'I can't go anywhere. I've got too much to do here, too many things to look after.'

He didn't tell her that he had no intention of going away for a month, or even a week, without Orla Corr.

'Delegate, Dad. *Delegate*. Isn't that right, Derek?'

Derek was a little surprised to be consulted.

'Yes, love.'

'Some things can't be delegated, Lucy.'

'What things?'

'Your mother's car, for instance.'

'Oh I want to talk to you about that. You leave the car to me. I'll look after it. We have a local sale coming up for cancer research. Everybody is bringing along something that will be auctioned off for the cause. And it'd be most appropriate for Mammy's car . . .' She faltered. 'Oh dear . . .'

Derek had his handkerchief out again. She knocked his hand away.

'I'm *not* crying, Derek.' She turned again to Robert. 'I'm sure Mammy would have liked her car to go to such a cause.'

'Exactly as I would have thought myself, Lucy.'

'Well, that's settled, then. In fact, I'll drive it home with me today.'

'Not quite. I have something to tell you. Come inside and we'll have a drink before lunch.'

They sat in the sitting-room with their drinks, while Robert told them about the Morris Minor and Babs's strange will. Again he said nothing about the big mileage; there was no point in sharing such unpleasant information with his daughter. When he had finished, there was a silence. Derek and Lucy looked at each other.

Then Derek said, 'That's very strange, Mr McGuinness.'

'I think so too,' said Robert. 'Totally out of character. We never had any secrets from each other.' He glanced at Lucy's face, but there was no trace of cynicism to be detected. This encouraged him. 'Tell me, Derek, what do you know about Hanley and Patterson?'

'Not a lot.'

'Are they genuine solicitors?'

'Oh I don't think there's any doubt about that. Kate Hanley has been in practice for at least fifteen years, probably more. As far as I know Herbie Patterson used to be a private investigator in a previous existence. He was a late vocation to the law.'

'A private investigator?' Robert was disturbed. He didn't like the sound of that at all. 'Investigating what?'

'Anything and everything. Industrial espionage. Installing hidden cameras to observe tradesmen at work. Finding heirs and heiresses. Investigating wives for husbands, husbands for wives. That sort of thing.'

'It all sounds a bit sleazy,' said Lucy.

'Oh I don't know,' said Derek. 'Think of Philip Marlowe and Sam Spade.'

'That's exactly what I *am* thinking of.'

'It sounds *very* sleazy,' said Robert. 'Ferreting about in dirty linen. But it doesn't surprise me one bit. I didn't like the look of that Hanley woman the minute I saw her. The point is, Derek, what can we do about it?'

Derek took off his glasses, breathed on them and polished them with his handkerchief, before he replied. He spent a lot of time in front of the mirror practising such deliberate professional gambits in order to offset his excessively youthful pink appearance.

'Well, as I see it, Mr McGuinness,' he said importantly, 'you have three possible options. The first one is, do nothing. Accept that the will is valid. Just let things take their legal course.'

'That's not an option.'

'I anticipated that. The second option is to contest the will made by Mrs McGuinness on her deathbed, on the grounds that the car was properly included in the wills made by yourself and your wife in my presence, even if not expressly mentioned, that it really belongs to you and therefore couldn't be put into any new will without your consent.'

'Could I win that?'

'There's certainly a case to be made, though not a very convincing one. But it would take a lot of time, years maybe, to reach a conclusion. We don't know what other information the Hanley woman may have up her sleeve.'

Robert reacted crossly.

'What information could she possibly have?'

'Who knows!'

'There is no other information, Derek,' said Robert, with increasing anger. 'There couldn't be any other information.'

'Let's hope you're right, Mr McGuinness.'

'I *know* I'm right!' Robert was now scowling at Derek. Lucy observed her father with interest.

'Of course,' said Derek hurriedly, the pink of his earnestness now several shades paler. 'But I couldn't guarantee that a court action would eventually go in your favour. And going to court could well bring some unwelcome publicity.'

'Publicity?' Robert hadn't thought about that.

'You have a high profile, Mr McGuinness. A high *moral* profile, if I may say so. It wouldn't look very good if you were seen to be opposing your wife's last wishes. Or that you were claiming to own the car yourself, even though you expressly bought it for your wife.'

Robert knew that, along with his high moral profile, he also had a lot of immoral enemies who would be only too happy to throw whatever dirt they could in his direction.

'What's the third option?'

'Do nothing until some buyer turns up to claim the car. And then refuse to part with it. Plead sentimental value. Throw the ball into Hanley and Patterson's court. Let them make all the moves. And fight each move separately as it happens. You'd cause them a lot of grief and they might give up the whole affair. Or the buyer might just back away from trouble.'

'If I were you, I'd wait to see who turns up to claim the car,' said Lucy, 'and then give him money to go away. Offer to buy it back from him.'

'Him?' said Robert. 'Where did this "him" come from?'

'Her. Whatever. At least then you'd know who Mammy intended to give it to.'

'I don't believe your mother intended to give it to anyone. I feel she was somehow tricked into making this will. Or at least signing it. Nothing else makes any sense.'

'The car isn't very valuable, is it?'

'It has great sentimental value to *me*.'

'Of course, of course.' Lucy didn't sound very convinced. 'But not to anyone else, except maybe to this mysterious third party. I wonder what the "reserve" is.'

'I asked that Hanley person and she point-blank refused to tell me. Said she was bound by professional secrecy, or some rubbish of that sort. Could you find out, Derek?'

'Me?' Derek was genuinely shocked.

'You're a solicitor. You know the way these things can be handled. I'm sure she'd listen to a little friendly persuasion from a fellow practitioner. Have a word with her. Offer her a few bob if necessary.'

'It doesn't really work like that, Mr McGuinness.'

'Everything works like that, Derek. *Make* it work. I don't mind how much you spend.'

'I'll do what I can, but I'm afraid I can't promise you any joy.'

'What am I paying you for, Derek? Apart from the fact that you're married to my daughter, that is.'

'Don't mind him, dear,' said Lucy. 'He's only taking the mickey.'

Derek essayed a smile, but looking at the set of Robert's pudgy face he wasn't at all sure that his father-in-law was playing any innocent game.

'I'll do my best, sir.'

'That's my boy.'

'Dad,' said Lucy thoughtfully, 'what possible reason could Hanley and Patterson have for tricking Mammy into doing such a thing with her car?'

'How the hell do I know!'

'It seems very odd.'

'Of course it's odd,' snarled Robert. 'It's bloody odd. That's why I want your husband to investigate it for me.'

'But supposing Mammy *did* intend to sell the car to someone in particular?'

'Don't be ridiculous, Lucy. Your mother wasn't like that. I told that Hanley woman we had no secrets and do you know what she did? She openly sneered at me! That's why I *know* that there has to be more to this than meets the eye. In case you've forgotten, I'm an important man. As Derek says, I have a high profile. There are a lot of people who'd like to do me harm. For all sorts of reasons. Look, Derek, even a sleazy outfit like Hanley and Patterson must have some office staff. If that Neanderthal woman gives you the fingers, buy one of her clerks. Only find out for me what's going on, who's behind this!'

He poured himself another drink, breathing heavily. Derek and Lucy exchanged glances.

'Don't excite yourself, Dad,' said Lucy soothingly. 'I'm sure there's a perfectly simple explanation.'

'If there is, I want to hear it.'

'I'll do my best, Mr McGuinness.'

'Make sure you do.'

Lunch was a rather silent affair. Despite the succulence of the roast pork, Robert sat there, staring angrily at his plate. Derek attempted to make small talk, but he really wasn't very good at it, and besides, he was worrying how he was going to extract information from another solicitor without contravening the legal ethics code, or at least without getting caught.

Lucy wondered what had got into her mother that had prompted her to put the car up for sale. Relations had not been ideal between her parents for several years and she suspected that Orla Corr was rather more than a secretary at ORMAX. Such unpleasant thoughts, however, she had endeavoured to keep at bay, while she was making her way through boarding school and college and garnering Derek Furlong in the process.

Those teenage years had been very selfish. She had taken all her mother's affection and had given very little in return. Oh she had loved Babs all right, but they had never been really close, principally because Lucy always had so much to do to keep up with her friends and the never-ending round of her social activities.

In the back of her mind there had been the vague assumption that, later on, when she was married and had a child of her own, she and Babs would get together and share womanly thoughts and experiences and perhaps do some knitting, or crochet-work.

Now the time had passed. Her mother was dead and Lucy realized with a great sense of guilt that she had never really understood Babs and that there would be no cosy chats in the future to help her make up that deficit.

As soon as lunch was over, she excused herself and went upstairs to her mother's room. This was the main bedroom and was located at the front of the house. Ten years before, her mother had gone to hospital to have an operation. Lucy hadn't been told what the illness was and, being a very self-occupied twelve-year-old, had never really thought to ask. She only knew that her mother had come home without any hair and wearing a wig. Robert had moved out of his wife's bed and had gone to sleep in the second bedroom. At the time, Lucy, when she thought about it at all, had considered this move a heroic sacrifice on the part of her father, one born from pure sympathy for his wife and a desire to leave her in peace to recover her health. However, even when Babs had regained something approaching full health, Robert had not returned to the main bedroom. The arrangement, entered into so quietly, had come to be accepted as normal by Lucy and she had attributed it to the different hours her parents kept and the separate lifestyles they led.

Now, however, as she opened the door of her mother's bedroom, quite other thoughts assailed her.

This was where Babs had seen out her last illness. Lucy remembered the last few weeks of her mother's life, the dimness of the room, the strange medical smells, the hushed comings and goings, Babs's white face and emaciated form melting deeper and deeper into the pillows as she gently relinquished her hold on the world. The oppressive sense of imminent death had spread its ripples around the whole house, even out into the garden, so that there was no hiding from it.

Now clearly a transition was in progress. All the medical appurtenances had been removed – the trolley, the oxygen cylinders, the metal stand holding the saline drip. That was understandable, but there were other signs of a less palatable nature. Her mother's wardrobe was empty, the doors flung wide as if to emphasize the fact. The other wardrobe was full of her father's clothes, which obviously had been brought back in from the second bedroom where he had slept for years. The dressing table held none of the familiar feminine objects she associated with her mother, but was now given over to masculine effects; the perfume bottles, the mother-of-pearl backed hairbrushes and the vanity boxes had been replaced by an electric razor and some aftershave lotions.

But most disturbing of all was the absence of Babs's chest of drawers. In Lucy's mind this was something inseparable from her mother. It had come with Babs from the farm in Galway where she had been born and reared, and was her most prized possession, so she had often told Lucy, apart from Lucy herself. During Lucy's childhood it had been the place that held all the most delicious and surprising surprises just waiting to be found by a little girl who had been very good and deserved such delights. Bars of chocolate, packets of sweets,

lollipops and suchlike lurked in its secret corners. It was also a wonderful treasure chest to rummage in on wet days, containing as it did old necklaces to be
worn during games of make-believe, little pictures in metal frames to be exam-
ined and identified as being of Granny and Granddad Needham from distant
Galway, and china ornaments and boxes full of spools and bobbins, which
could become whatever a child's imagination might invent.

Its disappearance now seemed to trumpet out the fact that Babs was dead.
Lucy had a vision of her mother arriving up in Heaven and being asked by St
Peter what she had done with the chest of drawers. It was a poignant picture
to have to look at, and made her want to cry.

She retreated to the corridor, closed the door behind her and stood there
blinking back her tears. For the first time she understood that her mother was
really gone. She felt like lying down on the floor, as she had so often done as
a child, and wailing her woes to the whole house, while the walls cracked
around her and the roof flew off and the chimney-pots banged about like skit-
tles in the sky.

Instead, she recovered her composure with an effort and entered the second
bedroom.

Because the curtains were closed, it was quite dark and gloomy inside. Lucy
pulled them apart and allowed the light to flood into the room. On the
stripped single bed lay her mother's clothes, neatly folded as if awaiting
disposal. There were several cardboard boxes stacked against one wall. She
poked in them and discovered that they contained the bric-a-brac missing
from the dressing-table in Babs's room, along with shoes and other items. The
shoes particularly attracted her attention. She picked up a small pair of black
patent leathers with a little gold strip around the toecaps. They looked as if they
had just been purchased, and much too tiny for an adult foot. Her mother had
loved shoes and always kept them immaculate, so that they never seemed to
wear out, but merely retired gracefully to a corner when past their fashionable
life.

Lucy returned the shoes to the box and stood up. She looked around the
room. There, standing against the other wall, was the chest of drawers.

She walked over to it and ran her hands along the mahogany surface, feeling the numerous scratches and scars it had accumulated with the passage of
time, some of them directly attributable to herself. One she especially remembered – a long scratch she had inflicted on the wood with a pair of scissors

during a burst of temper over some long-forgotten injustice, real or imagined. She opened the top drawer. Tears again gathered in her eyes as she surveyed the familiar contents. Nothing seemed to have been changed. She picked up a small picture and looked at the old man's portrait it held. Granddad Needham, whom she had never met, but about whom her mother spoke so often and so affectionately, stared back at her. Grandma Needham, in an even older and browner photograph, seemed to be looking at something far distant. And the china ornaments were still there, along with the spools and bobbins.

She opened a second drawer. It held some books. There was a hardback called *Nora, a Biography of Nora Joyce* by Brenda Maddox; two paperbacks, *Dubliners* and *A Portrait of the Artist as a Young Man*, by Joyce himself. And most surprising of all, there was a copy of *Ulysses*. There were also several books by James Barnwell. Lucy remembered these well. They were funny books and her mother used to read them to her when she was quite a small girl. Lucy hadn't understood them all, but she remembered how her mother used to laugh a lot at them and how her infectious delight in the writing had conveyed itself to her daughter. They brought a rush of nostalgia for the simpler happier days before she had gone away to boarding school, days spent in the company of her mother, often in her mother's bed, while her father was away from home, or otherwise occupied.

Lucy looked at the Joyce books in surprise. She had no idea that her mother read such things, especially *Ulysses*, which Lucy had attempted in college but had never quite got through. She knew that her mother's education had been severely curtailed and felt that, in the natural order of things, reading Joyce would have been beyond her. Yet there it was, with her name on it, hidden away in her most secret place.

And, even more surprisingly, there was a second copy of *Ulysses*. It was buried deeply beneath the other books. Lucy picked it up. It was an old copy, dog-eared, that had evidently been bought second-hand. She flicked open the cover. On the flyleaf was written, 'To Nora. From Jim. 1976'. And underneath was 'Séamus Creedon, St Fiachra's CBS'. There was also a telephone number, one of the old six-figure ones.

Lucy wondered who Séamus Creedon was and if he had ever guessed that his book, with his name inscribed, and perhaps that of his girlfriend, would turn up in a strange woman's chest of drawers twenty-three years after he had written in it. She felt sure that Nora, whoever she was, wouldn't have been over the moon at the thought. Of course, that was assuming that Séamus Creedon and Jim were one and the same person, which seemed likely, because Séamus was the Gaelic form of Jim and because everything on the flyleaf appeared to be written in the one hand.

She heard a footstep on the stairs and closed the drawer.

'Are you in there, Lucy?'

It was Derek.

'In here.'

He entered the room.

'What are you up to?'

'Do you see this?' she said, pointing to the chest of drawers, 'I'm going to ask Dad if I can take it home with me.'

Derek showed no surprise; he was used to giving in to Lucy.

'If you want to. Though I can't see where we'll put it.'

'Oh we'll find a place. If it's left here it'll only get thrown out.'

Derek put his arms around her.

'Do you miss her, love?'

She nodded against his chest.

'I'm only beginning to realize how much.'

TWELVE

He sat down heavily on the bench and closed his eyes. Then he opened them again and stared at the pond. The ducks had vanished and had been replaced by monstrous griffins hovering grimly, darkening the sky with their scaly wings. There was turbulence in the waters of the pond. In the distance rumbled the deep tones of impending thunderstorms.

He looked back at her. She was staring at him intently, a little smile playing around the corners of her mouth.

'Yours?'

'Of course. And she's lovely.'

He didn't want to hear about the loveliness of the baby. He didn't want to hear about anything. He wanted to run away somewhere and howl at the moon, but it was still only the afternoon and the moon wouldn't be out for hours yet, and then would probably be hidden by the clouds. Ireland was a bad country for moon-howling in.

'Oh shite,' he said.

'Ah no, don't be like that, Jim. I brought her out specially so that you could see her.'

'I don't want to see her.'

'Of course you want to see her. What man wouldn't want to see his own child.'

Now even the griffins took flight, beating the air with their clangorous wings. The world began to shake with thunder. Faintly through the reverberations he heard her voice.

'Don't worry, Jim. I'm not blaming you and I'm not claiming you. I just wanted you to see her, that's all, so that you could be as proud of her as I am.

Ah please, Jim, say something nice to me.'

He exploded into life.

'Nice?' he shouted. 'Nice? Holy bloody God, you really take the bloody biscuit! What the hell is there to say something nice about!'

He turned away from her and strode back along the path. When he got to the bend, he stopped and looked back. She was sitting on the bench with her head in her hands. Was she crying? It was impossible to tell. To hell with her. Let her cry.

Everything was telling him to keep on walking. All his instincts, all his sense of self-preservation. She had left him one night over a year ago and had never thought to get in touch since then. And now she had arrived back with a baby in tow and expected him to be nice about it. Even somebody like Sally Carmody, with her long tongue and her fat breasts, wouldn't do a thing like that to him. He'd be better off well away from this deceiving woman, even if it meant living the rest of his life in arid bachelordom. To hell with her. Let her cry.

He walked slowly back towards her.

She didn't raise her head when he sat down beside her. Her shoulders were shaking and he saw that she really was crying. The realization appalled him. He fumbled in his pocket and brought forth the clean handkerchief.

'Don't cry.'

She looked up at him, with tears streaming down her cheeks. When he thrust the handkerchief at her, she took it and made use of it to wipe her face.

'Is it true?'

'I thought you'd be pleased.'

'Is it *true*?'

'Of course it's true. What do you take me for?'

'I don't know. Honest to God, I just don't know what to take you for.'

She sniffed and then blew her nose into his clean handkerchief.

'Will you look at what I've done now! I always seem to ruin your hankies.'

God, didn't she realize that this was well beyond hankies!

'It's OK. Keep it.'

'I couldn't give it back now, that's for sure.' She stuffed the piece of cotton into the pocket of her raincoat. 'I'll send you a new one. Two new ones.'

'You'll do no such thing.'

'I'll probably forget, anyway.'

They sat in silence a moment.

'What is she – what did you call her?'

'What else only Lucia.'

'Lucia.' He savoured the name.

'The Nuncio was delighted. He comes from Santa Lucia di Piave. That's in Italy. I didn't tell him it was in honour of you. He thought it was in honour of *him*. Thinks I have a bit of a *grá* for him.'

'You know the Nuncio?'

'My husband does. He comes to our house sometimes.' Then she added, 'I shouldn't have mentioned that. Forget I said it. Anyway, we call her Lucy at home. But I call her Lucia inside in my head. Would you like to hold her?'

He had held babies before. His sister had babies. He shouldn't be afraid of a baby. But he was deadly afraid of this one.

'It's all right if you don't want to.'

'Give her to me.' His voice was muffled.

From the pram she took the bundle wrapped in a white crocheted blanket, and put it into his arms. He held it carefully, pushing the blanket aside from the child's face with his finger.

'Isn't she beautiful?'

It wasn't the word he would have used, but he nodded his head.

'How old is she?'

'Six months last Friday. She was born on the sixteenth of March. That was a Wednesday. We met on a Wednesday, if you remember.'

'Oh God,' he said, looking down at the little face. Lucia opened her eyes fleetingly. In that moment he could see that they were green, like her mother's.

'Green eyes.'

'No. All babies' eyes are blue.'

'I saw them. They're green.'

'That's only in your mind.'

'How can you be sure she's mine?'

'I'm sure.'

'She doesn't look like me.'

'She does sometimes. When she wrinkles her nose she's pure you.'

He was inordinately pleased.

'She is?'

'The spitting image of you. When it happens I feel very funny, because I'm the only one who knows. They're all seeing Uncle This and Aunty That and Cousin The Other, and the Nuncio is seeing second and third cousins back in Italy, eating spaghetti. And I'm seeing you.'

'But your husband and you . . . I mean . . . you must sometimes . . .'

'Yes, we do. *Sometimes*. Once in a blue moon. But Lucia is yours. I know that for an honest-to-God fact. All yours. Every little bit of her that isn't mine is yours.'

A great peace seemed to have descended on the world. The griffins were fled and the ducks were back paddling about the calm pond.

'I never thought of anything like this,' he said after a while.

'I never thought of anything else.'

Somehow that remark rippled the pond.

'How can you be really sure this is my child?'

'Because my husband doesn't – well, he *can't*, if you know what I mean. Anyway, he never wanted kids. We couldn't afford them. We couldn't this and we couldn't that. There were a million reasons. I cried my eyes out night after night. But when he makes his mind up! We fasted and abstained on all of the days commanded, and we abstained on other days too. He wouldn't use anything artificial. So it was counting and calculating all the time, marking days off on the calendar, doing sums, and doing penance. Praying. And the gas part of it all was that he didn't need to do any of the tricks, or the prayers. Only *he* didn't know. But I did. When the natural method failed, according to him, he thought it was a pure act of Holy God, a sort of a sign. God wanted us to have a child. So he accepted it. Even if she wasn't a boy. He would have preferred a boy.'

'How did you know about him? I mean, not being able to have a child.'

'I knew. I took tests and things on the sly, so I knew it wasn't me. Anyway, all that doesn't matter now. I have Lucia. *We* have Lucia.'

'Well, then, that settles it, doesn't it?'

'Settles it?'

'The only thing to do now is leave him and come and live with me.'

'No.'

'Why?'

'He's my husband.'

'Holy God, *we're* a family now. Us here. You, me and Lucia.'

'No, I can't. So don't ask me about it.'

'Tell me *why*. One good reason. Well? I can support you. I've got a job. It's not the best in the world, but it's not the worst. Lots of secondary teachers get married and raise families on what they earn.'

'It's not a question of money, or anything like that. I'm married and marriage is for life. So I can't marry you. And I can't come and live with you, because that would be adultery.'

He took several moments to digest that.

'And what about Joyce's tower?'

'That was adultery too, I know that. But it was a once thing. I could confess that and promise never to do it again and everything would be all right. But if I was to go and *live* with you, permanently, the priest would refuse me absolution unless I agreed to give you up. And if I was living with you, I couldn't promise to do that. Anyway, I wouldn't want to give you up. I don't want to give you up now. So it's best not to get into it.'

'That's a crazy philosophy.'

'Maybe it is and maybe it isn't, but that's the way I was brought up and there's no way I can change the way I feel about it.'

He looked down at the baby. Lucy had opened her eyes and was staring up at him very solemnly. He smiled at her. She stared back. He put his finger on her chin and flicked it gently. She smiled at him.

'She's smiling at me,' he said.

'Of course she is. She does that all the time. It's mostly wind. She's a very good-tempered baby, like her daddy.'

'Which daddy is that?'

'There's only one *daddy*.'

'Am I supposed to take comfort from that?'

'I wouldn't look a gift horse in the mouth. You can enjoy the thought of having a beautiful daughter without ever having to look after her.'

'I *want* to look after her!'

'No you don't. Looking after her means changing her nappies and blowing her nose and getting up in the middle of the night when she cries.'

'That sounds like a perfectly desirable occupation to me.'

'Don't be a daft eejit! She'll always be a nuisance in one way or another. Falling down. Getting sick with measles and things. Clinging on to you and whingeing. And then when she gets into her teens she'll go all moody and spotty and she'll hate you, and she'll start going after the worst kind of fella imaginable. All her fellas will be greasy and spotty, and you'll hate them and they'll hate you and there'll be hate all over the place. She won't do anything you tell her. She'll stay out, especially when you tell her to come home early. And you'll be up all night every night again wondering where she's got to and imagining all kinds of awful things happening to her. You don't want all of that.'

'I do, I do!'

'No, you don't. This way it'll be all plain sailing for you. You can watch her growing up. She'll grow beautiful and tall and she'll never learn to hate you.'

'How can I watch her growing up when you won't bring her to live with me?'

'I've been thinking about that. There's plenty of ways I can arrange it.'

'But she wants to be with me. She *smiled* at me.'

'Wind.'

'I don't believe a word of it. She looked at me and recognized the light upon her from her father's eyes.'

The baby started to whimper.

'That's what she thinks of you and your light. Give her back here to me.'

He handed her the baby without demur. She took the bundle and crooned over it, holding it close to her breast. He wanted to be there. It amazed him to see her in the role of a mother. She looked born for the part. He wondered why it had never crossed his mind that she might have got pregnant at Joyce's tower.

After a moment, she sniffed.

'Oh-oh! I thought it was too good to be true. I'm going to have to change her. Do you mind?'

'Why would I mind?'

'A lot of men do. If you like I can always slip up to the hotel above – they have a changing room for babies.'

'Can you do it here?'

'I'd rather do it here. She's only a wee scrap, anyway.'

She reached into the bottom of the pram and drew out a flowery bag with a zip on it. Inside she had powder and a couple of clean napkins and some cotton wool and other things.

'You can turn away, if you want to, Jim. She won't mind and I won't mind.'

'What father would want to turn away from his daughter.'

'You'd be surprised.'

'Just you carry on and leave me alone.'

She laid the baby in the pram and busied herself. He felt absurdly shy, not knowing where to look. What *do* you look at when a baby is being changed, especially a girl baby?

'Yuck!' she said. 'Don't look!'

He had no intention of looking at *that*!

'Gentlemen don't look at ladies in embarrassing positions.'

'Eejit. Here, make yourself useful.'

He stared at the jar of cream she pushed into his hand.

'What?'

'It's a new one. *Open* it, please.'

He opened the jar. His beard trembled with patriarchal pride. 'I have performed an act of service for my daughter. Without flinching.'

The baby had stopped whimpering. He stole a glance, admiring her deft fingers as she shook powder, fastened pins and tucked things in. The offending napkin was put into a bag and secreted in the nether regions of the pram.

'There we are. All sweet-smelling and pleased with yourself. I suppose you're looking for something else now, are you? Well, come on, then.'

Then she paused.

'Would this bother you, Jim?'

'What?'

'She's due a feed.'

'Why would that bother me!'

'Of course it wouldn't. My husband doesn't like it much, but I make him put up with it.'

'I hate that bastard.'

She put her hand fleetingly on his, squeezing gently. Then she unbuttoned herself and put the baby to her breast.

'Do you mind if I watch?'

'I want you to watch.'

He looked at the baby sucking busily on the nipple, one little fist curled against the white of the breast. He thought he had never seen anything so beautiful.

'I wish I had a camera.'

'You'd be arrested for taking dirty photographs,' she said happily, settling back on the bench.

'I'd willingly go to jail for the privilege.'

'And I'd come and visit you with the child under my arm. Look, love, there's your Daddy in there behind all the bars – for taking dirty pictures of babbies.'

'Not of other babies, only of you. I'm a one-woman, one-baby man.'

'I don't want you to be, Jim. I mean, I do and I don't. God, isn't it terrible! Imagine you got into all this with just one little squirt.'

'That's not the way it seemed to me.'

'No. Nor to me. I'll remember that night for the whole of my life.'

There was a long pause, while the baby sucked and the ducks paddled about. Some people passed, but nobody took the slightest notice of a woman suckling a child. He had an urge to stand up and announce to the passing world that this was *his* woman and *his* child, two of the most beautiful things that had ever been created. However, he doubted if anyone would understand, so he contented himself with clutching his wonderful news to himself.

She took Lucia from her breast, turned her over and patted her gently on her back. The baby burped.

'Good girl,' she said, putting her to the other breast. 'Now tell me what you've been doing with yourself since I saw you last.'

'Nothing much. Teaching. Moping about. Getting drunk occasionally.'

'What about women?'

'What about them? You've spoiled me for all the rest.'

'That's no way for you to talk, a young boy like you. You should be out and about finding yourself a wife.'

'*You're* my wife, Nora.'

'No, I'm not,' she said sadly, 'and I never will be. Not unless he dies, God forgive me. Not that I wish him to. But he won't. So there's nothing to do but for you to find a wife and make a family for yourself. If you leave me your address, I'll send you a picture of her nibs here every birthday, so that you can see how she's getting on and growing up.'

'Will you leave me *your* address?'

'No. I *can't*, Jim.'

'I'm sure there's some way I could find out.'

'If you do, you do. And that's that. I can't stop you nosing around. But I hope you won't, for both our sakes.'

'Maybe I'll see your picture in the paper one day, standing beside the Nuncio.'

'Oh my picture doesn't ever get in the papers.'

That didn't surprise him. He had already formed a mental picture of her husband: tall, supercilious, cruel in little things – and impotent. He took pleasure in that unworthy thought. The bastard was *impotent!*

'If you won't give me your address, how am I expected to get in touch with you if I change jobs? Or change digs.'

'Yesterday I opened a PO box. Well, I mean, I asked Kate and she did it for me. I have the number here somewhere.' She rooted in her handbag and brought out a piece of paper. 'There it is.'

He took the piece of paper from her.

'You've got it all thought out, haven't you?'

'Tear it up if you're not happy, Jim. It's up to you what you do.'

'I'll keep it.'

'I'm glad. You can write to me there if you decide to leave St Fiachra's and go somewhere else. You can give me your new address. If you want to. Do you want to?'

'I don't know. Yes, I do. No, I don't. When I'm standing here looking at you, I never want to let you out of my sight. But who knows what'll happen to both of us when we haven't seen one another for years, maybe.'

'We'll just have to do our best. Oh I have something else for you.'

She reached again into her handbag and took out a photo.

'What's that?'

'Look at it.'

He looked.

'It's a baby.'

'Your daughter, aged about half-an-hour. It was taken in the hospital the night she was born. Wednesday, the sixteenth of March 1977. I'll send you a photo every year on her birthday, so you can see her growing up.'

He put the picture carefully into his inside pocket.

Then, out of the blue, she said, 'Tell me about your MA. Have you finished it yet?'

'The MA is gone.'

'What do you mean, gone?'

'I gave it up.'

'Oh you can't, Jim.'

'Oh I can. I have.'

'But why?'

'For God's sake,' he said bitterly. 'How could I go on writing about Jim and Nora when it would only keep reminding me of you!'

'You can't give it up just like that.'

'I'll find something else. That's if I decide to do anything at all. Plenty of material out there. Poets are ten a penny.'

'But there's only one Joyce. Please, Jim. Please go back and give it a try. What will your daughter think of you if you don't have an MA?'

Eventually he gave in and made a promise that he would indeed 'give it a try'. But he didn't hold out much hope for himself, or for his resolve in the matter.

She put the sleeping baby back into the pram and tucked her in.

'I've bought myself a couple of Joyce's books,' she said.

He was delighted to hear that she had read *Dubliners* and was making her way through the *Portrait*. His enthusiasm for Joyce bubbled up and he forgot about the strangeness of the position he found himself in and the strangeness of the woman he was speaking to. They discussed the stories at length. He found she had a great appreciation of Joyce and a keen way of putting her finger on the kernel of a story.

As they talked, the day began to close in. There was a noticeable drop in the temperature.

'Good lord, is that the time?' she said suddenly, looking at her watch. 'I'll have to get this lassie home before it gets any colder.'

'That's a nice piece of machinery on your wrist. It must have cost a packet.'

'Things are better with us now, especially since Lucia was born. He gave me this as a present after the birth. And we're moving to a new house next month.'

'I don't want to hear about it.'

'No. I'm sorry. I shouldn't be rabbitting on about things like that.'

He said nothing. She stood up. He stood too.

'I'll have to go,' she said.

'Do I get a goodbye kiss?'

She leaned forward and kissed him on the lips.

'Goodbye, Jim. Till the next time.'

'If there is a next time.'

115

'There will be. I promise you.'

'Can I see you to your bus?'

'You know the answer to that. Say goodbye to your daughter.'

He put his hand into the pram and touched the little face.

'Goodbye, Lucia.'

They moved along the path and out of sight.

THIRTEEN

Derek Furlong was a nervous man by nature. He had been born like that. According to the nurses, his mother said, Derek had emerged from the womb twitching nervously and glancing furtively about the ward as if wondering what he was doing in this exclusively female gathering and what the whole affair was likely to cost him.

He had carried this nervousness with him into his adult life. It was very much with him when he went to Leeson Street to confront the two-headed Hanley and Patterson beast in its lair.

And, of course, that particular adventure, taken reluctantly at the behest of his overbearing father-in-law, had been more disastrous than even Derek's fearful forebodings.

Later, safely back in the bosom of his home and his wife, he described to Lucy the galvanic effect the name Robert McGuinness had had on the Hanley/Patterson bloc.

'I was doing reasonably well till I mentioned the name of my client. Then they blew up. I thought for one awful moment they were going to assault me. With heavy things. That dark room they lurk in is full of heavy things.'

'My poor darling.' Lucy smoothed his hair and pressed a vodka-and-tonic into his shaking hand. 'Do you think we should go to the police?'

Derek gulped at his drink.

'Not a chance. They didn't actually hit me, so I've no bruises to show. And they made sure there were no witnesses. But it was all very unpleasant. That Hanley woman scared the pants off me.'

'Dad seems to have got up her nose.'

'That's not a place I'd wish to go.'

'But Dad's like that. He doesn't care what he says to people.'

'I wish I were like that.'

'You're nicer as you are. Did you learn anything at all?'

'Only that they don't have a buyer for the car yet.'

'Well, that's good anyway. I suppose.'

'What am I going to tell your father?'

'Oh you'll think of something.'

She left him sipping his drink and composing his excuses, while she made her way upstairs.

Her father had raised no objections to her taking away the chest of drawers. In fact, he had seemed delighted to be rid of it. It now stood in one of Lucy's spare bedrooms, looking decidedly out of place in the minimalist surroundings.

Lucy hadn't yet made up her mind where she would eventually put it, but she was determined not to part with it. It reminded her so much of her mother. It had a rough honesty about it very much like Babs's own unpretentiousness. It stood solidly against the wall and seemed to say that here it was, that there was no nonsense attached to it, that it was 'up-front, in-your-face and what-you-see-is-what-you-get' in all its dealings, with nothing concealed or disguised.

'Not even a secret drawer,' sighed Lucy to herself, 'containing scented love letters tied with a blue bow. Oh Mammy, why didn't you hide something for me to find?'

Then, as she again rummaged among the odds and ends, she found the car keys. They were in a little blue Wedgwood vase standing in a corner of the top drawer. Her mother must have put them aside as spares. Lucy contemplated them with some interest and then returned them to the vase.

She took out the battered copy of *Ulysses* and sat on the bed with it. The inscriptions on the flyleaf stared back at her. 'To Nora. From Jim. 1976. Séamus Creedon. St Fiachra's CBS.' Then the thought struck her that perhaps the apparent similarity in the handwriting might be mere coincidence. Suppose that the sequence had been: Jim buys the book and gives it to Nora; later Nora and Jim split up and Nora sells it on. Then, later still, Séamus Creedon, a senior pupil, or a teacher, in St Fiachra's, buys it again. Then, later again, her mother buys it.

Not very romantic, but quite possible.

Lucy flicked through the text till she reached the end papers. Here she discovered the photograph. She hadn't expected a photo and the reason why she hadn't discovered it before was that it had been concealed inside the back cover. A sheet of white paper the same size as the back cover had been carefully taped over the picture and Lucy had to remove this before she found the print.

She moved to the window so that she might the better see the faces of the two people in the picture. One was certainly her mother, dressed in some kind of summer clothing, a white dress and white sandals. The other was a man, a narrow man with a dark beard. He was dressed in a pullover and what seemed to be grey slacks. They stood together, arms around each other's waist, looking a little self-consciously at the camera, as if afraid of it. Lucy guessed that they had used a camera with a timing device and had posed themselves with little more than a few seconds to spare. They were standing in the open. Behind them was some undergrowth, through which could be seen the gleam of water.

Both of them were smiling. They seemed very happy together. She stared long and hard at them, but particularly at the man. Who was he? And why had her mother taken such care to keep the picture out of sight?

She turned the picture over. On the back was written the date September 1989. She compared the handwriting on the photo with the signature 'Séamus Creedon' on the flyleaf. To her inexperienced eye they seemed very similar indeed.

She sat for a long time absorbing the significance of what she had found, not knowing whether to laugh or cry at the idea of her mother looking so happy and relaxed with another man ten years ago, when Lucy had been twelve years of age. September 1989, that was when she had started in boarding school in Athlone. She tried to remember that September, but found that she had been so preoccupied with her own affairs in the new school, that she had very few memories of what her mother had looked like at the time, let alone of any conversations they might have had.

When she roused herself from her reverie, she consulted her watch. It was 2.45 p.m. The school would still be open. On a sudden impulse she picked up the telephone beside the bed and dialled the number on the flyleaf. The moment she started dialling a recorded male voice told her that the number had been changed. She rang Directory Enquiries and got the proper number of St Fiachra's CBS.

She drew a deep breath and dialled again. A female voice answered.

'St Fiachra's. Can I help you?'

'Excuse me, is there a Mr Séamus Creedon on your staff there?'

'Who's speaking, please?'

'You won't know me. My name is Lucy Furlong. I've come across a book with Séamus Creedon's name on it and the name of the school. I'd like to return it. I just wondered if he is still teaching there, that's all.'

'Oh, I'm afraid we don't have a Mr Creedon on the staff. You've no idea when he was here, have you?'

'Twenty-three years ago.'

'That's a fair old time.'

'I know, I know. It was a long shot. Sorry for troubling you.'

'I'm just the secretary here, and I'm only three years in the job.'

'Ah well, thank you, anyway.'

'I tell you what,' said the secretary. 'We do have a couple of dinosaurs, I mean senior staff members, who've been here since the Flood.' There were noises in the background, a door opening, a man's voice. 'Hang on. One of them's just come in.'

Lucy sat on the bed, feeling more foolish with every passing second. She could hear muffled voices off. Then the phone came to life again.

'Hello?' It was a male voice. 'I believe you're looking for information about Séamus Creedon?'

'Did you know him?'

'I surely did. Years ago. Are you a relation of his?'

'No. I found a book belonging to him, that's all.'

'Oh? That'd be Séamus. Always had a book in his hand. He's gone from here this long time. But will I tell you something? I'm looking at his photo right here in front of me this very minute. On the wall in the office here. It was taken for the Year Book of 1978, the last year that he taught here. A staff photo. And there's your man looking out at me as if it was yesterday.'

'Do you know where he is now, Mr—?'

'Clancy. Bill Clancy. And the answer is no. Not off the top of my head. But give me a little while to ask around and I might be able to get you some information.'

'I don't want to put you to any trouble, Mr Clancy.'

'No trouble at all. I'm always willing to help a female in distress.'

'I'm not really in distress.'

'No matter. I'll help you anyway. Tell you what, you give me your phone number and I'll give you a ring in a day or two. How's that?'

Lucy decided that there couldn't be much wrong with that, so she gave him her number.

'That's in Howth, isn't it? And it's Ms Lucy Furlong?'

'Mrs,' said Lucy, just in case there were complications, or Mr Clancy got any funny ideas.

'Mrs. Game ball. One other thing – would you like a copy of the 1978 Year Book?'

'Oh I couldn't possibly put you to the trouble—'

'Nonsense. I'll send you a copy. There's a load of them in the press here. Séamus Creedon was a decent skin. Glad to help a friend of his. So if you give me your address?'

Lucy could find no excuse not to.

'Thank you. I'll bung that in the post immediately.'

'You're very kind, Mr Clancy.'

When she had hung up, Lucy carefully removed the photo from the book. She decided not to say anything to Derek about the phone call; Derek had enough on his plate at the moment. Anyway, it would all probably come to nothing, or at least would have no real significance.

She wondered again why her mother had wanted to sell the car. Lucy had no doubt in her mind that Babs had made the will because it was what she wanted done. She was not the sort of person to be swayed by some crooked solicitor, as her father seemed to think. Or pretended to think. And then there was the odd wording in the advertisement: 'the vintage car fuelled with love'. What could that possibly mean except the unthinkable – that her mother had had an affair.

The more she thought about it, the more the idea thrilled Lucy. She went back to the chest of drawers and poked about amongst the odds and ends it contained. But there were no letters, no other photographs of a strange man.

It would all come to nothing.

But two days later the Year Book arrived through the post. It was a glossy publication, dated September 1978, and seemed to be full of pictures of football teams and bright scholars who had done exceptionally well in the Leaving and Intermediate Certificates.

There was a note from Clancy.

'All I can find out about Séamus is that he left here in 1978 and went to teach in the CBS in Ballina. He stayed there for several years and then resigned. I can't find anyone who knows where he went after that. But I'll keep trying. In the meantime, you'll find his photo on page sixteen. He's on the left of the second row. The laddo with the beard. I'm the handsome fat fellow beside him.'

Lucy found herself looking at a slight, dark-haired, bearded man. He was undoubtedly the same man who was standing beside her mother in the photo from the book.

Séamus Creedon. Her mother's lover.

FOURTEEN

Séamus Creedon's father died very suddenly in the summer of 1978, when Lucia was one year old. One moment he was casting on the water, having promised Niamh and himself a couple of fat brown trout for the evening meal, the next he was dead and quietly slumped against a tree awaiting discovery by his wife. In the circumstances, it seemed appropriate that the name of the retirement cottage they had purchased on the shore of Lochcrideen was *Tóg bog é* – 'take it easy'. In death as in life, Colm Creedon seemed to have chosen the easy way.

When he heard the news, Séamus immediately hurried home from Dublin. He found a sadly changed mother. Niamh Creedon had regressed almost overnight into a timorous, apprehensive woman, lost without her husband. Séamus was the first of the family to arrive. He took one look at his mother and realized that he had to take charge. By the time his sister and brother reached Maaclee, all the funeral arrangements had been made. Not only that, but Séamus informed them that he was going to move in with his mother and take care of her.

Eithne and Ciaran put up little opposition to this plan. Indeed both of them welcomed the fact that their dreamy and rather feckless younger brother had so suddenly matured into a responsible adult. They protested, of course, but their protestations lacked conviction.

Anyway, Séamus had his mother's backing. Even in her distraught and confused state, Niamh knew that life with either Eithne or Ciaran would entail not only having to leave the cottage, but also having to endure the close proximity of their tiresome offspring. Séamus was a bit of an oddball, but he was clean and quiet about the house and easy to get on with. Moreover, he was single.

So it was decided. Séamus returned to Dublin and resigned from St Fiachra's. The Clarinet was surprisingly civilized about his unexpected departure. He took Séamus into his office, sat him down and produced a bottle of whiskey.

'A man has only one father, Séamus. We'll drink a toast to the old man.'

In fact they drank several toasts. By the time Séamus finally left the office, he was barely able to walk in a straight line. But he felt enriched by the knowledge that the Clarinet was a human being after all.

He departed with an unexpected bonus. As they were saying goodbye, the Clarinet said, 'Hold on a minute.' He opened the drawer in his desk and pulled out a wad of notes. He didn't bother to count them, but thrust the bundle at Séamus.

'Here, take this.'

Séamus protested, not very convincingly.

'Go on,' said the Clarinet. 'It'll help with the funeral expenses. And I'll get in touch with the school in Ballina. Tadhg O'Neill's an old friend of mine. If you want teaching hours there, he'll see you right. But one thing,' he added by way of an addendum, 'you'd better improve your time-keeping. O'Neill's a stickler for the time-keeping.'

Séamus made his unsteady way back to Drumcondra to collect his meagre belongings from his room. In his semi-inebriated state this was not a simple operation. He had to say goodbye to Mrs Maher, which entailed accepting her consolatory embraces while carefully avoiding a farewell fumble and tumble on the settee in the front parlour. However, he finally managed to escape unscathed, feeling a bit like a departing ambassador who has successfully wriggled out of a potentially embarrassing diplomatic incident.

Before he left Dublin, he dropped a letter into Nora's PO Box informing her of his change of address. She replied the following day.

Oh my dear dear Jim I'm so sorry to hear of your father's death and that you are going to have to leave Dublin but you must of course look after your mother she has nobody now only you. Lucia is getting so big you wouldn't recognize her she says ma-ma and da-da all the time in between dribbles. And when she laughs and her nose crinkles up all she needs is a beard I'm sending you another photo this one shows her standing holding on to MY finger in case you think its someone else's the next minute she sat down on her bottom. I think of you every day and I'll pray for your mother that she is able to put up with losing her husband after so many years together. I love you my darling Jim.

Life settled into an uneasy routine in the cottage. Niamh recovered her initiative sufficiently to cook for them both and generally keep the house in order, but she never asked him again why he wasn't keeping company with someone his own age. Instead she became jealously protective of him and glared at any female in the village of Maaclee who showed any interest at all in her son. For his part, Séamus gave her no cause for alarm. He seemed to have little interest in anything beyond his work and the odd bit of fishing in the lake.

Brother O'Neill, as forecast by the Clarinet, gave him sufficient hours in the Ballina school to enable him to live, but not too many to prevent his doing other things in his spare time. Once again he thought about and then jettisoned the idea of trying for an MA on Joyce, deciding that he didn't have the intellectual capacity to produce anything new or sufficiently worthwhile. Instead, he returned to his earlier love – writing stories. There was an old Remington typewriter in the cottage that had belonged to his father and he learned to operate this with a couple of fingers, so that he was able to convert his handwritten text into typescript. The stories he wrote were humorous, fantastical almost. He found it impossible to write anything else. Then, rereading his work, he found it equally impossible to imagine that anyone else apart from himself, and perhaps Nora, would want to read such rubbish.

The nom-de-plume he chose was James Barnwell. He thought that was very clever and felt sure that Nora would appreciate it.

Eventually a day came when he packed three short stories into a large brown envelope. He took the envelope down to the local post office to have it weighed.

'London?' said Sheila Delaney, the postmistress, peering at the envelope over her glasses. 'And what's *that name*, Mr Creedon?'

'A magazine.'

'*Prolix*. That's a very peculiar name.'

'They publish peculiar things. I'm probably a bit peculiar myself.'

'Oh I don't believe that. I'm sure you're perfectly normal in the things that matter.'

She looked longingly after him as he left the shop.

'A little dote,' she said to her husband, who was arranging the parcels in the back office.

'Who?'

'Little Mr Creedon.'

'My arse.'

'I'd sooner have his,' said Sheila wistfully.

A year later, Séamus's first story, about a quirky schoolteacher living on the western seaboard, was published in a prestigious London magazine. It was followed by two more in quick succession. They were very well received and, within six months, his first novel, *Quirke's Progress*, went to the printers. He sent a copy to Nora. She was delighted.

Dear Jim, *she wrote*, there's too much of you in *Quirke* for comfort but I nearly died laughing all the same. Lucia was sitting beside me looking at me not knowing what was up with her mammy at all she had a cough last week but it's better now her eyes are green after all. When she's old enough I'll let her read it for herself and I know she'll enjoy it as much as I do. You're a right eejit writing these things I keep thinking about that night in the restaurant and the story you made up about the flamenco dancers on the boat. Oh lord I DO miss seeing you. And thanks for writing on the flyleaf though I cut it out just in case but don't worry I'll keep it in a safe place and wear it next my heart when I go out. I send you my love and a big kiss. And a kiss from Lucia too. Your loving Nora.

Quirke's Progress sold so well that Séamus was commissioned to write a second novel and received an advance. Despite his best endeavours, however, it took him nearly two lean years to fulfil his contract and it was well into 1983 before *Quirke Rampant* appeared in the bookshops.

In the meantime the pictures continued to arrive every March. They were of Lucia, aged three, riding on her first three-wheeled bicycle; Lucia, aged four, at her birthday party, with a clown's hat on her head and a look of utter dismay, plus a great deal of birthday cake, on her face; Lucia, aged five, holding up a picture painted by herself; and Lucia, aged six, in jeans and a jockey's cap, astride a pot-bellied pony.

Nora's letters, or rather notes, which were always enclosed with the photographs, confined themselves to comments about Lucia's measles, Lucia's tummy bugs (especially after the encounter with the birthday cake), Lucia's cut knee which she had got trying, and failing, to climb a small tree in the garden, Lucia's first day at school. They read like the comments a wife might make to a husband coming home from his day's work, as she laid out his supper on the kitchen table.

But, alas, they came no more than once or twice a year.

In 1985 Quango Publishing published his third novel, *The Quirke Dynasty*, and James Barnwell became a literary mini-celebrity. Séamus Creedon, however, remained a shy, part-time teacher, living with his mother in a small cottage in Maaclee and being secretly lusted after by the postmistress. He asked his publisher for privacy and his publisher obliged, feeling that any intrusion into the writer's life might only result in a spoiling of the freshness that made his stories so acceptable to a growing readership. In fact, his mysterious reclusiveness became an added attraction and a valuable selling point.

By this time Lucia had made her first Communion and he duly received a picture of his daughter glowing in her white frock and veil, white handbag and little white shoes. The shoes in particular moved him, reminding him of Nora's white shoes on the strand at Sandymount and all the excitement of that unforgettable day. He wondered what Lucia's voice sounded like and decided that it must resemble her mother's, though no doubt the Galway accent was probably overlaid with the Dublin drawl that she must have picked up in school. Pictures filled his imagination of her doing all sorts of things, playing in the schoolyard, standing up in class to read for the teacher, skipping with a rope, being tucked into bed at night by her loving mother.

Mostly, however, he thought about Nora and her green eyes and the moist passion of her mouth.

Suddenly, in the spring of 1988, when Lucia was eleven years old, Niamh Creedon took a turn for the worse. It was as if the blinds had been pulled down on an already empty house. Séamus found her one day, standing by the sink in the kitchen. She had been preparing the dinner. On the chopping-board in front of her lay some neatly diced carrots and parsnips. In her hand she still held the knife she had been using, but she was standing there immobile, her eyes open but seeing nothing.

Three days later she was dead. He wrote immediately to Nora, just to keep her informed that Lucia's grandparents, on her father's side at least, were now no longer living. A Mass card arrived with the names Nora and Lucia on it, but no other message.

His mother left him the cottage and a small annuity, the fruit of careful investment by both his parents over the years. He resigned from the school and, when his sister and brother had taken themselves off to their respective homes, he plunged into a new book.

In the evenings, when his daily writing stint was over, he took to sitting in the dark with a glass of whiskey in his hand, trying to remember all the little incidents of the short time Nora and he had spent together and to make of them a continuous meaningful narrative, but found it more and more difficult to recall the details that had seemed so significant when they had happened. Regularly he fell asleep steeped in a maudlin glow of self-pity that was pleasant enough at the time, but invariably resolved itself into a bitter awakening with an ugly taste in his mouth and an unwillingness to get up and get on with the world.

On a visit to Galway he bought himself an ingenious wooden frame capable of holding a couple of dozen photographs. In this he carefully inserted his pictures of Lucia and hung the frame on the wall over his writing desk where he could look at it every day. He regretted that he had no picture of Nora to include in the collection. However, he screwed a hook into the corner of the frame and hung the gold pendant from it. That little symbol would have to do.

No Christmas card came from Nora. This was a devastating blow.

On Christmas Day he went to Castlebar and had dinner in a hotel, in a festive atmosphere that seemed to belong to another planet. His table companions for the meal were three obvious couples and a quiet, dark-haired girl in a green frock, who had been placed beside him by the sympathetic manageress to complement his own singleness. Her name, she told him, was Teresa. She was a hairdresser and she lived in Ballyshannon.

As the meal progressed, the wine went down and the paper hats and streamers were distributed, Teresa became more talkative. She was getting over a broken relationship.

'That's why I'm here on my own. The bastard broke it off just before

Christmas. Imagine that. Saving himself a present. But it left me stuck without any place to go.'

'I'm sorry to hear that.'

'Oh you needn't be. I'm better off without him.'

'That's a good philosophy.'

'What about yourself?'

'Much the same. She didn't even send a Christmas card.'

'Shitty old world, isn't it?'

'Tell me about it.'

After the dinner there was dancing, to music provided by a trio of musicians. Inevitably they found themselves shuffling around the crowded floor together. She held him closely, her body warm against his. He found himself responding to the pressure of her thighs and the soft caress of her fingers on the back of his neck. Her cheek nestled against his. After a while, as if by chance, her lips drifted along his cheek and settled on his mouth. Her tongue slipped gently through his lips. Hot desire radiated through his loins.

He closed his eyes, thinking, This is Sally Carmody all over again, but different. This is a well-practised woman. And what the hell. I will, if she will.

He tightened his arms around her and returned her kisses.

Later on, as they stumbled up the stairs together, her hand was firm on his arm, guiding him.

'What room are you in?'

'The key's in my pocket.'

She found his key and opened the door.

'I'd better see you safely in.'

'I've a bottle in the case. Would you like a nightcap?'

'Why not.'

They sat on his bed and drank the whiskey.

'Jesus, he's a terrible bastard.'

'Forget him. He's not worth it. Nobody's worth it. Not even a Christmas card. Think about that.'

'I know, I know.'

They lay on the bed, comforting one another with kisses. Soon the sentimental commiseration was dissolved by a stronger emotion. The kisses dipped deeper. Buttons became undone, fingers fumbled at zip-fasteners, nylon undergarments slipped and melted away. He found his hands on her smooth body. She was moaning softly and pulling him to her as he panted over her. A moment of sanity struck him and he tried to hold back, but she dug her fingers into his spine, clutching at him.

'Come on! It's all right. Oh God, oh God.'

Her voice rose to an importunate whine. There was no joy, no tenderness, merely an increasingly desperate urgency. He felt as if he were falling down a dark well into unimaginable darkness.

When he awoke, he was alone in the cold dawn. Of Teresa there was no sign, not a garment, not even an earring.

Groaning out of the bed, he staggered to the bathroom. The face in the mirror was haggard with guilt, impossible to look at. He crept back into bed and fell into a disgusted sleep.

Next morning, on his furtive journey down to the breakfast room for the last sitting, he rehearsed various topics of conversation and various excuses that might prove suitable to the situation he expected to await him. He found that he needn't have bothered. Teresa never appeared. It seemed that she was as unwilling as he to renew the intimacies of the previous night. As unobtrusively as he could, he finished his breakfast, vacated his room and stole away.

Two days later when postal services were resumed, there was still no letter from Nora.

He started a new book.

In spite of himself and his gloomy prognostications the book went well enough. After four months he had a first draft, which he sent off to the publisher.

Then, on an equable September morning three months later, the postman brought two letters. One was from Quango and he felt that he already knew what it contained.

The other was in Nora's unmistakable hand.

He put his coffee cup down and opened the letter from Quango. It was more or less as he had expected.

Delighted to see the preliminary draft . . . some rather black passages here and there . . . readers in general enthusiastic . . . perhaps you may like to look at . . . suggestions follow . . . cheque enclosed.

He drank his coffee and stared at Nora's letter. Waves of guilt washed over him as he remembered again the half-forgotten events of the previous Christmas.

It was almost beyond his powers to open the envelope.

FIFTEEN

'Shite,' said Noel Kerrigan.

His personal secretary looked at him in displeased surprise.

'Minister,' said Aoife Langan, 'please don't use coarse language in the office. It demeans you.'

She always called him 'Minister', even when they were alone together, sometimes even when they were at their most intimate, indulging in the pleasures of the bed. At certain moments he had even heard her scream out 'MINISTER!' Not now, however. Kerrigan recognized the reproach contained in her tone. His eczema began to ignite.

'Sorry. When did this summons from Her Royal Purity come?'

Aoife pointedly ignored this unbecoming reference to the Taoiseach.

'The Taoiseach rang half an hour ago, when you were in the . . . ah . . . little room, Minister.'

Kerrigan often retired to the 'little room'. It was his haven of peace and quiet when the responsibilities of his office hung heavily upon the beating of his heart. Today promised to be an especially difficult day. Today he would deliver to the Dáil his decision about the Gallery.

'How did she sound?'

'Very reasonable.'

'Oh Christ! Sorry, sorry. I shouldn't have said that.'

'You certainly shouldn't.'

'I know, I know. It just slipped out. But you know what it means when she sounds *reasonable*. I'll be lucky if she doesn't disembowel me all over that carpet

132

of hers. Did she say when?'

'As soon as you were available.'

'Did you say where I was?'

'I told her you were at a meeting.

'God, you're a treasure. Did you say with who?'

'Whom. I mentioned your principal officer.'

Kerrigan ignored the grammatical correction. He knew he could rely on Gilligan to back him up if the worst came to the worst, because Gilligan was one of the few people afraid of him.

'I suppose I'd better go and face Mother Frigidia.'

Aoife frowned at the appellation. She was very narrow-minded about things religious, though she seemed to find no difficulty in throwing such scruples out the window when she took her clothes off. Kerrigan had long since given up trying to understand women.

Éilís Ní Snodaigh sat in her office thinking about the chequered history of the country that she was privileged to serve as Taoiseach. History weighed heavily upon her shoulders. It occupied a great deal of her waking hours and sometimes even visited her dreams.

She was tall and thin, and had a long nose set in the middle of her saturnine face, dark eyebrows and dark hair. Although she was undoubtedly a woman, she looked like a man and, more important, she looked remarkably like de Valera himself.

With such attributes married to a lively intellect, she had found little difficulty in being accepted into politics and soon made her way up in that rarified world till she became party leader and, in due course, Ireland's first female Taoiseach, albeit at the head of a coalition that included The Radical Party, Labour, the Greens and six assorted Independents. The leader of the Radical Party, Martin Shevlin, was her Tánaiste, or deputy.

She disliked Noel Kerrigan. However, he was popular and pragmatic. Over the years he held his seat in Kildare with the greatest of ease and had enough intelligence to allow himself to be guided by his subordinates when he found himself out of his depth. He was also very good in Europe and got on well with a wide variety of foreign ministers from various countries, having demonstrated an ability to talk (or drink) even the toughest of them under the table when such was demanded of him.

Of late, however, she had noticed a certain unevenness in his demeanour that disturbed her. Something was amiss with her Foreign Minister and she couldn't put her finger on what precisely it was. This annoyed her and made her fearful. She smelt danger about him.

'Well, Nollaig,' she greeted him, when he presented himself at her office.

'You wanted to see me, Taoiseach?'

'I did, I did, In fact, I *do*. Sit down there and take the weight off your feet.'

This was intended as a folksy greeting, but the reference to his weight made Kerrigan flush. He knew he was too heavy and didn't need to be reminded of that sad fact, especially not by this abstemious beanpole.

'I'm trying to get it off, Taoiseach.'

'Just my little joke, Nollaig. I wouldn't dream of criticizing your physical attributes, as well you know.'

'Of course, Taoiseach.'

'You will be announcing your decision on the Gallery appointment in the House today, I believe?'

'*Our* decision, Taoiseach. It was approved in cabinet.'

'Of course, of course,' murmured the Taoiseach.

Kerrigan stared uneasily at the inscrutable face before him. He was disturbed by the implications of distancing contained in the Taoiseach's murmurings.

Having made her point, the Taoiseach devoted the rest of their brief discussion to other matters not in dispute. She was kindness herself in the praise she bestowed on Kerrigan for the work he had put in on Ireland's behalf during the last debate in Strasbourg concerning the appointment of commissioners. This irritated Kerrigan even further. He felt he was being patted on the head like a little boy, while something rougher was being shoved into another part of his anatomy.

He left the Taoiseach's office itching and burning all over.

It was a stormy afternoon in the Dáil chamber. Kerrigan, however, performed quite well. He normally performed well in acrimonious exchanges. He had the bulk and the voice that carried clearly over even the most raucous of heckling. He read his statement without a quiver in his voice.

'With reference to the appointment of the Director of the new European Gallery of Arts and Culture, the Government has decided to nominate for the position, as the most qualified and suitable candidate, the eminent businessman and intellectual, Mr Robert McGuinness.'

He sat down immediately, but before the backside of his broad breeches had reached his seat the chamber was filled with the sound of hooted laughter, booing and shouted questions.

Timothy Hogan, the Ceann Comhairle, banged his gavel and called for order, but the deputies were enjoying themselves and the row continued until he was forced to suspend the House for twenty minutes. After the resumption the mood became more serious and the tone of the speeches more virulent.

Kerrigan hugely enjoyed the cut and thrust of the debate, while it was confined to a straight contest between himself and the Opposition. He was up and down from his seat like a yo-yo, answering insult with insult, accusation with counter-accusation, outshouting and outsmarting all but two or three of the more experienced Opposition deputies present. The Government had made its decision, he roared, and there would be no rowing back on it to suit the bent politics and the unscrupulous opportunism of those on the opposite side of the House who wished to make political capital out of a matter of Art and Culture.

However, he soon began to notice that there was surprisingly little support coming to him from his own benches. One or two voices were raised in his favour, but that was all. The six Independents were conspicuous either by their absence from the chamber or by their inability to make their voices heard in the hurly-burly. He felt the sweat break out on his forehead and trickle down his red face. It caused his shirt to stick to his back and his underpants to knot themselves uncomfortably in his crotch. His eczema blazed and burned.

The Taoiseach sat beside him, an enigmatic little smile on her face.

But in the end all was well. Whatever about the presence or absence of the Independents in the chamber during the debate, the numbers were there when it came to the vote and the Government's decision was accepted. The session ended in acrimony and argument, however. The Opposition deputies left the house promising that the last had not been heard of the affair.

The Taoiseach swept out in true statesperson style, her long gown flowing about her thin frame. She smiled acidly at Kerrigan, but said nothing directly to him.

Kerrigan had a drink in the bar with some of his cronies. In fact, he had several drinks. Comforting words were exchanged through the alcoholic haze, backs were slapped and hands were clasped in affirmations of confidence and support. He could feel himself growing in stature. It was going to be all right.

He arrived back in his office agitated by bonhomie and wine. Aoife was preparing to go home. His sexual desires were aroused by the sight of her trim figure as she powdered her nose and reinvigorated her lipstick. He urged her to stay for a little overtime, a quick rummage in the annexe to his office, a release for him and, perhaps, a bonus for her.

In spite of all his pleas, she refused. She had a sodality meeting, she said. He knew she was big into sodalities, but he thought that for once she could give the religion a miss and concentrate on her boss and her career. He was unwise enough to say so.

This seemed to annoy her. Evidently she had not forgotten his taking of the Holy Name in vain. She gave him a cold goodbye and departed for her solitary apartment in Dalkey.

'Bugger you and your sodalities!' said Kerrigan aloud in his empty office. He thought about making a phone call and arranging a sexual rendezvous with one of the ladies in his private directory who were usually available for such purposes. He had even picked up the phone before wiser counsel prevailed.

While he was waiting for his car to arrive, he had another drink.

Outside Iveagh House he was accosted by a crowd of jostling protesters carrying placards containing unpleasant words like SLEAZE and CRONYISM and calling rude remarks at him. The crush included a large percentage of shadowy figures in anoraks, now wet with the late evening rain, their subdued chanting no more than a threatening rumble in the growing dusk. He pushed roughly through them with the aid of his driver and got into his car.

The effects of the alcohol had bolstered his courage and now enabled him to view the demonstrators with a measure of disdain once he was safely in the back seat of the Mercedes.

'Fuck the lot of you,' he said to himself.

The car pulled away around the Green and headed through the rain towards the Naas Road and the southbound motorway. Kerrigan lay back in his seat and thought about the events of the day. Everything would be all right, he decided. There'd be a bit of a rumpus for a day or two, the Opposition would try to use it to their advantage, but in the end it would all fade away.

When he reached his home in Newbridge, he found the house empty and in darkness. He took a bottle of whiskey and a glass from the sideboard, seated himself in the armchair in front of the TV set and turned it on. There was nothing of particular interest on the screen. He emptied his glass and then replenished it.

Gradually he drifted into sleep.

Kerrigan awoke with a start with Mollie's voice ringing in his ears. Her heavy hand was shaking his shoulder. She was holding a tray with cups on it in the other hand.

'Get yourself up out of that, you drunken, lazy heap. I've got some tea for you.'

As he struggled into wakefulness, he realized that he was at home in his armchair with the television tuned into the evening news. There was a lot of shouting and chanting going on.

'What do you think of that for a carry-on!' said Mollie. 'That is if you're capable of thinking at all.'

'Oh shut up, you fat bitch!' roared Kerrigan. 'Can't you see I'm trying to listen to the bloody telly!'

Her reaction startled him.

'Don't you shout at me!' Mollie screamed at him.

'I'll shout at you if I like!'

'I'm not one of your cheap floozies!'

'What? What? What the hell are you saying? What cheap floozies?'

'You heard me. Coming home here stocious drunk with her stinking perfume all over you. You needn't think that I don't know what you've been getting up to with that blondie hoor you call a secretary! I suppose you have to pay her to put a hand on your privates, because she wouldn't do it other-wise.'

Kerrigan was now beside himself.

'Shut up, shut up!'

'Look at you!' Mollie was matching him decibel for decibel. 'You drunken, fat, scabby piece of worthless dirt!'

He lunged at her and she hit him with the tray, scattering cups and saucers in broken shards on the carpet, while the teapot gushed a long line of wavering, scalding liquid over Kerrigan's face, chest and arms. He roared out in pain and staggered back, falling across a small occasional table and collapsing in a heap on the floor.

As he lay whimpering, he heard the door slam behind his departing wife.

'Oh God, God,' moaned Kerrigan to the demons perched on his shoulders. 'What in the name of God brought all that on!'

SIXTEEN

The morning rain had ceased and the September afternoon had begun to offer some promise, as he walked into Maaclee along the small country road between his cottage and the village.

Her letter had said that she would come in a red car. When he turned the bend at the church and could look the full length of Maaclee's main street, he immediately saw the car. It was parked outside Molloy's shop, red against red. As he approached the vehicle she became visible. She was sitting at the wheel, with her back to him. He could see her red-brown hair from a long way off, but he couldn't bring his legs to hurry down the street. Nothing unusual ever arrived in Maaclee without close observation, so he knew that he was being watched from both sides of the street – by Mrs Delaney in the post office and by the Lavelle family in the greengrocer's shop. Everyone except the post-mistress would especially relish the vision of a red-haired woman sitting in a red Morris Minor, waiting for quiet little Mr Creedon.

Séamus stopped beside the passenger door of the car. She turned her head and looked at him without surprise. Her eyes were wide and a little smile twisted her lips. He opened the door and sat in beside her.

'Hello, Jim.'

'You're different.'

She *was* different. Her face was much thinner than he remembered it, white and strained. There were lines around her eyes. Even her hair looked different, though it was the same colour. Her green eyes were tired.

'I'm happy to see you.' She paused, waiting for a response. When it didn't come she continued, 'Are you happy to see me?'

'Oh God.'

Her hand held his. Her fingers were thinner than he remembered them and cold to the touch.

'What in God's name has happened to you?'

'Not here. I'll tell you some place else. Show me where to go.'

'You're facing the wrong way. Go to the end of the street and turn at the petrol station.'

As the car moved away from the kerb, the watching eyes followed it from both sides of the street.

'We're being well watched. All the periscopes are up.'

'Do you mind?'

'I've learned not to mind a lot of things.'

They turned at the garage and drove back through the village again.

'Straight on for about a mile. Then it's on the right. I'll tell you when.'

After a pause, driven by his guilt over the episode in Castlebar, he added bitterly, 'I thought I was never going to see you again.'

'I thought the same myself.'

Her reply angered him and increased his guilt.

'You had a choice. I hadn't. I waited and waited. Not even a card at Christmas.'

'Please don't. I couldn't help what happened.'

'A card. Not even a bloody, miserable Christmas card!'

'Oh Jim.'

She stopped the car by the roadside and sat hunched over the wheel. In no mood for sympathy or forgiveness, he wouldn't look at her, but stared out through the windscreen at the empty road, driving nails into her hands and feet.

'Have you any idea what it's been like this past year? Surely to God you could have managed some sort of a message, just to let me know that it was all over, instead of turning your back on me like that? If you only knew how miserable I've been.'

'Jim. Look at me, Jim.'

He refused to move.

'Please look at me.'

He turned slowly. She was holding out something towards him. It took him a few seconds to realize what it was – a wig of red-brown hair. His eyes looked up and past it to her face. Contrition flooded through him.

140

'Oh Christ!'

'You see.' She was staring straight at him. 'Bald as a bloody egg. That's what it does to you, Jim. Pathetic, isn't it? Do you think I should have sent you a photo, or something? Would you have liked a picture of me looking like this? Well? Cat got your tongue?'

She put the wig back on her head. It sat a little askew, as if deliberately intended to provoke laughter. He wanted to yell out his misery, but instead took refuge in humour.

'You have it on arseways. Like a clown in a circus.'

He leaned forward and adjusted the hairpiece.

'You're worse than a child. I'll never be able to take you anywhere.'

The tears that had gathered in her eyes now spilled over. She put her head against his chest and they clung together, laughing hysterically.

'God, you're a hard-hearted bastard, Jim.' Her voice was muffled against his shirt. 'I don't know why I bother with you at all.'

He hugged her fiercely. The red wig went askew again. He freed one hand and snatched it off her head.

'I prefer you without the floor mat.' He nuzzled the skin of her head with its light incipient fuzz. She turned her mouth up to his and they kissed deeply and seriously.

After a while they heard a car approaching and broke apart.

'Come on, let's go home.'

He plonked the wig on his own head.

'How do I look?'

She burst into laughter at the sight.

'It doesn't match your beard.'

'We're a right pair. Kojak – and the only bearded red-haired whore west of the Shannon. That'll give the Special Branch something to think about.'

She drove along the road somewhat erratically.

'I don't know why I'm laughing. I was crying all the way down from Dublin.'

'Time for you to stop, then. We don't allow any tears in *Tóg bog é*. Turn right here. And don't hit my poor gate. The shagging butcher does it regularly.'

She negotiated the narrow entrance and edged the car up the dirt drive. Trees bent over them as they stopped at the cottage. The car stopped and she sat a moment, listening to the peace.

'*Tóg bog é*. It's beautiful,' she said.

'It needs a lick of paint and some of the slates want fixing. Dad was an easy-going man who didn't believe in exerting himself. Come on. It's nicer inside.'

He got out, came around the front of the car and opened her door for her with a hint of a bow.

'Madam.'

'Aren't you the little gentleman,' she said, stepping out.

She was wearing a dark grey costume with a long jacket over the skirt. A white blouse with a frilly collar was visible underneath. Her little feet were tucked into high-heeled grey shoes.

'My mother reared me well. But I'm not putting my coat on the ground, even for those posh shoes.'

'Take that wig off your head. You look ridiculous.'

'Wait till you see me in the shower.'

'Is that a threat or a promise?'

'A bit of both.'

He took her hand and led her up two wooden steps to the door. There he paused. He took off the wig with a flourish.

'There's just one more thing I've got to do. I hope you can take this. I hope *I* can take it.'

With one hand he pushed the unlocked door open, with the other he turned her around and then swept her up into his arms. She was feather light.

'What are you doing, you eejit?' she whispered, her arms tightly around his neck.

'Probably giving myself a rupture. Please, God, don't let me collapse.'

He carried her over the threshold.

'I was dreading this. I knew you'd be a ton weight.'

'God, you really know how to make a woman feel good.'

'Welcome to my castle. *Our* home.'

He lowered her till her feet touched the floor. Her arms were still around his neck and she kissed him again before she turned to look at the room. She laughed with delight.

They were standing in the main room of the cottage, a kitchen-cum-dining-room-cum-living-room. His father had had the original window knocked out and had replaced it with a large picture-window that took up half the length of the wall. Sunlight now streamed through and lit the tiled floor and the pine furniture.

'You're right. It really *is* nicer inside.'

A log fire burned brightly in the grate. The pine table was set for two. Glasses and a bottle of wine reflected the light from the fire. A candle stood in a silver candlestick and there were napkins in the glasses.

'I don't believe it.'

'There's a week's work in that lot. The napkins and the candlestick are my mother's. But I did all the rest myself.'

'Don't tell me you can cook as well?'

'I can *re-heat*. I'm a champion re-heater.'

He opened the oven door and exposed a large dish, with a roasted chicken sitting in gravy and surrounded by small potatoes.

'I bought that culinary delight in Lavelle's this morning. Ready cooked. Including the potatoes and the gravy and the mushy peas. If you look closely you'll see the peas lurking behind the chicken. Oh and there's stuffing up the chicken's fundament. The gravy came in a separate packet. All I had to do was add hot water and serve. The whole village was agog when the news of my order got out. Tom-toms sent messages up into the surrounding hills. Granny Lavelle, who is the matriarch of the tribe, came in person from her cave in the bowels of the premises to supervise the purchase. She was very curious about the chicken, especially when I asked her if it would be enough for two people. She wanted to know who the other person was. I told her an aunt of mine from Tory Island, a woman of advanced years with hair on her chin, but I don't think she believed me. Nobody in Maaclee believes me.'

'I wonder why.'

'All is now ready, madam: chicken, potatoes, peas, even gravy, just waiting madam's pleasure. You will notice that the Merlot – take note it's a *Merlot* in honour of a certain day in Dún Laoghaire thirteen years ago – is already open and is breathing gently in anticipation. I had to go to Castlebar to get a bottle of Merlot. I have a recollection that the waiter in the restaurant that night didn't let the wine *breathe*. The man must have been a philistine.'

'Jim.' She came close to him and took his hands. 'Stop it, please. I don't need any of this. I don't deserve it.'

'Let me be the judge of what you deserve. I'll get over my hysterics soon enough and revert to my usual surly self. Behind that door is the lav where you may go to wash your hands and freshen up before the meal. There is no charge, but you may leave a tip on the saucer for the cleaner. You may replace this floor mat if you wish, but personally I wouldn't recommend it even for private use on a long pole for taking cobwebs off the ceiling.'

The wig was left on the chair in the corner while they had their meal. He lit the candle, even though the day was still bright enough, and poured the wine gravely. They toasted each other equally gravely. The chicken was delight-ful, they said, a dish fit for a wedding feast, though in truth it was overcooked and dry. The stuffing crumbled, the peas congealed into a glutinous mess and the potatoes were underdone and *al dente* to the point of danger. But they both found the whole meal just millimetres short of absolute perfection.

'We're a right pair of liars,' he said, when they were relaxing with the final glass of wine. There was no sofa to share, so they took the two easy chairs and placed them together in front of the fire. 'That was a real dog's dinner.'

'I think it was great.'

'I love it when you lie in your teeth.'

'They're still my own teeth. And I'm not lying. I've got something here to show you – you can have it for dessert.'

She opened her handbag, took out a paper wallet containing photographs and laid it on the table in front of him.

'Lucia. All the ones you've missed this past year. She's twelve since March and she's gone to boarding school in Athlone. He insisted. God, the tears when I was leaving her in the convent. I'll miss her terribly around the house, but I suppose it's best for her. I mean, I'm not really able to give her the bit of polish she needs. And don't start arguing with me, Jim.'

'Have I said a word?'

'You're *looking*. And don't think I haven't been over all the arguments on both sides. This is the way it's got to be. Just look at her. She's a lovely child, isn't she?'

He couldn't disagree with that. They both pored over the pictures and she explained to him the exact time and place where each one had been taken.

'I wish I could meet her in person.'

'I know. I wish it too. Maybe we'll manage it one day.'

'And now it's my turn. Come along.'

He took her into his study and showed her his writing-desk and the pictures in the elaborate, extendable frame on the wall above it.

144

'So this is where James Barnwell writes all those funny books?'

'The very place. With his daughter looking down on him and her mother's letters in the drawer here.'

'You don't keep all *that* rubbish, do you? I don't even know where to put the full stops.'

'Pure literature. Someday they'll be sold at Sotheby's for vast sums of money.'

'You still have the pendant?' She fingered the gold chain. 'It's only a very cheap little thing. Hardly worth keeping.'

'Very precious. A souvenir from the night we made Lucia.'

'God, I was a brazen hussy, wasn't I? Taking advantage of a poor innocent boy like you.'

'I grew up that night, Nora.' He held up the photo wallet. 'Do I keep these?'

'Of course. I brought them for you.'

Back in the living-room he sat her down again before the fire, while he cleared the table and took the used dishes to the sink. She offered to help, but he wouldn't hear of it.

'No guest works in this house. Not the first night, anyway. By next week I'll have you scrubbing the floor.'

She sat quietly watching him while he washed and stacked the plates and the cutlery on the draining board.

'You're a real treasure. It's a wonder no woman has snapped you up.'

'They've tried. God help them, they've tried.'

'Go on! I don't believe you.'

'It's true. Many's the time in St Fiachra's I had to run screaming to protect my virtue.'

He told her about Sally Carmody and others he had come across during his not very successful career as a sex object, but carefully avoided all mention of Teresa.

'They find me cuddly, I think. The beard intrigues them. And then I have this 'little boy lost' appearance about me. I even notice it in the mirror when there isn't a woman in sight. A bit like a basset hound. All ears and slobbery jowls. It's pretty ghastly having to confront *that* every morning before I'm properly awake. But women seem to like it. They want to take me home and put me on the mantelpiece. Like a Toby jug.'

'Are you trying to make me jealous?'

'Ah, women are queer cattle. You wouldn't want to take notice of anything they'd do.'

When he had finished the dishes he turned and looked at her.

'We have decisions to make here.'

'Like what?'

'I presume you'll stay a day or two?'

'If you'll let me.'

'Well, that's settled. But that's for later. So what's it to be now? Bed? Or a walk around the lake?'

'It's only six o'clock,' she said, her head bent, not wishing to meet his eyes or to answer the question.

'A walk it is, so.'

The evening was still bright and warm, but he made her take a cardigan from the car to put around her shoulders. She wore the wig in case they bumped into anyone. They walked on the narrow path that followed the shoreline, close together, his arm protectively around her waist. The lake murmured gently and a blackbird in a tree gave notice that he was turning in for the night.

'A noisy hoor,' he said. 'He sits up there every evening and frightens the fishes. One of these days I'll buy a shotgun and send him to join his ancestors.'

'You wouldn't!'

'Don't underestimate me.'

'This is a beautiful spot. What's the lake called?'

'Lochcrideen.'

'The lake of the kingfishers.'

'If we're lucky, we'll see one.'

But they didn't. When they had gone no more than half-a-mile the evening began to close in and they sat upon a stone to rest, because she found she wasn't able to walk as far as she wished. He was very solicitous.

'Are you all right? You're not cold?'

'I'm fine. Really. It's just that I get a bit exhausted sometimes.' After a pause she asked, 'Do you want to know what happened to me?'

'You can tell me when you're ready.'

'I think I'm ready now.'

But still she hesitated.

'You don't have to tell me. I don't mind, really I don't. All that matters is that you're here now. From the day I first saw you in Leinster Street I've wanted nothing except to have you here with me.'

'You're very sweet, Jim.'

'I'm the world's champion liar, but we'll let that pass.'

'It started early last year. Nothing very much at the beginning. I was just a bit tired, that's all. A bit out of sorts. Irritable. I found the lump one morning in the shower. He was away at the time and Lucia had gone to school, so I was alone in the house. It was the most awful moment of my life. I was in a sort of a huge silence as if there was nothing in the whole world except me. There wasn't a sound to be heard except the thump of my own heart. And the dribble of the water out of the shower. I didn't know what to do, so I just sat down in a corner of the shower and held myself. I thought maybe I was going to die there and then, or at least before the day was out. Then I pulled myself up and rang Kate. She was great. She came over immediately and took me down to the doctor. Kate's a rock of sense.'

'Why didn't you call *me*?'

'Don't be an eejit. Anyway, the doctor sent me to the hospital and there were all sorts of tests. A biopsy. You know what that is? They take out a little bit and examine it. Then a mammograph. And the news was bad. It was malignant. I had cancer. I can remember the doctor coming into the ward to tell me. He was only a young fellow. The poor lad was as awkward as anything about it. You'd swear *he* had it, not me. He kept licking his lips and staring at a spot on the wall over my head and looking as if he was going to cry. I had to tell him it was all right. And somehow I was better able to cope with it once he put a name to it. So there had to be an operation, very quickly, to get rid of the lump. I woke up to find . . . I thought, thank God that's over. I was a bit lopsided, like a car with a flat tyre. But I was able to get up and walk about and think of coming home. Everything seemed to be working. Then, well, they found there were secondaries. That really softened my cough. They put me on the chemo. I was deadly sick with the chemo. I mean, really deadly sick. That's when I lost my hair.'

'My poor baldy Nora.'

'When *he* heard about it, he wasn't best pleased, I can tell you. Oh he paid for the doctors and all that kind of stuff. Only the best for his wife. But he wasn't able to look at me. I had a live-in nurse and consultants calling every hour of the day and the night. He knows an awful lot of important people. And priests. By the dozen. Even bishops and things. I had more prayers said over me and more anointing than *you've* had hot dinners. But he never came near me from the day of the operation. I mean *near* me.'

'What sort of a bastard is he!'

'He just couldn't bring himself to. I don't blame him. He's dead afraid of sickness. And anyway, he never really loved me. Not really. And he had someone else to go to. Very beautiful. Perfect in all departments. No bits missing on *her*. Before the op we used to sleep together the odd time. No, I don't mean *that*. But at least he'd lie beside me and sometimes put his arms around me. But all that ended when they . . . Anyway, after the chemo they told me I was in remission. Things had quietened down, as far as they knew. I might live to be a hundred, they said. Or . . .'

She paused with a little sigh. His arm tightened around her and she leaned against his shoulder.

'I'd even settle for ninety-eight,' she said.

'How did Lucia take all this?'

'Oh children are able to put up with a lot. They're selfish little bodies at heart. And I kept as much as I could from her. She was worried while I was in the hospital, of course, but when I came home with my wig on she sort of felt that everything was OK again, Mammy was up and running. And she thought the wig was great. That's the way it should be, Jim. There's no point in trying to burden the kids with our problems.'

'I don't know what to say to you, Nora.'

'Oh don't say anything. Just understand that I couldn't get in touch with you. I wanted to. I kept thinking of you all the time. But there was nobody I could send out, nobody I could trust. No, that's not true. Kate would have done it for me. I just *couldn't* bring myself to write to you. I didn't know what to say. How could I tell you that I'd lost all my hair like a shorn sheep? That they'd cut this big piece of me away. That I was maybe going to die. Then I thought that it would be best to say nothing. I knew you must be feeling let down, if you thought about me at all. But I felt it would be easier on you if it was all over. I didn't want you to have to carry this thing. Better if you forgot all about me.'

'I thought about you day and night.'

'I couldn't stop thinking about you, hard as I tried. And I didn't want you to imagine I'd just cut you off. Oh God, I was torn in two. I couldn't bear to have you thinking badly about me. That's me. Selfish. So when he bought me the car for myself—'

'That was bloody big of him.'

'I chose it myself. He would have bought me a Rolls if I'd wanted one.'

His face was set in stone.

'I really shouldn't be here at all,' she said.

'This is where you belong!'

'Look, Jim. You've had two deaths to put up with—'

'You're not going to die! I won't let you die!'

'I'll do my best not to, I promise you. My da always used to say, "Live as long as you can and die when you can't help it." That's what I intend to do. But it isn't fair to come here and inflict myself on you.'

'Don't you *ever* listen to anything I say?' It was almost a shout. 'This is where you belong. With *me*. I love you. That bloody wanker of a husband you have doesn't know what love means.'

'You're worse than the blackbird. You'll frighten the fishes.'

'Feck the fishes!'

They sat quietly for a while, until he felt her shiver.

'Come on,' he said, 'let's get you in out of the night air.'

When they reached the cottage they found the fire still glowing. He sat her down with a blanket around her and put on some more logs. From a press he produced a bottle of brandy.

'What do you think?'

'I'd love a drop.'

'It has your name on it. I bought it specially when I got your letter.'

They sat in front of the fire and sipped the brandy. There seemed to be little left to say, but there was great comfort in their closeness.

'You get to a stage, don't you, that's way beyond words? All I want to do is sit here and hold your hand.'

'I'm ugly.'

'There's no way you'd ever be ugly to me.'

'Ugly. Cut up. A big bit of me missing. Will you be able to take it, Jim? Looking at me?'

'I'll gladly take it.'

Later on he stirred.

'Have you a case with you?'

'In the boot of the car.'

The case was a fat leather one. He brought it in and put it on the floor beside her chair.

'Now, there are two bedrooms. One double and one single. I've been sleeping in the double since my mother died, because it's at the rear of the house and overlooks the lake. Where would you like to sleep? I've changed all the bedclothes. And whichever you choose is OK with me.'

'I'd like the lake view.'

'On your own?'

'With you, if you can bear it.'

'God, Nora, how can you ask!'

While she was preparing herself for bed, he went outside to look at the sky. There was a quarter moon, with wispy clouds drifting across it. The trees murmured in the light wind.

As he stood there, Séamus Creedon wept, a mixture of guilt and sorrow and joy.

SEVENTEEN

The morning papers were full of it. Most of them led with the stormy scenes in the Dáil. There were pictures of the crowd outside Iveagh House showing the artist, Oonagh McCantley, being cut free from the chains binding her to the railings. Not a pretty sight, according to many. One tabloid ran the head-line, OONAGH IN BONDAGE. On the inside pages of the broadsheets there were full accounts of the speeches, charges and counter-charges made by TDs from all sides. The leading articles carried titles such as, A Disgraceful Episode, Shameful Behaviour, and Whither Democracy? each vying with the others in righteousness outraged.

Robert McGuinness savoured the attention of the Press. True, it wasn't all complimentary, in fact, it was mostly denigratory, but he liked to believe that he was at one with Behan in his contempt for the begrudgers. And they would be dealt with. Orla Corr was already compiling a list of those journalists (and their nearest and dearest) whose contributions were most poisonous, with a view to having them suitably looked after in the future. Robert had a way of 'looking after' people. He never encouraged, or even suggested, any violence – an unobtrusive sacking, a gentle withdrawal of credit, a quiet curtailment of supply, these were the effective means by which his disapproval was translated into action.

In the meantime, it was essential to accentuate the positive. The important thing was that he was now the Director of the European Gallery of Arts and Culture. That was the indisputable truth in the day's news. He said it aloud to himself many times. He had made it.

The telephone seemed to confirm his assessment of the situation. Since the late bulletins of the previous evening it had been ringing constantly as well-wishers hurried to extend their congratulations to the new Director. Most were self-serving customers and worried debtors of ORMAX, but some clerical friends and acquaintances had also sent their kindest regards. These included the Archbishop of Dublin and the Lieutenant of the Knights of St Nicodemus, who were rather unfortunately advised to do so by their PR people. As the morning progressed and they became aware of the mounting tide of criticism, there was a troubled fluttering in the clerical dovecotes and some anxious phone calls were made.

Orla Corr, of course, was delighted. They spent the night together in the penthouse, drinking wine, listening to the late news broadcasts, making love and generally talking about themselves, concocting plans for the glittering social future they saw stretching in front of them. Robert already had on his payroll an eminent, impecunious scholar, who had agreed to coach him on the finer aspects of artistic appreciation before he took up office, and to remain with him as a consultant thereafter. For her part, Orla was contemplating the prospect of early trips to the fashion houses of Paris and London and the even more entrancing prospect of playing hostess at dinner parties attended by the finest artists on the continent.

It was one of their most sublime nights together. Even Robert's subsequent hangover was worth it.

When he arrived back in Silverglen the following morning, he was pleased initially to see a small group of media people outside the gates of his house. The gates were locked, of course, in the tradition of rich people the world over, and could be opened only from the inside or by remote control from the car. As he approached and counted no more than a dozen people, including a young lady in a short skirt and provocative knee-boots, and a man from RTE carrying a TV camera, Robert toyed with the idea of inviting them in for a drink and a comfortable interview in the lounge. He was wearing a new grey suit and had already selected the exact spot in the lounge that would provide an appropriate background to the pictures. The impromptu 'few words' he had thoroughly rehearsed for just such an occasion were suitably modest and humble.

He stopped the car and lowered the window, with a broad, welcoming smile. The group immediately crowded around him and a whirring camera was pushed to within inches of his face.

'Good morning, ladies and gentlemen,' said Robert. 'What can I do for you?'

The knee-booted young lady with the spiky blonde hair pushed herself forward.

'Angela Turley, RTE. Mr McGuinness, in view of the widespread objections to your appointment as Director of the European Gallery of Arts and Culture, have you considered withdrawing your name?'

Robert's smile disappeared, as if it had been painted over. His face went bleak.

'Absolutely not.' He tried to keep his voice even and statesmanlike. 'What gave you such a ridiculous idea?'

The questions now came fast and furious. There were cameras clicking everywhere and microphones lined up like mourners at a wake.

'Did you see what happened outside Iveagh House last night?'

'Would you like to comment on the editorial in the *Independent* this morning?'

'Do you know that The Friends of Civilization have applied to the High Court for a judicial review?'

'What is your answer to Mr Quigley's assertion that you have no qualifications for the post?'

Robert allowed the ghost of a patronizing smile to return to his face at this mention of the leader of the Opposition.

'Mr Quigley is entitled to his opinion, now that he has finally discovered that he has one. I have nothing further to say on the matter. Good morning.'

He closed the car window and pressed the remote control. As the gates swung open he could see Matt Sweeney, his general dogsbody, coming down the drive. When he was safely inside the gates, Robert stopped his car.

'Matt, don't let any of that shower set a foot on my property.'

'Leave it to me, Mr McGuinness.'

Robert drove carefully up to the house. Here he paused for a few moments to regain his composure. He could see his brother's hired car parked to one side. Declan McGuinness, Bishop of Tamishni, had arrived in Ireland the day before and Robert didn't wish to meet him with a face looking like a dish of cold porridge.

He closed his eyes and meditated a moment on Orla's incomparable body. The vision steadied him. Blood flowed through his veins again. God dammit, he had something the bishop could only dream about.

The Bishop of Tamishni, big and bulky in physical appearance, was an easy-going man. He went about his diocesan duties quietly and unobtrusively, gave no trouble to anyone, and created about himself an atmosphere of peace and tolerance. His Bishop's Palace in the small north African country he now called home was no more than a modest two-storey building on the outskirts of the capital. Faced with the heavy opulence of his brother's home, he found in his breast a stirring of nostalgia for the uncomplicated life he had left behind him.

There was also an uneasy feeling troubling him since the telephone call he had received that morning from the agitated Archbishop of Dublin.

By the time he was crossing the carpet to shake Declan's hand, the glow had returned to Robert's countenance.

'I'm sorry I wasn't here last night, Dec, to greet you on your arrival. But you know the way it is. Business is a devil.'

'I'm sure.' The bishop wondered what 'business' would keep his brother out all night and send him home looking like a cat that had guzzled the last drop of the cream, but he refrained from turning over that particular stone.

'I hope they looked after you well?'

'Absolutely. The bed is very comfortable and Mrs Kirwan provided me with an excellent supper.'

'You'll have a drink?'

'It's a bit early for me, Robert.'

'Oh come on,' said Robert, expansively. 'This is a special day. It isn't often your brother is all over the papers for something as prestigious as this. It demands a special drink. Will brandy be all right?'

'Just a small drop, if you insist.'

The golden liquid gurgled sinfully into the glasses.

The rain of the previous evening had spent itself. Rays of weak morning sunlight poked through the tall windows, glinting on the otherwise dull frames of the dull paintings, picking out the odd piece of brassware designed and carefully placed (by no less than Designer of the Year, Oliver d'Arcy) to be thus highlighted. Sunlight now also twinkled in the multifaceted brandy goblets.

The bishop found the room oppressive and pretentious, but he appreciated that Robert probably felt a statement of his wealth was necessary in order to impress visitors.

'There you go.'

Robert handed the bishop a glass. As he did so he threw a watchful eye out through the window. The gates were already securely closed and Matt was standing on guard.

The two brothers sat and contemplated each other, neither of them taking much pleasure from the activity.

'Congratulations,' said the bishop, with as much sincerity as he could muster. He raised his glass.

Robert smiled the gracious smile he had spent some time cultivating.

'Thank you. I've been waiting a long time for something like this.'

'You think you'll be able for it?'

Robert's face darkened.

'You think I won't?'

'I'm your brother, Robert.'

'What the hell does that mean?'

'Precisely what it says. I know you. I know your personal qualities. You're a good organizer. You thrive in the market-place. You know how to make money. But you know damn all about art. I just hope you haven't bitten off more than you can chew, that's all.'

'I know what I'm doing.'

'I hope you do.'

'You're very worried about me all of a sudden, Dec. I don't remember getting daily bulletins of concern from whatever arsehole of Africa you hide yourself in.'

The bishop refused the invitation to take part in a vulgar slanging match.

'I'm always worried about you. I'm particularly worried now that Babs has gone. I've always felt that she had a great steadying influence on you. You must miss her terribly.'

'I do,' lied Robert. He stared sombrely at his fingernails, trying to look suitably sad at the mention of his bereavement, unhappy at the way the conversation was going. He sincerely hoped he wasn't going to be compelled to listen to a sermon on bereavement. 'But life has to go on.'

'Of course, of course. I'll say no more on the subject. But what about this furore in the papers on your appointment?'

'Hot air. Politicians will make whatever use they can of it in anticipation of the next election. They'll be full of it for a day or so, until the next murder or the next air disaster, and then it will all die away. I've seen it happen again and again. Believe me, I know how these things work. In a couple of weeks people will have forgotten that there was any argument about the appointment.'

'You don't feel hurt when they say nasty things about you?'

'If I did, I wouldn't survive a day in business.'

'Business insults tend to be impersonal. Some of the things I've seen in the papers are quite different.'

'The people who matter are behind me. I can put up with bad mouthing from no-hopers who don't count.'

'The archbishop is concerned.'

'What does that mean? I had a ring from the palace last night to congratulate me.'

'Even so. He feels, in the light of today's reaction, that you might like to reconsider.'

'No bloody way.'

'I envy your ability to be so single-minded.'

'In your heart, you probably despise me.'

'No, no, no. I'm not in the business of despising. It's not recommended in my line of work.'

'Neither is envy.'

'True. But I don't know another word that fits the way I feel about you. I suppose I secretly admire you. I'd never be able to put up with some of the things they've said about you.'

'You were always soft, Dec. That's why you went into religion.'

'Very probably, though Mother had something to do with it as well. And God was also a consideration.'

'She tried to push me in the same direction,' said Robert, ignoring the reference to God, 'but I wasn't having any of it.'

The bishop nodded.

'You always seemed to be certain of the way you wanted to go.'

'That's why I didn't waste my time going to college.'

They both knew that this was a lie. Robert hadn't gone to college because his parents couldn't afford to send any of their children to university. Declan had managed it only through the good offices of the missionary order he had initially joined as a lay brother.

At first, Robert hadn't worried about his lack of a college education. Later in life, however, as he had accumulated wealth and wealthy friends, he had begun to resent his inability to mention casually his days in Trinity or UCD.

Now he felt that his appointment to the directorship would make all things whole. He sat back in his armchair and smiled coldly across at his brother.

The bishop, for his part, was thinking with increasing nostalgia of Tamishni and the graceful figure of Imdur, his housekeeper, as she worked about the house. Her deft movements, the way her figure swayed under the colourful clothing, filled his mind for a few moments.

The phone rang. The bishop started guiltily from his reverie, dismissed the image of Imdur and made a little confession to God. Robert excused himself, left the room and lifted the phone in the hall.

It was Kerrigan. He sounded frayed.

'That you Robert? This is Noel.'

'Who?' Robert liked to keep his clients in their place.

'Noel Kerrigan, dammit.'

'I was wondering when you'd ring.'

'What do you think?'

'Think?'

'About the coverage in the papers.'

'You did fine, Noel.'

'Fine?' The tepidity of the adverb irritated Kerrigan and the tone of his voice showed it. 'I worked my arse off for you.'

'You won't find me ungrateful, Noel. Or ungenerous.'

'Christ, the stuff I had to put up with in the Dáil yesterday.'

'It's your job, Noel. It's what you're paid to do. And I know you have the thick skin for it, or you wouldn't be in politics. Believe me, I appreciate all you've done on my behalf.'

'What in God's name did you say to Mollie?'

'Mollie? What would I say to Mollie?'

'Did you tell her about Aoife?'

'What would I do that for?'

'That's what I want to know. She's left me. In the name of God, you didn't have to do that, Robert.'

'Are you drunk, Noel?'

'Bloody sure I'm not drunk. How could I be drunk at this time of the day? I was drunk last night, but I know what happened. The minute I got home she laid into me about floozies in the office. She never said anything like that to me before. I never even thought she knew a word like "floozie". And "blondie hoor". She called Aoife a "blondie hoor". How the hell would she know anything about Aoife unless somebody told her? She threw tea all over me. You should see my face this minute. And then she walked out of the house and she says she's not coming back.'

'You think I told her?' Robert was full of righteous indignation. 'You're mad, Noel. I didn't tell her: I have no reason to tell her. You're playing the game all right. I'm happy with your performance. You're important to me. Why would I want to harm you? Think about it.'

'Then who told her?'

'Why don't you ask her?'

'She won't even talk to me. She's staying with the daughter and she got her to pass on the message.' Kerrigan sounded genuinely distressed. 'Imagine saying things like that to the kids! What's that going to do to them? I'm in bits here. Can you imagine what this is going to do to me if it gets out? Can you imagine what Mother Frigidia is going to say?'

'Look, Noel.' Robert was becoming tired of the conversation and of Kerrigan's professed concern for his 'kids', the youngest of whom was nineteen years of age and living in a flat with his girlfriend. 'I'm very sorry for your trouble, but I had nothing to do with it. Give Mollie a couple of days on her own and she'll come back. Women always do.'

'What the hell would you know about it!'

'If you're going to start abusing me I'll hang up the phone right now.'

'No, no, no. I'm sorry. But if you didn't spill on me, who did?'

'I don't know. Maybe Mollie just guessed. Women guess these things sometimes. Maybe you talk in your sleep. Maybe you left a letter hanging around. Maybe she doesn't know anything, but was just trying it on.'

'Christ, trying it on? Trying it on? D'you think I just fell for something?'

'Better men than you have been taken in by women. Calm down. Give her a few days to think about it. I know Mollie. She's all right. And she must love you, or she wouldn't have put up with you all these years. Buy her flowers, why don't you.'

'Flowers, for God's sake! I never bought her bloody flowers before. What would I buy her flowers for! She'd know I was feeling guilty.'

'That won't do any harm. She'll think you're sorry too. Tell her there's nothing in it. That it must have been a rumour deliberately spread by the Opposition.'

'I wouldn't put it past some of those bastards!'

'Tell her you'd never do anything like that in a thousand years. Tell her you love her.'

'God.'

The thought of telling Mollie he loved her appalled Kerrigan. He could hear the vacuum cleaner being used in the living-room, where his daughter, Siobhan, was doing her best to get the stain out of the carpet. Siobhan had come over from her own home with the message from her mother and had grudgingly attempted to clean up the place. She had barely spoken to Kerrigan, however, her set face and tight lips indicating her extreme displeasure with him. Life was going to be difficult in the Kerrigan household for some time to come.

'All right, I'll do what I can. You wouldn't put in a word for me yourself, would you?'

'I'll think about it.' Robert had no intention of doing anything of the sort. 'But you're her husband. You're the one who'll have to make your apologies. Nobody else can do that for you. What do I hear about a judicial review by that Friends of Civilization crowd?'

'Oh them! They're looking for an injunction to stop me actually appointing you. But they won't succeed.'

'Are you sure of that?'

'I'm sure of nothing this weather.'

When Kerrigan had finally hung up the phone, promising to go and make his peace with his wife, Robert walked thoughtfully back to his brother.

'The Foreign Minister,' he said in answer to the Bishop's enquiring look. 'Just a call to tell me in person of the appointment.'

EIGHTEEN

Sunshine spilled across the cottage kitchen. He moved the bacon in the pan with the fork, turning the rashers over to crisp the other side. The mushrooms sizzled in the melted butter, the tomatoes bubbling beside them. On the work-top sat two eggs awaiting their moment of truth. He reached to the shelf above and took down a small jar of tarragon, which he sprinkled into the pan. The appetising aroma permeated the kitchen and beyond.

Much earlier he had heard the birds waken in the trees and on the lake, all the stirring sounds of life beginning again with a new day. In the darkness he had listened to her breathing softly beside him and had savoured the perfec-tion of it all. If the Angel of Death had come at that moment to signal the end of the world he wouldn't have minded in the least. 'Now more than ever seems it rich to die.' He had said that line to her in Sandycove, just before they had made love beside Joyce's tower. Now he felt that he knew the real meaning of it. He had longed to touch her again, to show her how much he valued her being there beside him, but instead had decided to let her sleep.

The story of his life.

So he had crept from the room and busied himself in the kitchen, whistling while he worked, like one of the seven dwarfs. He was a happy man.

The bedroom door opened and she stood there, wrapped in a blue dress-ing-gown.

'God, that smells lovely.'

'Tastes even better. I hope you're decent.'

'How decent do you want me?'

'Whatever.' He turned and looked at her.

'I must look a sight.'

'You'll do. You can make yourself useful as well as beautiful. There's cups and

160

saucers on the dresser and you'll find knives and things in the drawer.'

She began to set the table.

'Are you always this bossy?'

'Only with women.'

'That's a relief.'

'You can cut some bread too. There's a bread-knife over there somewhere.'

'What plates do you want out?'

'I have them heating in the oven.'

'You're fierce organized. I'll never be able to keep up with you.'

'You don't know the half of it. Everything here is done by the book. Standing orders are pinned on the back of the door.'

He spooned bacon, tomatoes and mushrooms on to two plates, then returned them to the oven. With one expert hand he cracked the eggs and dropped them into the pan.

'I don't see anything on the back of the door.'

'I must be losing it. Getting old. Forgetful, But don't worry, I'll have them up tomorrow. How do you like your egg?'

'Soft.' She was cutting bread.

He stopped his work for a moment and turned to face her.

'Do you know something?' he said. 'I'm so blindingly happy it hurts me inside. Like an ulcer.'

She stopped what she was doing and went to him.

'Thank you for being so kind last night.'

'Let not the word gratitude be so much as mentioned between us, unless it goes from me to you. I love you.'

He gently pulled open the lapels of her dressing-gown and kissed the scar where her breast had been. She held his head tightly to her.

'That was not an invitation to idleness. Get back about your chores, wench, before you make me destroy the eggs.'

'Yessir,' she said happily.

They ate their breakfast at a table that he carried out to the edge of the lake. The morning was soft and moist. There was some weak sunshine, but no rain.

She had changed into a white dress and whiter sandals. He was busy setting the table when he saw her come out of the cottage and he stopped what he was doing, remembering the day on Sandymount Strand. She laughed at his surprise.

'Exactly what I wore then. I kept the frock specially. I can still fit in it, so don't go accusing me of getting fat. And I've got the special bra on. You'd never know, would you?'

She extended her arms and pushed her chest out.

'Hold on. Before we eat.'

'I'm starving.'

'It'll only take a minute. Stand over there with the sun on your face.'

He put the camera on the table, while she stood with her back to the lake.

'I'm not very good at this yoke.' He fiddled with the timer. 'In fact, I've never used it before. There we are. I hope.'

He scurried around to her side and they faced the camera together, laughing self-consciously as they waited for the flash. When it came, he kissed her lightly.

'I'll send you a copy. We can call it our wedding photograph.'

As they ate their breakfast their talk at first was about nothing more than the food, the morning, the lake, and other inconsequential things. They smiled a lot at each other, as if they had only just met. They touched hands often across the table. However, as they reached the end of the meal the conversation gradually died away and a silence descended. They had a last cup of tea and sat there for what seemed like an age, saying nothing.

Then she broke the silence.

'You haven't asked me how long I'm staying.'

'For the rest of your life, I hope.'

'The only answer is as long as I can.'

'And who decides that?'

'Lucia, mostly. She's at school now, so I won't be needed at home until the mid-term break.'

'That's over a month away.'

'I'll have to fetch her then and take her home. Could you put up with me here for three or four weeks?'

'To coin a cliché, I can put up with you here till death us do part. But I know I have to compete with . . . *him*.'

'He doesn't even come into it. I've told you that before.'

'I wish I could believe you.'

'You'll have to take my word for it. He's never at home. At the moment he's in Prague, setting up some deal or another. After that it's Dusseldorf. And somewhere else after that. When he *does* come home, he'll barely talk to me. He doesn't *care*, Jim. When I was taking Lucia to school, I told Mrs Kirwan, that's the housekeeper—'

'Of course.'

'Don't be like that.'

'It's just strange to be eating breakfast with a lady who has a staff at home.'

'Two maids and a gardener as well as Mrs Kirwan. It's not much.'

'God, what a life of deprivation!'

'We have money, you know that. Lots of money. I could have an army of servants if I wanted. But I don't want.'

'I admire your restraint.'

'You're spoiling this, Jim.'

'I'm sorry. You go ahead.'

'What I'm saying is, I told Mrs Kirwan that I might be away for a few weeks. That I was going to visit some friends in the west of Ireland. I even invented a few names. If he rings, she'll tell him that, and he won't give a damn. That's the way we are now.'

'Then leave him and come and stay here with me.' He became animated as he pursued the thought, jumping up from his chair and moving excitedly about. 'Here, or anywhere you like. We can go away together. I'm earning enough from the books now to take care of the two of us. The *three* of us. We can go to France, Germany, any place in the world we fancy.'

'And what about Lucia?'

'I said the *three* of us.'

'I mean what about her school? What about her life?'

'She can have a new life with us. We can find her a new school, no matter where we go. The world is full of schools.'

'She's only twelve.'

'Kids are very resilient. They can adapt to anything.'

'No, Jim.'

'I'm telling you,' he insisted. 'I've been working with children. I know what they're like.'

'I'm not going to tell her that Robert isn't her father.'

'Robert!' He seized on the word. 'I knew it. I knew he'd bloody well be called Robert. I hate the name Robert. Robert, Robert, Robert! Six hundred and sixty-six. The number of the Beast. God, what a name! Robert, you bastard,' he shouted across the lake through the trees, 'may you rot in hell for a lousy specimen of humanity. Do you hear me? I want you in Hell for all eternity.'

His voice echoed over the water. A frightened duck lifted itself off the lake and fled, wings smacking the air.

She sat watching him, as he brandished the name to the sky. After a while he stopped moving about and sat down again and put his head in his hands.

'Are you finished?'

'I'm sorry. I've been saving that up for years. Like a large vomit that just had to come out. It's over now. And I don't really hate the name Robert. Just *your* Robert.'

'Well, listen to me. When she grows up, I'll tell her. But not until then. If you love me, you'll go along with this. For my sake and for her sake.' She paused, looking at his bowed head. 'Do you love me?'

He raised his head.

'I love you. God help me, I don't know how to do anything else.'

'I love you too. I've loved you ever since the day you followed me up Grafton Street. From the first moment I saw you walking along with your blue folder under your arm.'

'You didn't see me *then*?'

'I saw you a lot sooner than you think. And I knew you were following me long before we even reached Bewley's. I fell in love with you then. Well, actually the real moment was when I sat across the table and looked at you over a sticky bun. You had crumbs on your beard.'

'They call me the Sticky Bun Kid.'

'No one had ever followed me before, just for me. It was the best moment of my life. Well, the *second best*. I want to be with you. I want to share your bed and your food and your life. I want to grow old with you. But I love Lucia too. And I don't want to do anything that will hurt her. When she's grown up and ready to leave home, I'll tell her then. And then I'll come to you, if you still want me. In the meantime, we can have time together.'

'Time? What time?'

'Kingfisher time. Whatever we can manage. A week here and a week there. Sometimes several weeks together. Days when I can't see you, I'll write to you. I'll phone you. It won't be so bad. I'll send you pictures of her. You'll find it'll work out all right, Jim. When I'm not here, you'll have space for yourself, time to write, to be alone. It'll be like a marriage, like two people living in a big house, who don't see each other every day, but they know that they belong to each other and that the other one is always there, waiting.'

'Waiting for how long?'

'Only a few years.'

'Till Lucia is grown up? We're talking about nine or ten years.'

'And what's that in a lifetime?'

They argued about it, but he knew that he was going to lose the argument. He knew that he was never going to win an argument with this implacable woman. He had only two choices – to agree with her, or to lose her. And he knew that he didn't want to lose her.

They spent the rest of the day alternately walking around the lake and making love in the cottage. They argued a lot. They even found time to eat a little. He took her out in the boat and showed her the spot where he had composed the ridiculously obscene poems he had written about her. She made him recite them and he shouted out the vulgarities, while she clapped her hands and laughed. They heard the *chee-chee* of the kingfishers and saw the flash of the blue and orange plumage as the birds went about feeding themselves. They found the hole in the bank where the birds had nested and they watched them diving from a branch into the lake in search of fish. They disturbed magpies and numerous smaller birds as he splashed his oars and they scraped in against the bank of the lake.

That night, as they sat in front of the fire, he read her the kingfisher poem by Hopkins.

'As kingfishers catch fire, dragonflies draw flame;
As tumbled over rim in roundy wells
Stones ring . . .
Each mortal thing does one thing and the same:
. . .*myself* it speaks and spells,
Crying *What I do is me: for that I came.*'

'This is *me*,' she said. 'Here with you. This is what I was born for.'

It was a day to remember.

Next morning she woke him up and told him that she had an idea. She was going to take him out for a drive in her car. He protested that he had a car of his own and showed her the silver Mazda he had bought the previous year.

'The sensible thing is to use my car and save the Ancient Minor.'

'Ancient? What do you mean "ancient"?'

'Ancient, as in old. Liable to pack it in on the least pretext. Wheels fall off. Clutch seize up. Things like that. We don't want to find ourselves out in the middle of Connemara when the old girl has a stroke. Or four.' He chuckled at his joke. 'God, I'm so clever it's unbelievable.'

'Have you looked at the clock?'

'That female was made long before clocks were thought of.'

'Typical male talk. There's only about twenty thousand miles on it.'

'In human terms that's about a hundred and two years.'

'She's barely run-in. So I don't want to hear any stupid arguments from you, thank you very much.'

'There's even less mileage on my Mazda. And it has the advantage of youth.'

'Stuff your Mazda. We're going to use my car. I want to do the driving and take you around some of the little towns in Connacht you haven't even heard of yet. Anyway, I need the practice.'

They dawdled over their breakfast. There was a sublime air of lack of urgency about the second day, as there had been about the first. Limitless time seemed to stretch before them, as though they were on honeymoon. When they finally started out on the journey, it was already into the afternoon. She dressed herself in a woolly white sweater and slacks and tied a green scarf around her neck. She exchanged her white sandals for a pair of walkers.

'Will I do?' she asked, presenting herself for his approval.

'You'll take the sight out of their eyes.'

She drove down through Maaclee to take the road to Connemara, but pulled in when they reached Molloy's shop. Eyes peered at them from windows on both sides of the street.

'Don't tell me she's given up already?'

'I want an ice-cream.'

Obediently he got out of the car. Young Chrissie Molloy was minding the shop for her mother.

'Two large cones, please, Chrissie. Stop grinning. And stop squinting out the window at the car.'

'That's a right oul banger you have out there, Mr Creedon.'

'I hope you're talking about the car.'

'Oh Mr Creedon!' screeched Chrissie.

'That automobile is vintage, Chrissie. Pure vintage.'

'Yeh.'

'If you were to put that car on the market,' he said, thrusting his beard over the counter at her, 'there'd be a million millionaire collectors queuing up to buy it.'

'I wouldn't be one of them.'

'You've no taste, Chrissie.'

'Who's the lady, Mr Creedon?'

'My granny.'

He took two cones out to the car and they sat eating them.

'That young strap in there says your car is an old banger.'

'Children nowadays know nothing.' Ice cream dribbled down her chin. 'Even your own daughter. When I took her to the convent in Athlone, she wanted me to leave the car at the gate so that the other kids wouldn't see it. You've reared her badly.'

'That's what comes of being an absentee father.' He leaned over and wiped her chin with his hankie. 'You're eating that like a kid yourself. If Chrissie sees me wiping your chin, she'll really believe you're my granny.'

'I'm excited. Must be all the sex.'

'Oh lord, don't remind me.'

'What d'you mean?'

'I'm not much good at it.'

'Don't be an eejit. You're great.'

'Keep talking, you wonderful woman.'

'I could eat you this minute.'

'Not in front of all the neighbours. Just drive the car.'

'Yes, boss.' She started the engine. 'But I'll get you again.'

He waved at Chrissie's face staring out the shop window.

'I feel like an absolute bloody beginner at the love-making,' he said. 'But I intend to improve my ratings by diligent application and constant practice.'

'I can't wait.'

'Have you no shame, woman?'

'Not a bit, where you're concerned.'

They drove into the dying sun, through Castlebar to Westport, then further west past Croagh Patrick and the Mweelrea Mountains, and around Killary

Harbour into Connemara.

'Be careful now, paleface,' she cautioned, 'the minute we cross this border, you're in my part of the world.'

'I know. Savage Connemara men will rise up in their sweaty millions and tear me limb from limb. And God knows there's not much on me to begin with.'

They found a B+B in Ballyconneely where they stayed for the night. He made a great show of signing Mr J. and Mrs N. Joyce in the visitors' book and they giggled together long into the night. On the following day they drove to Rossaveel. Here they boarded a trawler, the *Íosagán*, captained by a certain Michael Pats, a solemn, dark, wizened man with a mop of curly hair, who was running an unofficial service to the Aran Islands. He had with him a young helper he called Páidí.

There were no seats. They shared the deck and a number of crates with some Americans, a couple of English, a Swiss and two Germans. As soon as the *Íosagán* had cleared Cashla Bay and entered the North Sound *en route* for Inishmore, they hit a strong south-wester that caused the small boat to pitch and roll in a most alarming way. He had put her sitting on a crate and now he crouched on the deck beside her, a protective arm around her waist.

'Maybe this isn't such a good idea,' he said.

'Rubbish,' she said. 'I've done this more often than you've had hot porridge. All I'm worried about is the wig.'

She tied her scarf around her head to make sure the hairpiece didn't shift itself.

'Can you imagine what this crowd would say if they saw my baldy head!'

When they landed at Kilronan, she knew where she wanted to go and pulled him away from the others.

'Up here. There's a fella I want to see.'

At the top of a short hill they found a small shop where there were bicycles for hire.

'You've been here before.'

'Not for ages. Let's take two bikes and ride down to Dún Aengus.'

'Are you sure? Will you be able for it?'

'We'll just have to find that out, won't we?'

And she rode away before him down the narrow road, so that he had to push himself to catch up with her.

'You're a bloody divil,' he shouted through the wind, when he was finally alongside her. 'If we're to make anything of this relationship, you'll have to remember to respect my grey hairs.'

'Come on, you old softie,' she yelled at him.

But half-a-mile down the hilly road her strength suddenly gave out. They pulled over and he helped her to find a place to sit.

'Are you all right?'

'I'll be fine, but I don't think I'll make it to Dún Aengus. Not today, anyway. Just doing too much too soon, I suppose. You think you can climb a mountain and then you find you can't even get over a tiny hill. Now, don't fuss. Just give me a little time to get myself together again.'

They sat watching the Atlantic waves frothing and tossing on the rocks below them. After a while, she said, 'It's dawning on me what an awful thing I'm asking you to do, Jim.' He started to speak, but she stopped him. 'No, listen to me. I want to say this. And I want you to listen. Are you listening to me?'

'I'm all ears. Well, mostly ears. I'm thinking of having a job done on them.'

'Be serious, you eejit. What I'm saying is, any time you want to end our . . . arrangement, you're free to do it. I won't object. I'll die, but I won't object. I mean it, Jim. Another woman may come along that you'll want to be with. That's OK. You're free to do whatever you like.'

He tightened his arm around her.

'Shut your gob, woman.'

She leaned her head against his shoulder. They sat there for a long time and he knew that no matter what happened he would never again be free.

NINETEEN

Lucy was wearing her breakfast face. She hunched over a cup of tea, listening to the radio.

'Most of the papers agree on their attitude to the appointment. The head-lines vary between "ridiculous" and "shameful". All carry comments from the Friends of Civilization about their impending visit to the High Court to have the Government decision overturned.'

'Oh shut it up, for God's sake!'

Derek Furlong obliged and the radio died.

'They're giving your old man a hard time, all right.'

Lucy sipped her tea.

'He probably deserves it, but I just can't listen to any more. You'd imagine there'd be even one hack in his favour.'

'The Catholic papers support him.'

'Hah!' After a pause, Lucy added, 'What do *you* think, Derek?'

'Me? I'm not paid to have opinions about the boss.'

'When I was young I thought the sun shone out of his ears.'

'Most kids are like that about their fathers.'

'Were you?'

'I was an exception. I had an analytical mind. I saw the old fart for what he was.'

'I had Daddy nearly canonized. A sort of Saint Daddy. I didn't see him too often, but whenever he was home he gave me loads of money. And he never told me off for acting up. He left all the dirty work to Mammy. And then there were those robes and uniforms he wore any time he got the chance. He loved dressing up. Oh he was really *big* in the church. Will I tell you something?

When I made my Confirmation, there were dozens of girls with me, all dolled up, powdered and painted and wearing their finest, but nobody was looking at them – everybody was staring at Daddy. He really was gorgeous. Like a bloody peacock.'

'Yes, dear.'

'I'm telling you! Every night when I was saying my prayers and I came to the "God bless Daddy" bit, I used to think that God would have been shit scared not to!'

'Don't let it eat into you, pet.' Derek glanced at his watch. 'It's time I was hitting the road.'

'Oh you've got buckets of time. He won't be in the office today. He'll be at home with the bishop. You know that.'

'I don't *know* anything of the sort, Lucy. He might just come in to catch people out.'

Lucy looked at her husband thoughtfully.

'You're scared of him, aren't you?'

'Even more scared than God is.'

'Why?'

'Because he'd sack me as soon as he'd look at me.'

'But you're his son-in-law.'

'That makes no difference. If it suited him, he'd squash me between his thumb and forefinger like a beetle.'

'Yes. He would, wouldn't he!'

When Derek had departed for ORMAX, Lucy showered and dressed. In a thoughtful frame of mind, she looked at her slim body and wondered to what unimaginable vastness it would progress as the pregnancy advanced, how awkward it would become to shift about in confined spaces, how wretchedly it would react to the almost inevitable morning sickness. However, it was early days yet. Only she and her doctor suspected that she was in an extremely interesting biological condition.

Derek could be told later, when the opportune moment arrived. The thought of how he would respond to his new status brought a little smile to her lips. Something like mild hysteria, she fancied. Pink panic. Pure pink panic. He would probably need more TLC than she would in the months ahead.

She rang Twin Cedars several times, but got the engaged tone. Obviously others were clamouring to pat her father on his receptive back.

Finally she gave up on the phone, took out her Fiesta and drove from Howth to Silverglen. She didn't particularly want to see her father and congratulate him on his appointment, but she felt that she ought to. She was, after all, his only child, as Derek often reminded her.

When she saw the group of reporters outside the gates of Twin Cedars, her first impulse was to turn back, or to drive on past as if she had no connection with the house. But she did neither. She stopped the car and flashed her lights at Matt Sweeney, whom she could see inside. He noticed her immediately and came to admit her.

Lucy ignored the hands tapping on her closed windows and stared straight ahead as she drove through the gates. She paused only to exchange a word with Matt Sweeney.

'They didn't bother you, Mrs Furlong, did they?'

'Why would they bother me, Matt?'

'I think they gave the boss a bit of a hard time this morning.'

'Oh.'

It was a thoughtful Lucy who walked into Twin Cedars.

She found her father and her uncle in the sitting room, facing each other over brandy glasses. Something about their posture reminded her of a stand-off in a Western movie, though both of them were smiling.

Robert immediately jumped to his feet and embraced her.

'Ah my dear,' he said. 'You're looking very well and happy this morning.'

He was really rather pathetic in his desire to be congratulated. Lucy grudgingly obliged.

'Why wouldn't I?' She kissed the proffered cheek. 'Isn't my famous dad all over the papers? Congratulations. I'm sure you're as pleased as a dog with two tails.'

Robert made a dismissive gesture with his hands, which she could hardly bear to look at, so she turned to the bishop.

'Hello, Uncle Dec. It's lovely to see you again.'

'Good morning, Lucy,' said the bishop, embracing her. 'How's Derek?'

'Oh fine. Out working for his crust. Not like his boss. I've been trying to ring you all morning, Dad, but I couldn't get through.'

'The phone has been hopping off its cradle since yesterday evening,' said Robert. 'A great many people seem to be very excited over the appointment. I don't know why. I mean, it's not all that important.'

Lucy hated his patently insincere effort at self-deprecation.

'I see you have a reception committee at the gate.'

'Don't tell me they're still there. Did you speak to them?'

'No. I hope they haven't been giving you a hard time?'

'Oh heavens, no. Very polite. Very respectful. But I decided not to give any interviews for the time being.'

Lucy looked at the bishop in time to catch the little smile on his face.

'Matt seems to think they're a hostile army,' she said. 'He won't let them past the gate.'

'The Nuncio rang,' said Robert. 'He was asking how you were. And Canon Finnegan wants to say a special Mass next Sunday in honour of the occasion. I tried to put him off, but he's dead set on it.'

'Trust the canon.'

Robert looked at her sharply.

'And what does that mean?'

'Oh nothing.'

'Come on,' insisted Robert.

'Well, he's always hopping around, waving his arms. Looking for a band wagon to jump on.'

'The man is only doing his job.'

'Let me guess what his line was,' said Lucy. She struck an attitude and imitated Finnegan's sonorous tones. ' "The parish of Silverglen feels the need to rejoice when one of its sons reaches such eminent heights". Is that close?'

Robert's face reddened.

'I don't think that's called for, Lucy.'

She was suddenly contrite. He looked so pudgy and defenceless that even his pomposity was in its own way endearing.

'I'm sorry, Dad, But that old chancer feeds me up to my tonsils.'

'He merely follows his vocation, Lucy, to serve his flock. He has his finger on the pulse of the parish and knows what his parishioners want.'

'His parishioners want what he tells them to want.'

Robert looked at the bishop, shaking his head.

'Young people today have no respect for anything, Dec. When I was her age, I'd never have dared to criticize even a priest, let alone a canon.'

'As long as she's interested enough to want to criticize a priest, there's hope for the Church,' said the Bishop.

'Good for you, Uncle Dec.'

'Whatever kind of Catholicism you're teaching them in Africa, Dec, it's not the same religion I was taught in school.'

There was a discreet knock at the door and Sally, the maid, insinuated herself into the room.

'Excuse me, Mr McGuinness, there's someone here to see you.'

'Who is it?'

'It's Miss Hanley, sir.'

'Hanley?' The word in Robert's mouth sounded like an expletive.

'Oh goodness,' said Lucy.

'The one that came the day of the funeral,' said Sally helpfully.

'Where is she?'

'I put her in the little room, sir.'

'The *reception*-room, Sally. How many times have I told you that it's the *reception*-room!'

'Yessir, The little reception-room.'

'I'll be there in a minute.'

'I'll tell her so.' Sally disappeared out the door.

There was a silence.

'Well, now,' said Lucy. 'Miss Hanley. There must be news about Mammy's will.'

'I'll *will* her!' Robert stood up purposefully. 'She has a cheek coming here!'

'What are you going to do, Dad?'

'I'm going to throw her out.'

'You can't do that!'

'Just watch me.'

'But somebody in your position doesn't go throwing solicitors out of his house. Think how it would look in the parish magazine.'

'I'm going to pretend you didn't say that, Lucy.'

'And what would that crowd of reporters at the gate make of it. You ought to call them in to witness the eviction.'

Robert swung angrily on her as if he were going to hit her. Lucy stepped back, suddenly afraid of this manifestation of a new side to her father. The bishop came to his feet. Robert glared at him.

'I suppose you've already heard about this stupid carry-on?'

'What carry-on?'

'You're better off not knowing.'

'It's about Mammy's will, Uncle Dec. Somebody must have turned up with the reserve. If that's the case there's nothing you can do, Dad, except let him have the car.'

'To hell with that!' snarled Robert. 'If you think I'm going to let some perfect stranger walk away with Babs's car on the say-so of a crooked lawyer like that woman, you'd better think again!'

'Tread carefully, Robert,' said the bishop.

'I'll tread on *her*!' said Robert. 'I'll grind her into the floor.'

'Oh no, Dad—!'

But Robert was already out the door and stamping his way to the reception-room. The bishop and Lucy looked at each other.

The bishop spread his hands.

'He seems quite disturbed,' he said. 'Tell me what's going on.'

The first thing Robert was aware of when he opened the door to the reception-room was the unprepossessing smirk on Kate Hanley's face. She looked positively and evilly triumphant. She was clutching her briefcase in front of her as if to ward off evil spirits.

'Good afternoon, Mr McGuinness.'

'What do you want?'

'Please don't raise your voice to me. All I'm doing is my job – on behalf of your late wife, if you remember.'

'I have only your word for that.'

'Come off it, Mr McGuinness. You've seen the document. You will have recognized your wife's signature. You know, as well as I do, that the will is genuine.'

'I've no desire to spend any more time with you than is absolutely necessary, so say what you have to say and then get out.'

'Nothing will give me greater pleasure.' Miss Hanley assumed the measured tones of counsel addressing the court. 'You will remember that there was a reserve placed on your wife's car when she put it up for sale. I can now tell you that I have received a communication from a person who is in possession of the article your late wife explicitly mentioned as the reserve on her car.'

'Have you seen this . . . person?'

'Not yet. I have the name and address.'

'Have you seen the reserve?'

'No.'

'Then how do you know the claim is genuine?'

'He has described the article to me in great detail. I'm quite satisfied that he's telling the truth.'

Robert gritted his teeth. He felt an urgent desire to assault this woman and throw her out of his house.

'What article are we talking about?'

'A small pendant in the shape of a cross on an imitation gold chain, given to him by your wife.'

'That has to be a lie. Any jewellery owned by my wife was the real thing. I wouldn't insult her with imitations.'

'This was a gift to her from her father when she made her Confirmation in 1963. As you probably know, he was not a rich man. Unlike you, he had to make do with imitations.'

'I never saw my wife with any such pendant.'

'Be that as it may, it undoubtedly exists. Mrs McGuinness described it to me when she made the will. I have all the details written down in your wife's hand. A small imitation gold cross on an imitation gold chain. Mrs McGuinness gave it to this gentleman in Dublin in June 1976, at the corner of O'Connell Street and Middle Abbey Street.' She opened her briefcase and took out a sheet of paper. 'This is a copy of her original statement. I'm sure you will have no difficulty in recognizing the handwriting as genuine.'

She extended the sheet to Robert. He made no attempt to take it. Miss Hanley placed the sheet on the table beside her.

'I'll leave it there, in case you want to look at it later on.'

'Is that all?'

'My partner is outside in my car. If you wish, I can take your late wife's car with me now and—'

'Lay a hand on any of my property and I'll call the Gardai.'

Miss Hanley's smile grew broader.

'Suit yourself, Mr McGuinness. I was merely trying to do you a service.'

'The best service you can do me is to get yourself out of here immediately.'

'Very well. In that case I'll be on my way. I'll ask the gentleman who has bought the car to come and take it away at his convenience. And don't worry: he'll have a letter from Hanley and Patterson authorizing him to remove the vehicle.'

'Tell him not to bother. Tell him he'll be wasting his time.'

'Oh I see. You intend to deliver it yourself? In that case, I'll leave you his name and address.'

She took another sheet of paper from her briefcase and laid it beside the first one.

'I have to warn you that he lives in Mayo, Mr McGuinness. It would be quite a trip for you.'

'Get out, before I throw you out.'

'I wouldn't do anything like that if I were you. It's never advisable to hit anyone in the legal profession. We know our way around the law.'

She moved to the door and paused.

'I'll ask the gentleman in question to give you a ring before he comes here.'

'Get out!'

'Merely a precaution in case you find the prospect of a trip to Mayo too daunting.'

Robert raised his voice.

'Sally!'

Sally appeared in the doorway.

'Yes, Mr McGuinness?'

'Show this . . . *woman* out.'

'Yes, Mr McGuinness.'

'One final thing,' said Miss Hanley, 'you don't have to worry about the papers for the car. Your late wife left all the documents with us, plus an ignition key, so the new owner will be in full possession of the lot when he calls. Thanks for your courtesy, Mr McGuinness. I hope to do the same for you one of these days when you call at our office.'

Robert stood where he was till he heard the hall door close behind his unwelcome visitor. He drew several long, shuddering breaths.

'What happened, Dad?'

He turned to face Lucy.

'What?'

'I heard you shouting.'

'I wasn't shouting. I was merely kicking that bloody woman out of my house.'

He was in no humour to speak to his daughter. He wished she would go away.

177

'What did she want?'

'She had some cock-and-bull story about your mother's car.'

'What story?'

'Nothing for you to bother about— Leave them alone!'

But Lucy already had picked up the papers from the table and was scanning them.

'This is Mammy's handwriting—'

'Give them to me, Lucy!'

Robert snatched the papers roughly from his daughter's hand.

'Why are you carrying on like this, Dad?'

'I'm not carrying on. I'm angry, that's all. This woman marches into my house with her lies and—'

'That *is* Mammy's writing, isn't it?'

'How the hell would I know!'

'You *must* know! *I'd* know her scrawl anywhere.'

'Are you calling me a liar?' She didn't answer, but she didn't flinch from him. 'For all I know it could be some sort of a forgery.'

'Oh, come on, Dad!' She laughed at him. 'Get real. You know it's Mammy's writing. Anyway, who'd want to forge something about Mammy's old banger.'

'I don't want to talk about it!'

'But *I* want to talk about it.'

'It's none of your business.'

'She's my mother!'

'And she's my wife!'

'That's why this is so awful. You don't really give a damn about her, do you!'

'What the hell is that supposed to mean?'

'Mammy made a will about her car. She *wanted* it to go to this special person. If you cared about her at all you'd want to see that her last wishes were carried out. Her *last wishes*, Dad! And you can't pretend that you don't know the will is genuine. Derek told you all that in his report.'

'That was a confidential report. Derek had no right to tell you what was in it.'

'For God's sake, Dad! Derek's my husband. He tells me everything.'

'I'll fire the little bastard!'

'Now *that* will make a very good story in the papers, won't it? Knight of St Nicodemus fires his lawyer for telling the truth!'

'Don't you dare talk to me like that!'

'I'm grown up now, Dad. I can talk to you any way I like. As a matter of fact, we could go outside now and have this conversation in front of those reporters. How would you fancy that?'

'Damn you!' hissed Robert. He was white-faced with anger. 'Damn you, Lucy! I'll never forgive you for speaking to your father like that.'

He stalked past her and out of the room, the papers clutched in his hand. Lucy suddenly felt weak at the knees. She sank down into a chair, trembling all over.

Some minutes later the bishop found her there. He came and sat beside her.

'What was all that about, Lucy?'

She lifted her head to look at him.

'I feel sick, Uncle Dec. I've just had a terrible flare-up with Dad.'

His face was full of concern.

'Don't worry about it. By this time tomorrow it'll all have blown over.'

'I don't think so.'

'These things have a habit of disappearing with a good night's sleep.'

She shook her head at him.

'Uncle Dec, I saw something just now, something Dad didn't want me to see.'

TWENTY

They sat in front of the fire in the kitchen, very close together, looking into the flames and listening to the splash and gurgle of the overflowing gutters. The rain had been falling since early morning and showed no sign of abating.

It was the end of July 1998. She had to leave early. Lucia was holidaying in France and was expected home within a week. There was the long drive to Dublin ahead and the going would be slow because of the bad weather. There were puddles everywhere around the cottage and the little stream that ran past the gable end and into Lochcrideen was swollen to a miniature yellow torrent pulsing away above the splatter of the raindrops through the trees.

'It's time I was saying goodbye,' she said.

'This is the sort of day that's good for nothing except tears.'

'Isn't it.'

'Or maybe saying "to hell with it" and jumping back into bed again.'

'I don't want to go.'

'Then stay. You know what the man said – "Summer's lease hath all too short a date." '

'Is that Keats again?'

'Shakespeare.'

'Oh *him*!'

It was always like this. Every parting since the beginning had been difficult and had become progressively more so as they had grown into what they liked to call their kingfisher time. Each visit had further cemented their relationship by creating new habits to be shared and new memories to be remembered. He felt he had known her forever, though the number of their weeks together totalled no more than a couple of years.

He ran his hands through her red-brown hair, now flecked with white. It had grown again over the years and was almost as luxuriant as it had been that first day in Nassau Street. When she had felt able to dispense with the wig, he had insisted on taking it to hang in his study beside the pictures of Lucia and the imitation gold cross.

The arrangement they had made nine years before on Inishmore (rather, the arrangement she had proposed and he had agreed to) had been kept ever since as the situation had allowed. She had come whenever she could and he had always made himself available to spend the maximum amount of time with her by rearranging his writing schedule. Sometimes her visits were very short, no more than a day or two, but others had often extended to a couple of weeks, on one or two memorable occasions to a month and a half.

She had always come armed with plans, itineraries and road maps, and together they had explored all the western region of the country, particularly the 'little towns in Connacht' so dear to her. She knew Pearse's poem *The Wayfarer* off by heart and loved to recite it to him just to show that she could.

Or children with bare feet upon the sands
Of some ebbed sea, or playing on the streets
Of little towns in Connacht.

The little red Morris Minor had taken them again and again through the spectacular wildness of Connemara, from town to town, from boarding house to boarding house. Everywhere they went they signed the visitors' book as James and Nora Joyce. They always called each other Nora and Jim, though she had revealed that her name was Brigid Mary, aka Babs. She addressed her letters to Séamus Creedon, but never used the name otherwise, nor did she tell him her surname. This was as she wished it and, as usual, he deferred to her desires.

When he was tied into a period of concentrated writing, or had serious deadlines to meet, she would bring wallpaper and paint and devote herself to refurbishing and decorating the cottage while he worked. Despite her frail constitution, she seemed to have boundless energy to spare for this kind of artistic expression and she would often work for hours on end sanding and painting. When he told her to take it easy, she always protested that she never got the opportunity to do work of this kind at home in Dublin.

'Since he got rich Robert always brings in professionals for any decorating job. He thinks it's a mark of class.'

'I hate that creep more whenever I hear his name.'

'You shouldn't waste your time. He doesn't count.'

Gradually under her careful ministrations the cottage had changed in appearance and in spirit. It no longer had the rather gloomy atmosphere that Colm and Niamh Creedon had brought to it. Only the happier items of *their* tenancy now remained – the large picture window in the kitchen, the crockery and linens in the dresser, the battered old typewriter in the study. Everything else had been transformed by the lightness of Nora's touch. There were now brighter colours on the walls and gayer hangings on the windows. In one remarkable fit of energy, she had even re-tiled the rather dull green of the bathroom in whites and blues.

On the practical side, she had seen to it that he bought a washing-machine, a vacuum cleaner and other modern necessities and learned how to use them. She had dismissed his protests at these gross libels on his personal hygiene.

'If you were left on your own, you'd live in a tip and you'd never even wash your face.'

As the years had passed she had brought him regular reports and photographs of Lucia's progress. He had followed his daughter's career through school and into Trinity College, where she took a respectable, though not spectacular, degree. He had heard of her meeting with Derek Furlong and had seen a picture of the young man who seemed destined to steal away his little girl before her father had even met her.

'This romance with the Derek fella – it's serious, then?' he asked, while the rain came down the chimney and spluttered in the fire.

'I'm afraid so. One look was all it took, as far as she was concerned. When she makes up her mind, there's no turning her.'

'Like her mother.'

Though she laughed at the comparison, her eyes were watchful. He noticed this, but didn't dare push the questioning any further.

'And do you approve of this cradle-snatcher?'

'Oh Derek is only a *garsún* himself. And he's all right. No, *more* than that. He's a good man and he'll make her happy, as well as I can judge. If he doesn't, she'll skin him alive.'

'I suppose I'd better give my consent, so?'

'I'd like that.'

'Consider it done. Arise, Sir Derek, and ride off into the sunset with my daughter. But not just yet.'

'I'm afraid she wants to marry him right away.'

'How soon is right away?'

'Before the end of the year.'

'God, that's quick. She'll have come and gone before I can blink. Any chance I'll get an invitation to the wedding?'

'Oh my love.' She touched his cheek. 'You've had to do without so much.'

'And when the wedding is over, what then?'

'I'll come to you, if I'm able. And if you still want me.'

'I'll give the matter full consideration and let you know by registered post as soon as I've reached a decision. Have you told her about me?'

'Not yet.'

'You promised you would when she was grown up. She's surely grown up if she's getting married.'

'I'll do it, Jim.'

'When?'

'When the time is right.'

And she refused to be budged on it.

Finally she stood up to go and they walked to the door together. Outside the red Morris Minor seemed to crouch under the onslaught of the rain.

'Baby, it's wet outside,' he said.

'Wet or not, I'll have to go.'

'That's a sorry looking creature of a car, but I'll miss it when it's laid to rest.'

She looked at the Morris, then turned to him with the air of having made up her mind.

'If anything happens to me, Jim, I want you to have the car.'

He was struck with dread.

'What are you going to do? Run off with a sailor?'

'One of these days I'm going to die.'

His heart missed a beat.

'Me too. It's the common fate of mankind.'

'I'm serious about this, Jim.' She tied a plastic bonnet over her red-brown hair. Then she added, almost as an afterthought, her gaze carefully averted, 'The cancer has come back.'

He put his hands on her shoulders and turned her around to face him.

'When did you find this out?'

'I had a check-up last month.'

'And you never mentioned it.'

'I'm mentioning it now.'

He was quiet for a few moments, his fingers clenched on her shoulders.

'What precisely is the prognosis?'

'I'll have to have more chemo. I'll lose all my hair again.'

'Ah well, we'll get you a new wig this time. I want to keep the one inside on the wall. Just to remind me of the day you flung it at me in the car.'

'I did *not* fling it at you.'

'You felt like it.'

'That's different. I've often felt like flinging heavier things than that at you, but I never did.'

He suddenly clutched at her and held her close.

'Oh my God, Nora, I don't think I can take this.'

'You must, my love. We both must. There's nothing else to be done.'

They clung together for a while. Then she pulled herself away.

'About the car . . .'

'Forget the car.'

'Don't you want it?'

'I want *you*.'

'If I had to go, I'd like you to have it. God knows, I've nothing else to leave you.'

'Christ, I can't stand this sort of talk.'

'I've been making up a plan. If anything happens to me suddenly.'

'Nothing sudden is going to happen to you.'

'Pay attention, Jim. Listen. I want you to have it. So, in case he starts digging ditches or raising walls, I'm going to do it legal. I'm going to make a will about it.'

'For God's sake!'

'*He* made *me* make a will. The minute he heard what the doctor had to say, he said we ought to make our wills, leaving all we have to each other.'

'The smarmy, greedy bastard.'

'Oh he's not cheating me. I've nothing, anyway. Nothing of my own. Except the car. And that's for you. So I've been thinking I'll make a will about that. Kate said she'd look after it for me. She's a solicitor now. She'll know what to do.'

They left it at that. He knew she hadn't told him everything that the doctor had said, but he knew also that she didn't want to be pushed on it. And, in truth, he didn't want to hear whatever bad news she might be concealing from him.

'Before you go, Nora.'

'What is it?'

'I've something I want to tell you. A confession I want to make.'

'You don't have to make any confessions to me, Jim.'

'I must. I need to. I want you to forgive me.'

'My darling, I forgive you now, whatever it is. No, no, no. Please.' She put her hand on his lips. 'I don't want to hear it. After all I've put you through . . .'

'You've given me my life, Nora.'

'There you are, then. Let it be, my love. Just let it be.'

As the red car pulled away through the rain, he stood on the steps at the door watching it chug down the little lane to the road. In fact, he stood there long after the sound of the engine had faded. The rain fell on his face, but he wasn't aware of it.

'I was unfaithful,' he called into the wet world. 'I was unfaithful. And I'm sorry.'

Next day he immediately plunged himself into what he had decided would be the last book in the *Quirke* series. It was to be called *The Quirke Retrospective*. He found it a sad book to write, because it entailed saying goodbye to some characters he had lived with for several years, and he felt that he had had enough farewells in recent times. He also had to contend with his publisher, Quango, who disliked the idea of bringing the series to a close. After numerous phone calls, he went to London for face to face negotiations. He was glad to go, to have his time determined for him.

The trip took the best part of a week to organise and another week to execute.

When he returned to the cottage in Maaclee he was dismayed to find that there was no word from Nora. He fretted about the place for a long time before he could motivate himself to get back to work on the book. Finally he started to write, but found it very difficult. He tore up and otherwise scrubbed out draft after draft, filling his wastepaper basket with crumpled sheets and the recycle bin on the computer with washed out text. The thought that she might be really ill, perhaps even dying, filled him with a panic he had never before experienced.

Two months after they had parted, a letter came from Nora. It enclosed a photograph of Lucia in her wedding dress, with her new husband beside her. He looked long and hard at the beautiful young lady in the shimmering white satin, before he could bring himself to read what Nora had written. The deterioration in her handwriting distressed him. Where it once had been strong and forceful, it was now spidery and timorous.

'My dearest Jim you would be bursting with pride to see your lovely daughter now <u>Mrs Furlong</u>. Thank you <u>thank</u> you so much for giving me such a pretty child. We brought the wedding forward because well just because I'm not too good of late. This thing is eating me up so fast. There will be an ad in the <u>Tribune</u> about the car watch out for it the <u>RESERVE</u> is the little gold cross and chain you have hanging up in your room. I haven't told Kate who you are or where you live I thought it would be best to keep that our secret in case you didn't want her to know but when you come to collect the car Kate will give Lucia a letter from me explaining everything. Oh my darling whatever happens or wherever I go you will always be with me and I will do my best to look after you if they allow such things in Heaven if there is such a place and they let me in. I can't tell you how much I love you <u>but I do I do I do</u>. Always your own Nora.'

For a long period he stopped working altogether. Every day whatever the weather he went out walking along the lanes and across the fields around the lake. Most of the time he walked blindly, pausing only to hold agonized conversations with whatever specimens of wildlife he happened to interrupt in their predatory activity around the hedgerows and in the undergrowth. On such occasions he spoke aloud to the startled creatures and waved his arms a lot. This gave him some relief, but failed to impress his audience, which scattered before the animated scarecrow with the impassioned beard and the suffering face.

Small boys who witnessed some of his odd behaviour spread the word around Maaclee that old Creedon had finally flipped his lid and was up to all sorts of strange antics involving unnatural advances to little birds, lesser mammals and waterfowl, and shouting out loud like a madman. This caused a great deal of concern to the ladies of the town and especially to the lately widowed postmistress, Sheila Delaney. Sheila's solicitude was coupled with a vague hope that a time of stress, such as Mr Creedon was undoubtedly undergoing, might present an unexpected opportunity for a willing female to make herself useful as a comforter. It had not passed unnoticed that the brazen strap in the red car had been conspicuous by her absence for a long number of weeks and Sheila therefore reasoned that the trouble with the little man might have something to do with sexual deprivation.

One day she turned up at the cottage to enquire after Mr Creedon's health and to ask if there was anything she might do to improve his situation. When the door was opened to her knock, she was shocked by the emaciated, wild creature who stood before her.

'Oh Mr Creedon, what are you doing to yourself at all?'

He stared at her as if she were an alien from outer space.

'What?'

'God love you.' Before he could close the door again, she walked past him into the cottage. 'Will you just look at the place! It's easy seeing it hasn't felt the touch of a woman's hand for ages.'

The cottage certainly was untidy, things were thrown about, there were unwashed dishes in the sink, but he couldn't see that it was any of her business.

'Please get out. I haven't been eating my young.'

'I couldn't possibly leave you like this, Mr Creedon. You don't look as if you've had a decent meal in days.' She opened the fridge and stood aghast. 'Good heavens, there isn't a pick of food here. How can you be neglecting yourself so completely! I'll tell you what. I have the car outside. Why don't I skip down to Lavelle's and pick up something nourishing for you. Then I'll be back here and I'll have a good meal on the table before you can say Jack Robinson. Tell me what you like to eat and—'

'No.'

'Oh don't be silly, Mr Creedon. I was married long enough to the late Mr Delaney to know what is essential to keep a man happy. A nice strong fella like you needs his sustenance. And it's no trouble at all to me. In fact, it'll be a pleasure. So I'll—'

'No!' said Séamus again, this time moving several tones up the scale. It wasn't quite a shout, but it was only marginally less.

Sheila Delaney stared at him in surprise.

'Ah now, Mr Creedon,' she began.

He was quivering inside, but he held himself in check.

'I know you mean well, Mrs Delaney, and thank you for it, but all I want is to be left alone. Please.' He held the door open. 'Please. Just go. And thank you for being so thoughtful.'

'Oh well, if you're sure that's what you—'

'I'm sure. Goodbye.'

He closed the door behind her and leaned against it. He exhaled strongly. Then he walked into the bathroom and stared at himself in the mirror. The face that stared back at him was not beautiful to behold.

'She'd kill me if she could see me now. I'm in flitters. Inside and outside.'

He undressed himself, got into the bath and lay there steeping himself till the hot water ran out. Later he dumped his used clothes into the washing machine and put on a clean shirt and a fresh pair of jeans. Then he went around the cottage with the vacuum cleaner, whistling loudly and singing songs to drive out the demons. When he finally sat down to drink a cup of tea he was exhausted.

'Dear God,' he said, 'why did you invent cancer?'

He went to the cupboard, took out a bottle of whiskey and poured a generous dollop of it into his tea.

Thus fortified, he composed a letter to the Box No. It was a mad letter, full of all sorts of extravagances and outrageous puns. In the margins he drew little pictures of crazy men with spade beards. There was at least one preposterous limerick included in the wild whirligig of text and drawings. When he had finished, he found it impossible to look his letter over, so he put the sheets into an envelope and sealed it. Then he took it straightaway down to the post office. As he pushed the envelope into the post-box, he could see Sheila Delaney peering at him from the recesses of her shop, but he retreated before she could come out and accost him.

Afterwards there was nothing for it but to get back to the book. For the next couple of months he worked his way feverishly through another seven drafts, until he felt he had reached a stage where he could do no more. It was tedious and unrewarding work, but at least it kept him busy and away from the cap on the whiskey bottle.

Christmas came and went and there was no letter, not even a card. However, he remembered that the last time he had drawn conclusions from such an event he had been completely wrong. And he knew now that whatever was going on was none of Nora's fault.

He finished the book as the spring came with the daffodils. A new cycle of life began around the lakes. Trees sprouted, buds formed, birds mated and began to build their nests.

Then, one morning, deep into the summertime, there was the advertisement in the *Tribune*. The birds stopped singing on the trees outside.

And he knew that his life was over.

TWENTY-ONE

'Will you listen to me!' he shouted. 'Tell your mother I'm on the phone.'

'She doesn't want to talk to you, Dad,' said his daughter.

'Bloody hell! She's my bloody wife. She *has* to talk to me.'

'There's no use abusing *me.*'

'I just want to know what's eating her.'

'I can't tell you that. Well, I can, though maybe I shouldn't.'

'Tell me what?'

His daughter's voice lowered.

'Can you hear me?'

'I can hear you.'

'Well, she got a letter.'

'A what?'

'God, don't make me shout, Dad. She'll hear me. She got a letter. Full of stuff about you.'

'Stuff? What stuff?'

'Dirty stuff.'

'Dirty – Oh Holy God!' Kerrigan was rendered speechless for a moment. All sorts of dreadful images swam before his eyes. 'What bloody liar has been saying things about me?'

'Dad, what in the name of God have you been up to?'

'Shut up!' yelled Kerrigan. 'Shut bloody up before I caramelize you!'

The phone went dead.

Kerrigan sat staring at the receiver. He jiggled the cradle as he had seen innumerable actors do in countless movies, but the phone refused to be jostled from its implacable silence. He slammed down the useless instrument. He prayed. That is, he mentioned several holy names, but with a conspicuous lack of reverence. His eczema threatened to overwhelm him.

He was sitting in what had been his lounge, though it no longer resembled the neat room it once was. Since Mollie's departure, apart from the short visit paid by his daughter, no female hand had been laid on the house, and it showed. There was dust everywhere. Things lay untidily about the place. Kerrigan's overcoat was crumpled over a chair. His cap lay on the floor in the hallway, where he had thrown it the previous night. In the adjoining kitchen, unwashed dishes filled the sink and spilled over on to the drainer, the worktop and the table. Upstairs in his bedroom, *their* bedroom before his unfeeling wife had taken herself off, the bed was unmade and his dirty clothes were strewn uncollected across the floor.

Kerrigan's world was falling to pieces. Kerrigan felt as if he himself were falling to pieces.

From the beginning the media had been relentless in their pursuit of the decision to award the Gallery directorship to Robert McGuinness. Whatever hope Kerrigan had entertained that it would all go away was now in tatters. Newspapers, radio and television, urged on by the Opposition, without exception seemed determined to bring down the plan. The Letters pages were full of derogatory comments, ranging from derisory criticism to unadulterated abuse. Oonagh McCantley went about chaining herself to various immovable objects, attracting ever-larger swarms of enthusiastic supporters. The High Court had granted The Friends of Civilization an injunction preventing the implementation of the Government's decision pending a judicial review of the case. In the meantime pickets proliferated everywhere – outside the Dáil, the Department of Foreign Affairs, and the houses of Kerrigan himself and Robert McGuinness. Even the Taoiseach's residence had its quota of placard-carrying protestors, much to Éilís Ní Snodaigh's chagrin. Kerrigan's home phone rang so constantly that he had taken it off the cradle. Initially he had answered the calls, but the comments were so vitriolic that he had soon given up listening to them.

Who in God's name had sent a letter to Mollie full of lies and slanders! All he had ever done was have the odd little fling, apart from the Aoife affair, and that had only come about because . . . well, just because they had found themselves away together in Brussels and had had too much to drink. That's what had started it. A perfectly natural human response to a tempting situation.

There was nothing in it at first. Afterwards it just became a habit. There was still nothing in it, he told himself. Not a bloody thing. But of course Mollie wouldn't believe that. Women were a damn nuisance, the way they looked at things. Why couldn't Mollie have gone out and had a bit on the side herself?

'Because nobody would bloody have you!' he shouted aloud.

The phone rang.

'Feck off!' he snarled at it, knocking it to one side.

He stamped back up to the bedroom, kicking unwanted objects out of his way. When he had showered and shaved, he felt better, or at least calmer. Then he rang Aoife.

'The Taoiseach wants to see you,' were her first words, before he could say anything. 'She's been ringing you all morning. Apparently she can't get through to you at home. I rang you twice myself.'

'I had it off the hook,' said Kerrigan. 'Look, tell the bitch that I'm on my way in the next half-hour.'

'She's not going to like that.'

'She'll bloody well have to lump it.'

'Will I tell her that?'

'You'll do no such thing. What you'll do is buy the biggest bouquet of flowers you can find and give it to Joe Downes to bring with him when he calls for me. Spare no expense on this one, Aoife.'

'Do I put a note on it for her?'

'For who?'

'For the Taoiseach.'

'Don't be a gobshite. I'll look after any notes myself.'

He knew she was wondering whom the flowers were for, but he wouldn't give her the satisfaction of telling her that they were for his wife.

He hung up the phone and dressed himself in the best shirt and suit he could find amongst his things. While he was rummaging in one of the drawers in search of a suitable tie, he came across the gun. This was a small automatic pistol that had been issued to him for his personal protection. He was entitled to carry it with him at all times, but usually he didn't bother with it, relying instead on the professionalism of those about him who were entrusted with the job of protecting him.

Now, however, the weapon seemed suddenly attractive as he thought of the letter-writer who had had the temerity to send the letter to Mollie. He hefted it in his hand. This little thing could kill a man with ease, in response to no more than a gentle pressure on the trigger. A Garda marksman had shown him how to do it. You stood this way with your legs apart and your left hand supporting your right. Bang! Simplicity itself.

He heard the car pull up outside the house and reluctantly returned the weapon to its place in the drawer.

The visit to his daughter's house to try to make peace with Mollie was an unmitigated disaster. True, Aoife had procured an immense bouquet of flowers (which could later be paid for out of allowable expenses) and the fragrance and colour had filled the car beside the smiling face of Garda Joe Downes. The countryside was splashed with sunshine as they drove to the city. It was a good omen. Perhaps God was in His Heaven, after all.

But when they pulled up outside the semi-detached, mock-Tudor-fronted house where Siobhán lived with her husband and two children, Kerrigan was disturbed to see a couple of men, one carrying a camera, standing at the gate.

'Oh Christ,' said Kerrigan. 'Is that the bloody Press?'

'The long-haired one is O'Malley from the *Indo*.'

'Can you get rid of them, Joe?'

Joe got out of the car and a heavy discussion ensued between him and the pressmen. The long-haired O'Malley waved his hands a lot and seemed unwilling to be moved. The photographer hung back and busied himself with his camera. In a moment Joe returned to the car.

'They won't budge, Minister. They say they're within their rights. I don't know what else I can do. Unless I make a big deal of it and send for a squad car.'

'Get the hell out of here, Joe.'

Joe put his foot down and the car spurted away. Through the rear window, Kerrigan could see that the cameraman was already taking pictures of both the departing vehicle and the house.

All he could think of was, What the hell is happening to me?

When he arrived in his office, his bowels were in chaos. He immediately wanted to head for the small room. He felt he needed some time to think. But Aoife forestalled him.

'You'd better go straight over, Minister. They've been waiting for you for nearly an hour.'

'They? Who the hell is they?'

'An Taoiseach and An Tánaiste.'

'That Creeping Jesus? What the hell is *he* doing with Frigidia?'

'The Taoiseach asked him to come in this morning specially for the meeting.'

This was unpleasant news. It was bad enough having to face Éilís Ní Snodaigh on her own, without the spectacle of Martin Shevlin's snivelling face leering at him too. Shevlin was leader of the Radical Party, the second largest party in the coalition, and therefore held the position of Tánaiste, or Deputy Head of Government. He was a little man with lank greasy hair, who drank only ale shandies on his infrequent visits to the Dáil bar. In Kerrigan's eyes anyone who infected good beer with lemonade was more than a sad hoor, he was a blasphemous sad hoor with the taste of a dung beetle. Shevlin was a good enough politician and a hard-working, honest man, but these were mere peripheral virtues to Kerrigan.

'I hate that little bollocks,' said Kerrigan fervently.

'No, you don't, Minister.' Aoife brushed his hair back from his forehead with her long fingers. 'And *he* doesn't hate you. Now, be a good man and go and get this sorted out as quickly as possible.'

Kerrigan stared at her narrowly. Lately, she had rarely been as affectionate as this. Then it dawned on him. She obviously thought that the flowers he had asked her to buy that morning were intended for herself. He couldn't tell her that he had told Joe Downey to do what he liked with the bouquet. He reached out absentmindedly and fingered one of her breasts.

'You're a sound woman, Aoife. But I've a pain in my gut.'

'Now, now,' she said gently, allowing his hand to linger a moment, 'first things first. Off you go and make your peace with the Taoiseach.'

She kissed him lightly on the cheek and he squeezed her breast in acknowledgement.

'Come in.'

The Taoiseach's modulated voice never failed to pierce the thickest of doors. Kerrigan braced himself and entered the bright office. Though sunlight was streaming through the windows and the two people who faced him were both smiling, he was immediately conscious of a cold blast of air.

'Ah, Nollaig,' said Éilís Ní Snodaigh. 'You're welcome, my friend. Sit down.'

Michael Shevlin nodded his head and smiled his wintry smile. He said, 'Fáilte.'

Kerrigan sat. Suddenly his legs felt weak and he longed for the solace of his little room.

There was a silence, while the Taoiseach shuffled some papers that lay on the desk in front of her. Kerrigan reckoned that this was a deliberate ploy to make him feel even more uncomfortable than he already was. His mouth went dry. When he attempted to speak, he could manage no more than a feeble croak.

'Yes?' The Taoiseach raised her eyes.

Kerrigan swallowed.

'I . . . ah . . . I'm sorry to be so late in, Taoiseach. Things were in a bit of a shambles this morning.'

'Yes?'

Kerrigan realized that he was expected to explain the shambles, so he decided to say nothing more. He waved a dismissive hand.

'It's all sorted now, Taoiseach. No problem.'

'I'm glad to hear it. It seems there have been some difficulties for us all lately.'

'Difficulties?' Kerrigan hardly recognized the squeak as his own voice.

'We have decisions to make, Nollaig.'

'Ah yes,' said Shevlin.

Keep out of this, you little bollocks, thought Kerrigan, though he didn't dare voice his sentiments aloud.

'Decisions,' continued the Taoiseach in her unnaturally even voice. 'Difficult decisions,' she added, in case Kerrigan was not fully aware of the seriousness of the situation.

'Very difficult,' said Shevlin. He knew that the Taoiseach tolerated him as Tánaiste only because of the exigencies of the political situation, but he was determined to insert into any conversation involving the two of them as high a percentage of words as it was possible for him to attain without actually being rude. 'Extremely difficult.'

'Thank you, Tánaiste.'

'My pleasure, Taoiseach.'

'Yes,' said the Taoiseach heavily. She addressed herself directly to Kerrigan. 'Nollaig, this decision of yours to appoint McGuinness to the directorship of the Gallery seems to have created more problems than you anticipated.'

'Very much more,' said Shevlin.

'But, Taoiseach—' began Kerrigan.

She silenced him with a raised hand.

'I realize that the decision was passed in Cabinet, but I am sure you will admit that we bowed to your assurances of the rightness of the course you outlined only because of the vehemence with which you gave them.'

'Very vehement,' said Shevlin. 'I know for my part I had my misgivings when I went into that meeting, but you convinced me, I say, convinced me, by your assurances. I was very convinced by your assurances. Very.'

The Taoiseach looked down at her folded hands. The thin knuckles glowed white. Kerrigan glared at Shevlin. He longed to launch himself across the room and kick the little shite out the window.

He began again, 'I think it's very unfair—'

'Unfair?' The Taoiseach's voice went up a minor third. Kerrigan knew the danger signs and closed his mouth. 'Hear me out, Nollaig.'

'Yes, Taoiseach.'

'We are in difficulties. The opposition to the appointment shows no sign of diminishing. Indeed the latest opinion polls indicate that it is growing in strength.'

'Daily,' said Shevlin. 'Growing daily.'

'Thank you, Tánaiste.'

'Opinion polls!' exploded Kerrigan. 'For God's sake—'

She transfixed him with her steely gaze and he went silent again.

'We live in a democracy, Nollaig. We must listen to the voice of the people. And that voice is telling us clearly that your appointment does not meet with general approval. Then there is this legal delay in the High Court. Even if that goes in our favour, The Friends of Civilization seem determined to take it as far as the Supreme Court, if necessary. Besides—'

Ah, here comes the clincher, thought Kerrigan.

'—our independent friends are deeply unhappy.'

'If we don't keep them on board, they'll screw us to the floor,' said Shevlin.

The Taoiseach exhaled deeply through her long nose.

'I . . . we . . . have decided that McGuinness must be persuaded to withdraw his name.'

'Persuaded,' said Shevlin. 'Or forced.'

'We prefer persuasion,' said the Taoiseach. 'As he is your personal friend, you will have more influence over him than anyone else.'

'Oh I don't think—'

'We believe that you are the best person to advise him.' There was finality in the Taoiseach's voice. *Roma locuta est.*

'A climb down,' said Kerrigan hoarsely.

'The rationalization of a difficult situation, Nollaig,' said the Taoiseach. 'Do you think you can do it?'

Kerrigan was beginning to see things through a red haze. His head ached. His whole body was throbbing as the eczema joined the rest of him in reaction to the crisis now confronting him. He knew full well that he would never persuade Robert McGuinness to withdraw his name voluntarily. The pudgy little pig had his miserable little heart set on the post and would never relinquish it this side of death. And he also knew that to stand up in the Dáil and retract his earlier statement would spell the end of his career.

'It'll be difficult,' he muttered.

Shevlin leaned forward. Kerrigan turned his bleary eyes towards the Tánaiste. Say something nasty, he thought. Just give me the excuse to spread your guts over the Taoiseach's carpet. Go on, you sad hoor. Provoke me!

But Shevlin was consideration personified.

'Whatever help we can give you, Noel,' he said, 'we'll give you gladly. We're all in this together.'

'But we must follow the proper procedures, Nollaig,' said the Taoiseach icily.

She leaned back. Evidently in her mind the meeting was over as far as Kerrigan was concerned.

Kerrigan stood up with difficulty. His legs felt very uncertain. He clutched at the back of his chair to steady himself and asked the question he already knew the answer to.

'If McGuinness won't withdraw, Taoiseach?'

Éilís Ní Snodaigh stared at him silently. The tableau continued for some seconds: the stony Taoiseach, the furtive Tánaiste, the large, crumbling Foreign Minister.

Then the Taoiseach rose and walked around her desk. She took Kerrigan by the arm and led him to the door. Here she held him a moment and spoke softly, so that Shevlin couldn't hear.

'I'm told that you have been having some marital trouble lately, Nollaig. Perhaps it will be all for the best if you have to relinquish some of your onerous public schedule and concentrate on your family. After all, Nollaig, the family is the cornerstone of the nation, and it is there a man's first duty lies.'

She patted his hand. It was the kiss of death.

Kerrigan stumbled down the corridor. His world was in pieces. The only image that loomed large before his was the face of the one who had brought him to this sorry pass.

TWENTY-TWO

Séamus Creedon was up and about before 6 a.m. He washed and dressed himself very carefully in a dark suit, a dark overcoat and a dark tweed cap, as if he were going to a funeral, which in a sense he was. At 6.45 a.m. the local taxi-man, Sylvester Connolly, called to the cottage and drove Séamus to Manulla Junction, where he caught the 7.15 a.m. Westport train to Dublin. While eating breakfast in the dining car, he read the morning paper and learned in passing that the Foreign Minister was expected to make an important statement in the Dáil that afternoon. Some difficulty to do with an appointment to some Gallery or other was apparently exercising the collective mind of the Dáil, chiefly that of the Opposition. He glanced over the report idly, but found little of interest in it.

He had other things on his mind. The visit to Hanley and Patterson in Dublin promised to be a painful one, involving his hearing something of Nora's death. He was torn in two on the matter, wishing and not wishing to know the details of her suffering, dreading the effect it might have on him in front of strangers. Since he had read the advertisement in the *Tribune* and realized that she was certainly dead, he had found it extremely difficult to get himself out of bed in the mornings, to sit at his desk and push one reluctant word after another across the page. Collecting the red Morris Minor and driving it back to Maaclee promised to be even more painful. However, it was what she had wished and he knew he would have to obey her instructions, or spend the rest of his life in a purgatory of guilt over his disobedience.

The countryside clanking by the carriage window was clothed in the gentle radiance of late summer, but he could find nothing of his normal enjoyment in the little stone walls and the tiny fields tucked between them.

He wished it were raining for this dismal journey, but nature refused to co-operate.

You're taking pleasure in this, aren't you? he said to God, though not aloud, and avoided meeting the eye of a young nun who was sitting opposite him and who clearly imagined she was confronting a tormented soul in need of spiritual sustenance.

At 9 a.m., as the Westport train was pulling out of Roscommon station, Noel Kerrigan pulled himself out of bed. Most of the bedclothes came with him and deposited themselves in an untidy heap on the bedroom floor. He kicked them away from his feet and lurched into the bathroom to relieve his kidneys. As he stood there urinating he surveyed his image in the mirror.

'Jesus, Noel, you're rightly shanghaied.'

He knew this was true, certainly as far as his political career was concerned. That bastard McGuinness would never withdraw his name. It wasn't in his nature to make such a gesture even on behalf of a man who had done him much service over the years. He would stick it out to the bitter end and allow Kerrigan to be shot down in flames and ignominy.

He staggered into the blessed relief of the shower. The water cascaded over his body, cleansing away the physical dirt, but doing nothing to cleanse the black mental excrement that clogged up every pore of his mind.

Some time later, having shaved and dressed, Kerrigan poured himself a breakfast of whiskey, water and wheatflakes, and gradually restored himself to membership of the human race. As the alcohol lifted his spirits momentarily, he decided that he would make one more attempt to appeal to the better nature he knew McGuinness didn't possess.

However, when he phoned Twin Cedars, he was informed by a pert little maid's voice that Mr McGuinness was not at home, but was in his office in the ORMAX Tower in Dublin. No, she didn't know when he would be home, but she would take a message if the gentleman liked.

'No message.' Kerrigan slammed down the receiver.

There was nothing for it but to go to the ORMAX building and confront McGuinness in person. He rejected using the ministerial car. It would signal his arrival too clearly and anyway there was no point in dragging Joe Downes into his plans. He couldn't use his own car. Already he had had more than enough to drink and he felt he needed another couple of scoops before setting out, which would render him almost incapable of driving.

He took the gun from his bedroom drawer. It was unloaded. A small box of bullets stood beside it and for a long moment he contemplated using them. Then he closed the drawer.

He called a cab.

Lucy Furlong made a decision. She was alone in the house. Derek was safely on his way to work in the ORMAX Tower and would be away from his home until the evening. The breakfast was now over, the used dishes had been consigned to the dishwasher. She switched off the radio and looked around her spotless kitchen. Everything was tidily in place. Just one task remained to be performed. She realized that what she intended to do would cause a serious breach between her father and herself. It might even entail her being cut out of any form of inheritance, and it would almost certainly cost Derek his job. But she felt she had no choice in the matter.

She picked up the phone and called Hanley and Patterson.

'I'd like to speak to Kate Hanley,' she told the young lady who answered the phone.

'May I say who is calling?'

'My name is Lucy Furlong. Tell Ms Hanley that I'm the daughter of Babs McGuinness. Tell her that I want to help.'

'Hold on, please.'

Lucy waited with some trepidation. She really had no idea how Ms Hanley would greet her. Going by Derek's experience in Leeson Street, Lucy felt it was quite possible that the solicitor would attack her, or refuse to take her call. And when Kate Hanley finally came on the phone, her tone certainly was sharp.

'Hello?'

'Ms Hanley, before you jump to any wrong conclusions, let me say that I'm ringing you because I'd like to help Séamus Creedon get my mother's Morris Minor car.'

There was a considerable pause before the answer came.

'I see. May I ask how you know Mr Creedon's name?'

'I saw it on some papers you left with my father a couple of evenings ago.'

'I see. Am I to take it that Mr McGuinness has had a change of heart on the matter?'

'He doesn't know I'm ringing you.'

'That's very interesting.' Kate Hanley's voice was suddenly warmer. 'How do you propose to help?'

'If I knew Mr Creedon's address, I could deliver it in person.'

'Well, well, well.' A little suspicion was creeping in. 'I've already given the address to Mr McGuinness. Along with the name.'

'I'm sure you did, but I only got a brief look at the papers. I didn't get time to see the address.'

'Mr Creedon isn't at home today. As a matter of fact, he is at present on his way from Mayo to Dublin, and specifically to this office, to collect the car documents and a set of keys. He should be out in Silverglen sometime this afternoon.'

'Tell me something, Ms Hanley.' Lucy was now full of excitement at the action she proposed to take. 'Have you parking facilities in Leeson Street?'

'There is a little lane beside the office. Coming from the south you make a left. There's a car-park in there. It holds about eight cars.'

'Keep a space for the red Morris Minor.'

'I will indeed,' said Ms Hanley, with evident satisfaction.

Kerrigan made his unsteady way downstairs. The morning paper was lying in the hall. He picked it up and glanced through it. Already the hacks had him dead in the water. They were of the unanimous opinion that in the Dáil this afternoon he would back down before the outraged masses ensconced on the high moral ground and rescind the decision he had made a short time ago. Obviously the news had been leaked that the Foreign Minister was being hung out to dry. This leak probably emanated from the Department of An Taoiseach, though this was strenuously denied by 'Government sources'. The papers labelled Kerrigan 'arrogant' and 'stupid' and 'pig-headed', and it was clear (at least to the 'informed' hacks) that the decision to appoint McGuinness had been his alone, that he had misled his cabinet colleagues and had brought them into the unpopular mess where they now found themselves. Clearly Pilate was occupying government buildings and it was hand-washing time.

The doorbell interrupted his black thoughts. He flung the paper back on to the floor and opened the door to the cab driver. For a moment the cabby thought he was about to be assaulted, so ferocious was the scowl on Kerrigan's face, but the minister merely grunted, slammed the hall door behind him and stumped out to the cab.

★

Lucy drove her little Fiesta through the gates of Twin Cedars and parked it up close to the house. Matt Sweeney, who had been pottering about in the garden, came up to greet her.

'There you are, Mrs Furlong,' he said. 'I'm afraid you've missed the boss. He was away out of here a couple of hours ago.'

'That's all right, Matt. I've just come to take the car for a run.'

'What car is that?'

'Mammy's old banger. I promised to keep it in working order.'

'Fair enough,' said Sweeney, 'but the boss took the keys with him this morning. And he told me to put the run on anybody who might come looking for it. But I'm sure that doesn't apply to yourself.'

'Of course not,' said Lucy. 'And don't worry – I've my own set of keys.'

Sweeney watched her as she drove the Morris out of the garage. While she didn't imagine that Sweeney would try to prevent her taking the car, she was still on edge until she was safely out the gate and heading for Dublin. Her father would be very angry when he discovered what she had done, but Lucy decided that she no longer cared what Robert McGuinness thought about anything.

In his plush office overlooking the River Liffey, Robert McGuinness sat facing the Bishop of Tamishni. He was not a happy man. Twice that morning he had had to use his puffer to quell the rising pain in his arm and chest. He had read the morning papers and was very conscious of the fact that the media had continued to fan the flames of public outrage at his appointment. They showed no sign of ceasing their efforts to drag him down. For those papers that favoured the Opposition the real target was, of course, the Government. They wished to see the end of what they considered a wretched coalition and had no compunction about sacrificing an innocent man like himself in such a worthy cause. However, even those papers that backed the Government were now attacking the appointment as well. Evidently they too were prepared to throw him to the wolves to make sure the coalition did not fall. Injustice was being piled on injustice.

But he was damned if he was going to withdraw his name. Even if the Government *did* fall over the affair, a new coalition would soon be cobbled together and he would certainly find a way to exert his influence on them. He wouldn't be sorry to see Lizzy Snoddy out of office. She was a true incorruptible and he could do without her sort in power.

The row with Lucy was another matter entirely. It hurt him acutely to see his only child standing up to him as she had done, flashing her eyes in anger at him, being disobedient in a way that offended the moral teaching he had espoused all his life. After all the money he had lavished on her! And then to tell him he didn't give a damn about his wife! That really went beyond the limits. How in God's name could she say such a thing.

And now here was this ridiculous brother of his invading his business premises to announce his immediate departure for Africa, as if anyone gave a damn. He stared at the fat face of the Bishop and suddenly realized how much he hated the man.

'That was a quick decision,' said Robert.

'Not really. I've spent too much time here already. And this morning, after you had left the house, I got a phone call from my assistant, Father Hurley. It seems I'm needed urgently back at the ranch.'

'Oh well, if you've got to go, you've got to go. We all have our duties to perform.'

He stood up, to signal that he now had other things to do, and held out his hand.

'Have a safe journey.'

However, the bishop did not stand up.

'I want to say something before I go, Robert.'

Robert remained standing. He looked down at his brother stonily.

'Say away.'

'Two things, rather. First, you have had a row with Lucy—'

'My business.'

'You're my brother and she is my niece.'

'Still my business. I don't want any lectures from you about how I deal with my own child.'

'You really are an impossible bastard.'

'What's your second point?'

'You've been an impossible bastard ever since we were children together.'

'If that's all you have to say, then I suggest you get off back to your African savages and leave me to live my own life.'

'My second point is that you really ought to understand your limitations and withdraw your name from that ridiculous Gallery appointment.'

'Goodbye, Dec,' said Robert.

The bishop leaned closer.

'I've had a phone call from the palace. The archbishop is gravely disturbed at the way the situation is developing. He wishes you to withdraw.'

Robert could hardly believe what he was hearing.

'You're lying.'

'No, I wouldn't lie about a thing like this. His Grace thinks you ought to reconsider you position. For your own sake and for the sake of the Church.'

Robert couldn't bring himself to speak. He turned away, resumed his seat and flicked a switch.

'Miss Corr,' he said into his microphone, 'this interview is over. Please come in for some dictation.'

'Bless you, anyway,' said the bishop. 'I'll ask some of my savages to pray for you.'

'Don't throw your hypocrisy at me, thank you.'

As he left the room the bishop met Orla Corr on her way in. She smiled at him warmly.

'Have a nice trip, your Grace,' said Orla sweetly.

'Bless you,' said the bishop.

As he walked to the elevator, Declan McGuinness felt a great weight lifting from his shoulders. He was going home. The sunlight and the simplicity of Tamishni beckoned him and he knew that the people there, *his* people, would welcome him with open arms. With the help of God he would never again need to return to the seedy world occupied by his brother.

During the long drive into the city, Kerrigan said nothing at all. He sat back in his seat, his face red and scowling. Sometimes he snorted violently through his nose. The driver, normally a loquacious man, took one look in his mirror, saw that it was not a time for small-talk and wisely kept his own counsel.

When Séamus Creedon reached Heuston Station in Dublin, it was only eleven thirty. He took one look at the queue of people waiting for taxis and decided that he had more than enough time on his hands to walk the few miles to his destination. Kate Hanley wasn't expecting him until early afternoon, the morning was still sunny and bright, so he set off down the south quays of the Liffey. He had always liked walking by the Liffey. It wasn't a particularly clean river, but it was a friendly one, good for thinking by.

Not that he wanted to think too much on this day. Her image dwelt in the corner of his mind, but he couldn't bring himself to contemplate it with any degree of clarity. He walked briskly, head back, swinging his arms.

The red car drove sweetly, like a bird, Lucy thought. No sign of old age in this venerable lady. She remembered being driven to and from school in Athlone in what she then thought an old banger, something to be ashamed of in front of her schoolfriends. I must have been an impossible little pain in the neck, she thought, with a twinge of regret. Her mother had made those long journeys several times a year and had never once complained when her ungrateful daughter turned her nose up at the car. Of course, Mother, Lucy added wickedly to herself, perhaps you had another call to make on your way back home . . . to somewhere in Mayo! And she further added, Good for you, woman! I hope you had more happiness there than you ever had at home.

She drove down Leeson Street from the southern end and had no trouble at all in locating the narrow lane to Hanley and Patterson's car-park. She squeezed the Morris in and found the expected space awaiting her.

As she was locking the car, a voice called out, 'Hello, there.'

Lucy turned and saw a woman approaching. She was dressed in dark clothes and she had a formidable look about her, but she was smiling.

'Ms Hanley?'

'My God, you're Babs McGuinness all over again. Do you mind if I give you a hug?'

Lucy didn't mind at all accepting the unexpected embrace, though for some unaccountable reason she felt like crying.

'Come on inside,' said Kate Hanley, who wasn't far off tears herself, 'and we'll have a cup of coffee together to celebrate the occasion.'

'Is Mr Creedon here yet?'

'Not yet. Soon.'

'What's he like?'

'You won't believe this. I knew your mother for over twenty years, but I've never met the man in her life. I've never even seen a photo of him.'

'I have,' said Lucy, feeling thoroughly pleased with herself at the distinction.

'We're going to have loads to talk about. And I have a letter to give you – from your mother.'

'Oh God.'

Lucy's tears now really spilled out.

When the cab reached the outskirts of the city, Kerrigan leaned forward suddenly and spoke to the driver.

'Can you hear me?' asked Kerrigan.

'Yes, sir.'

'What would you do, if I stuck a gun into the back of your neck – like this?' said Kerrigan. He pushed a huge stubby forefinger against the back of the driver's head.

'Jesus!' said the driver, clutching the steering wheel. He was afraid to look in the mirror.

'What would you do?' snarled Kerrigan.

'Christ Almighty, I'll do anything you want me to.'

'Only joking,' said Kerrigan, withdrawing his finger. 'That was only my finger.'

'You shouldn't do things like that. You put the heart crossways in me.'

'Shut up and drive,' said Kerrigan.

He said nothing else till they reached the corner of Butt Bridge. Then he ordered the driver to pull over against the kerb.

'I can't stop here mister. There's a double yellow line. I'll have to go across the bridge.'

'Here!' shouted Kerrigan. 'Don't you know who I am! I can stop the whole fucking city, if I want to.'

The driver knew perfectly well who was in his cab. He pulled in against the kerb, ignoring the angry horn blasts all around him. Kerrigan stepped out unsteadily on to the pavement. He fumbled in his pocket for money, took out a handful of notes, made an effort to count them, then gave up and shoved the whole lot into the driver's hand.

'Now get the hell out of here,' he said.

The cab pulled away with great haste. Kerrigan turned up the collar of his coat and pulled his cap down over his eyes in an effort to make himself as inconspicuous as possible. He didn't wish to be recognized.

As he crossed the bridge and turned right down the north quays, he still had not fully thought out what he was going to do when he confronted Robert McGuinness, beyond making an impassioned, but dignified appeal to the financier's good nature and sense of decency. Though he tried to reassure himself with such noble phrases, he felt in his deepest heart that looking for decency or good nature in someone like McGuinness was like looking for a sweet smell in a slurry pit.

What would he do in the event of the inevitable refusal? He didn't know. Walk out with his head held high? That was it. Dignity at all costs. Show the bastard that there were some honourable men still to be found in the country, men of integrity and innate decency, the type of men who had made Ireland what she was, able to take her place in the community of nations. Damn bloody right, there were! And you're looking at one of them right now, McGuinness. Not that I'd expect you to recognize decency if it pissed on your shoes.

Before he entered through the ornate glass doors of the Tower, Kerrigan turned down the collar of his coat again and readjusted the set of his cap to present himself openly and fearlessly to the world. He strode into the foyer like the leading politician he was. He wasn't drunk and he had no eczema on his body and no gun in his inside pocket.

The receptionist recognized him immediately.

'Hello, Mr Kerrigan.'

'I'm here to see Mr McGuinness,' said Kerrigan. As she moved to lift her phone, he added, 'Don't tell him. It's a surprise.' He grinned conspiratorially at her. 'I've got good news for him and I'd like to tell him myself before he suspects.'

She smiled back at him.

'You'd better go straight up, so, Mr Kerrigan. You can use the private lift. Do you know where it is?'

Kerrigan knew. He had used it before. He raised a finger to indicate his satisfaction and then placed it on his lips.

'Not a word, now,' he said.

She watched with an indulgent smile as he entered the elevator. She thought, Men are such big children.

Kerrigan stood alone in the ascending elevator. Something sublime seemed to be happening to him. It was as if he had been born into the world for just this moment. He took a small flask from his inside pocket and applied it to his lips. The sublimity increased with each passing floor, each red number flashing in its dark recess. And there was music too. Something banal and unsuited to the greatness of the occasion, but music nevertheless. Better than nothing.

He hoped the receptionist wouldn't spoil things by phoning ahead.

TWENTY-THREE

Robert McGuinness was going through correspondence with his secretary, Orla Corr, when they both became aware of raised voices outside the door of the office in which they sat. The next moment the door was thrown open and Noel Kerrigan, Foreign Minister, stood there. He held his cap in his hand. His face was sweaty, his hair untidy, but he was steady enough on his feet. To Robert he seemed to be a little the worse for drink. Beside him a flustered young Delia Reid appealed to her employer.

'I'm sorry, Mr McGuinness, but Mr Kerrigan insists on coming in.'

'It's all right, it's all right,' said Kerrigan. 'Tell her it's all right, Robert. I'm not going to burn the place down. I just want a quiet word with my friend Robert. Isn't that OK, Robert? I hope you're not too busy to see me?'

'Of course not.' Robert rose to his feet. Orla Corr stood too. 'That's fine, Delia. Come and sit down, Noel.'

'Good on you,' said Kerrigan. 'Government business, sweetheart,' he said to Delia, placing a finger on his lips. 'Very important. Hush-hush stuff.'

Delia threw her eyes to heaven as she pulled the door shut after her.

Orla said, 'Do you wish me to leave too?'

'If you don't mind,' said Kerrigan. 'I just want a private word in your boss's ear.'

'Off you go, Miss Corr,' said Robert. He felt a little uneasy parting with her, though there was no sign of truculence in Kerrigan's face.

'Are you sure?'

'Yes, that's OK.'

'I'll be outside. Press the buzzer if you need me.'

She smiled a golden smile at Kerrigan as she left the office.

'That's a real looker you have there, Robert. I'll say that for you. You know how to pick them.'

'I presume you haven't come here to discuss my staff.'

'You don't mind discussing mine when the mood takes you. When you're putting the boot in.'

Robert ignored the reference to Aoife Langan. He walked across to the drinks cabinet against the wall.

'Would you like a drink?'

Kerrigan sat down in the chair in front of Robert's desk. He opened his overcoat carefully.

'A drop of whiskey would go very nicely.'

'Or have you had enough already?'

'It's very hard deciding what's enough. I'll take the drop, unless you have it rationed.'

Robert poured out two small portions. He put soda in his own glass, but left Kerrigan's unadulterated by any mixer.

'There you are.' Robert placed a glass in Kerrigan's trembling hand and resumed his seat behind the desk. 'What's troubling you?'

'Jesus, as if you didn't know.'

'Tell me.' There was no warmth in Robert's voice.

Kerrigan swallowed his drink in one gulp and put the empty glass on the floor beside his chair.

'I'm here, Robert, to ask a favour of you.'

'What favour?'

'I'm in diabolical trouble.'

Robert looked at him, but said nothing.

'It's a big favour and I wouldn't ask you if I didn't have my back to the bloody wall.' Kerrigan took a deep breath. 'I want you to withdraw your name for the directorship of the Gallery.'

There was silence for a moment.

Then Robert said, 'You're joking, of course.'

'Do I look as if I'm joking? D'you think I'd come in here just to make a joke? I'm in the shit, Robert. Sister Frigidia has me by the balls and she won't let go. The independents have her by the balls. Believe me, she has balls. This whole Gallery thing has blown up in our faces. If you won't withdraw your name, I'll have to go into the Dáil today and withdraw it for you. Then I'll have to resign and the government will probably be run out. You're not going to get the job either way.'

'I have been promised the job,' said Robert in a cold, even tone.

'No way. It's gone. Kaput. I've done all I could and it's no good. If you withdraw your name we can all get out of it with a bit of dignity. The government will stand up, I'll still be in the cabinet. There'll be other fucking jobs.'

'I don't want any other jobs,' said Robert, still in the same deliberate voice. 'I want this one. I want the one I was promised.'

'Are you listening to me? I can't give it to you.' Kerrigan's composure was fast slipping away from him. Dark clouds were gathering. Dark fingers were scratching at his tortured body. He was finding difficulty in focusing on Robert's face.

'You promised it to me.'

'For fuck's sake! What are you, at all? Do you understand English? I know I promised it to you. And I'd give it to you if I could. But I can't. I can't do it!'

'Don't shout at me,' said Robert, his voice still cold and emotionless. 'Nobody comes into my office and shouts at me. Nobody. Not you, not Lizzie Snoddy. Not God Almighty. Nobody.'

'Look.' Kerrigan lowered his voice again. He caught his shaking body in a tight grip. 'I'm begging you, Robert. Jesus, do you want me on my knees on the floor? I've lost my wife. I've lost my family. I'm going to lose my job. If I go down now, I'll have to get out of politics altogether and there's nothing else I know how to do. I'm finished if I have to go in there and eat my words. I'm asking you – please do the decent thing and withdraw your name.'

Robert stared at him with contempt.

'My heart bleeds for you, Kerrigan, but you can go to hell.'

He pressed the buzzer on his desk. Kerrigan stood up, his self-control now fast ebbing away. He put his hand in his jacket pocket and pulled out the gun. Robert's eyes widened in horror when he saw the weapon.

'For God's sake, Noel!'

A light shone in Kerrigan's brain, suddenly illuminating the stupidity of what he was doing. He stared at the gun in his hand and then put it back into his pocket.

'It's bloody empty, you little shite!'

The door opened and Orla Corr entered.

'Come in, come in,' Kerrigan said. As she hesitated, he added, 'It's all right. I'm going.'

Orla shut the door behind her. Then she crossed calmly to the desk and stood beside Robert, who had somehow pulled himself to his feet. He clutched at her in terror.

'I always knew you were a bollocks, McGuinness,' said Kerrigan. 'Now I know you're a windy bloody bollocks as well. And one thing is certain − if I have to cut my own throat, you're never going to get that job.'

He picked up his cap and put it on his head. He buttoned his coat and reassembled himself into an approximation of dignity. Then he turned and walked stiff-legged out of the office.

'Jesus,' whispered Robert. He sank back into his chair, beads of sweat running down his face. 'Did you see it, Orla?'

'See what?'

'The gun. He had a gun.'

'I didn't see any gun, Robert.'

'I tell you he had a gun!'

He felt drained and sick in his stomach, as if he were going to vomit. His hands were trembling. The pain in his arm was becoming intolerable.

'Are you all right?'

Her beautiful face, full of concern, leaned close to his. He nodded dumbly.

Séamus Creedon reached O'Connell Bridge. Before he turned right into Westmoreland Street, his eye was caught by the sweep of the Liffey as it flowed towards Ringsend and the sea. He was struck by how different the view was from what Nora and himself had seen when they had walked in that direction twenty-five years before. The buildings, for instance. Liberty Hall was still there, though growing shabbier by the year. The ugly Loop Line Bridge with its strident advertisements still spoiled the view of the Customs House and the expanse of the sky where the river met the open sea. Beyond the Customs House were the new flashing glass façades of the Irish Financial Centre and, right alongside, vying for attention, the assertion, aggression almost, of the ORMAX Tower.

He shook his head and walked along Westmoreland Street, past the new statue of Molly Malone, called locally *The Dish with the Fish*, or *The Tart with the Cart*. Grafton Street had changed mightily over the years. It was now paved with fancy tiles. New foreign shops occupied old sites. Switzer's Store was gone, its body space now filled by the more upmarket Brown Thomas. However, Bewley's Café, though wearing a new face, was still a source of friendly coffee smells and a bustle of customers coming and going, all looking indecently young and very prosperous. He did not dare to enter. It was for him now a place of painful memories. He hurried by without even looking at the entrance where he had waited for her.

Crossing St Stephen's Green was almost as bad. The impatient ducks were still being fed by screeching children. Not the same ducks, obviously, but exact copies, still splashing madly about, fighting fiercely for scraps of bread, as if the whole world were precisely as it had always been. Most unfair that they should survive Nora. Woman passes, but the ducks remain, he thought bitterly. Oh Nora, where are you now when I need you? Where, where, where?

The phone rang. Orla picked it up.

'Hello? Just a moment, please.' She covered the receiver with her hand. 'Hanley and Patterson. Do you want to take it, or shall I tell them you're not here?'

Robert's throat was dry. He spoke with difficulty.

'I'll take it. Bring me some hot coffee.'

She nodded, put the receiver into his flaccid hand and left the office. He swallowed, but was unable to clear the lump in his throat.

'What?'

'Mr McGuinness?' The hated voice grated on his ears.

'What the hell do *you* want?'

'I see you recognize me, Mr McGuinness. I just want to let you know that your wife's wishes have been granted. The new owner of the red Morris Minor is expected here any moment now.'

The pain in his chest was building. He groped in his pocket for his puffer, fumbled and dropped it. It rolled away across the floor. His voice seemed to come from a long distance away.

'There is no new owner.'

'Would you like to say hello to him when he comes? I'm sure he'll be willing to say hello to you.'

'Tell him to go to hell.'

'Whatever you like.'

'Tell him he'll never get the car as long as I'm alive.'

'A bit late for that kind of talk, Mr McGuinness. The car is already here.'

'You're lying. The car is at home where it has always been.'

'I'm afraid you're mistaken. It's standing here in the car-park at my office. I can see it through the window.'

'That's impossible.'

'Nothing is impossible, Mr McGuinness.'

He roused himself to some semblance of authority.

'If you, or anyone belonging to you, have trespassed on my property, you'll never practise law again in this city.'

'We never break the law, Mr McGuinness. The car was brought in here this morning by your daughter, Lucy Furlong.'

'Lucy?'

'She's still here, if you wish to—'

His throat dried completely. He tried to speak, but no words came. He reached forward to put down the receiver, but it slipped from him and fell by the side of the desk, dangling on its flex. He lay back in his chair, oblivious to the thin distorted voice coming from the earpiece. After a moment the phone at the other end of the line was put down and the voice became a tuneless whine.

Orla Corr brought a cup of coffee into the office and put it down on Robert's desk.

'Coffee, Robert.'

The recumbent figure in the swivel chair didn't move. Orla put her hand on Robert's shoulder and pushed him gently. The chair slowly swivelled around.

Her eyes widened in horror.

He was glad to leave the Green and cross into Leeson Street. As he negotiated his way through the traffic, he heard the siren of an ambulance fading somewhere in the distance.

He walked slowly past the Georgian buildings, counting the numbers off in his mind. He reached the lane and paused to compose himself for the meeting ahead.

A taxicab had pulled up outside the next door. As he stood there a young woman hurried out of the building and ran down the steps. His heart almost stopped at the sight of the familiar red-brown hair.

'Nora,' he said aloud.

But she didn't see him. She jumped into the taxi and it sped away.

He let out a long slow breath. Then he crossed the lane to the building with the brass plate on which were the names *Hanley and Patterson*. He became aware that there was a woman standing at the open door on top of the steps. She looked down at him.

'Mr Creedon?'

'Ms Hanley?'

She nodded.

'You've just missed her,' she said.

TWENTY-FOUR

When Robert McGuinness was laid to rest the stars of the select suburb of Silverglen came out in their glory to pack the Church of the Archangels for the funeral Mass.

They came in even greater numbers than they had a month earlier for Brigid McGuinness's interment. *That* had been a run-of-the-mill funeral; sad, no doubt, but not exceptional, to be expected, following the natural order of things. A woman of no apparent distinction died of cancer. End of story.

This, however, was a special occasion, this was the burial of a hero, the sort of event that happens rarely in the history of a parish. A man of distinction had died at his desk, working tirelessly for his community and his Church. Ravaged by grief at the recent death of his life's partner, he had been snatched away by the cruel Grim Reaper just as he stood on the threshold of elevation to the pantheon of the arts. This had the characteristics of an epic. So Canon Laurence Finnegan told them at every Mass celebrated in the church since the death of Robert McGuinness, and Canon Finnegan was a man who knew what he was talking about.

The facts were clear enough. Robert McGuinness had died from a heart attack. A first-class and very articulate witness had been present at the scene and had given a clear and concise account of what had transpired.

Orla Corr was a resourceful and intelligent woman. In her statement to the police and later to the Press she neglected to mention that Robert had told her that Foreign Minister Kerrigan had produced a gun in the office. Yes, she told all those who asked her, Mr Kerrigan had called to see her employer and they had had a discussion, but as far as she was concerned it was an amicable discussion between friends of long-standing.

She was well aware that the death of Robert McGuinness signalled the end of her association with ORMAX. She could see that the new owner, Lucy Furlong, was no fool and would not tolerate her father's former mistress about the place. Orla decided to move on.

Robert had left her a decent settlement, so she did not depart penniless. She also took with her some personal insurance in the form of certain confidential papers, receipts and bank statements which she felt sure would come in handy if the cash settlement should run out.

In the event, she met a handsome, wealthy Swiss industrialist with whom she set up home in Zurich. It was a mutually advantageous arrangement. He was happy, because she graced his arm with her undoubted physical charms and looked after his bedtime needs with calm assurance; she was happy because he had more than enough money to finance the most extravagant shopping trips.

In the meantime, and unbeknown to her husband, she made ready to send off letters to various Irish politicians, indicating that she had in her possession certain documents pertaining to their relationship with her deceased employer. She would say no more than that, make no threats, ask for no money, but simply wait for cash transfers to flow into her personal account on a regular basis.

The coalition government did not fall. Noel Kerrigan did not have to go into the Dáil and eat humble pie before resigning. News of Robert McGuinness's sudden death reached the Taoiseach's office just in time to save the Foreign Minister's skin. He presided over a sombre afternoon in the chamber, where the assembled politicians meditated on death and the transience of life, and many tributes were paid to the dead man by those who had been ready to vilify him while he was still alive. In truth, the opposition parties were glad to be off the hook of a motion of no confidence. They did not really want an early election, they had made their point on the subject of nepotism and they were content to let the matter rest there.

The impecunious scholar who had been retained by Robert to instruct him in matters artistic, a man of no political affiliations but of proven expertise, was appointed as Director of the Gallery. The choice was widely approved and applauded. The scholar sighed at the inscrutable ways of God and settled down to a safe and secure future.

Kerrigan counted his blessings. The Taoiseach swallowed her distaste for the man and contented herself with moving Aoife Langan to another department and insisting that Kerrigan patch up his shaky marriage. Mollie Kerrigan, placated by the removal of 'the blondie hoor' from the immediate vicinity of her husband professed herself willing to give him another chance and Kerrigan was more than happy to take it. The letter from Orla Corr was still in the future.

The Bishop of Tamishni sent his condolences to the canon and the parish, and a personal note to Lucy. He told the canon that he regretted that pressing episcopal duties in Tamishni prevented his attending the funeral. He told Lucy simply that he couldn't face it.

When Lucy and Derek Furlong arrived at the church in the mourning-coach, along with Robert's two sisters and their spouses, the crowd that met the young new owner of ORMAX and her newly appointed chief executive was almost overwhelming. Yet Lucy looked strangely detached. There was no sign of tears on her face and Derek's white handkerchiefs remained undisturbed in his pocket. Sympathizers marvelled at the young woman's bravery and composure under such trying conditions, though some of the more cynical averred that inheriting such a fortune must have made things a little easier to bear.

Lucy held her head high as she made her way through the clutching hands and murmured condolences. She scarcely seemed to notice the people about her, but her eyes constantly moved here and there, as though searching for a particular face among the faces in the crowd.

Inside the church, Canon Finnegan marshalled his troops around the altar. If he resented the presence beside the coffin of the Guard of Honour from the Knights of St Nicodemus, he was careful to conceal the fact. One had to endure such things. Because the Bishop of Tamishni had again been unable to get home in time for the interment, the canon was the undisputed ruler in his own church and spoke the eulogy himself.

'A veritable saint,' he thundered, his white hair dancing around his red face, 'a man who epitomized the greatest virtues known to mankind – love, compassion, honesty, integrity and devotion to his God. This was a *man*! Whence comes there such another?'

There was applause in the church – the canon's hands demanded it.

Lucy sat with her hands on her lap, wondering where Robert was. She was sure that, if Heaven really existed, he would have found a way of wangling himself into a prominent position there. She thought she could feel the infant stirring in her womb, though she couldn't be sure. Derek sat beside her protectively. He had developed a gravely paternal appearance (and practised it regularly in front of the mirror) since hearing of the new role he was destined to play in the world. Robert's sisters, Rita and Joan, wept tears of intermingled pride and sorrow. Their husbands comforted them and savoured their own elevated status by association with their blessedly deceased brother-in-law.

The organ thundered and the choir sang. The Knights of St Nicodemus, in their gaudy uniforms, flashed their swords in salute.

For years afterwards parishioners spoke with nostalgic awe of that tremendous moment with its outpouring of love, respect and admiration for one of their very special sons. One local historian even published a small book on *The Hero of Silverglen* that included souvenir pictures of the historic event.

Lucy did not see him until they were leaving the graveyard on their way back to Twin Cedars for the reception. By then she was tired of shaking hands and saying 'thank you' to people she had never seen before and she had given up hope that he had come to the funeral, accepting the fact that he had little inducement to attend. She understood why he might wish to avoid her and was determined not to blame him in the least.

And then, suddenly, there he was. He was standing a little back from the pathway through the cemetery, out of the stream of people moving along it. She stopped in her tracks when she saw him.

Derek placed an anxious hand on her arm.

'Are you all right, Lucy?'

'Yes, Derek. I'm fine. Go on down to the car and wait for me there. I have someone I want to talk to. Go on. Really, I'm OK.'

Derek left her reluctantly and she walked slowly over to the man who stood watching her. She paused in front of him and stared into his face.

'Are you who I think you are?'

'I hope so.'

She held out her hand.

'I'm very pleased to meet you.' Then she added, 'Jim.'

His thin, serious face broke into a smile.

'Lucia. You are so like Nora that it's hard to believe she's not still alive.'

'My mother was called Babs.'

'That was in another country.'

'I know what you mean.'

They stood in silence for a few moments, as if each were trying to fathom how much the other knew.

'You got the car all right?'

'Yes, thank you. Miss Hanley told me you brought it to Leeson Street yourself.'

'I was hoping to meet you then, but I got called away unexpectedly.'

'I saw you. You were leaving just as I arrived.'

'Oh dear. So close?'

'Inches.'

'Why didn't you call me?'

'I was afraid to. And you obviously had somewhere urgent to go to. But I knew you immediately. You're so like your mother. Of course, I've seen you many times since I first saw you in your pram. You were six months old that first time. In Stephen's Green.'

'I don't know what to say to you. I don't even know what to call you. Is "Jim" all right?'

'Jim will do very nicely indeed. And we don't have to say anything to each other. Not now. We have plenty of time ahead of us.'

'Will you come back to the house?'

'No. I don't want any of that.'

'Another country?'

'Yes. Please don't think I'm being awkward about it.'

'Oh I don't. I think I know how you feel.'

'I'm very sorry about how your . . . how Mr McGuinness died.'

'It's going to take some getting over.'

There was a long pause before he spoke again.

'You know where I live?'

'Kate Hanley told me.'

'Perhaps you'd like to come and visit sometime?'

'I'd like that.'

'I mean, of course, your husband as well. Does he know about me?'

'Yes. And I'm sure he'll be happy to come.'

She held out her hand again. He took it almost reverentially.

'I look forward to seeing you in Maaclee,' he said.

She smiled and turned away. Then she stopped and turned again to look at him.

'By the way,' she said, 'I'm pregnant. I think you ought to know that. You're the first to know, apart from Derek.'

'Thank you.'

He watched her slim figure as she walked away.

'Ah well,' he said aloud to himself. 'You did a good job, Nora, my love.'

He made his way across the cemetery to the newly filled grave with its mountain of flowers. The gravediggers had gone away for the moment and all was quiet, except for an inquisitive robin perched nearby, studying the freshly dug earth for unsuspecting worms.

Séamus looked at the gravestone, which lay flat at the top of the grave. The name of Robert McGuinness, the latest occupant, had not yet been added. All that was written on the stone was the name McGuinness. Below this was:

Brigid Mary, beloved wife and mother,

born 1951, died 1999.

Fair as a star.

He stared at this for a long time. The robin chirped and flew away.